I0630348

FAE PLANES DRIFTER

OTHERWORLD OUTLAWS 4

TAMMY SALYER

FAE PLANES DRIFTER: OTHERWORLD OUTLAWS 4

Copyright © 2023 by Tammy Salyer

All rights reserved.

No part of this book may be reproduced in any form or by any electronic or mechanical means, including information storage and retrieval systems, without written permission from the author, except for the use of brief quotations in a book review.

Cover by Miblart.

Hello and thank you for being here! Should you enjoy the words on these pages (and I hope you do!), I encourage you to join my Book Club and visit me at:

www.tammysalyer.com

I occasionally send newsletters to my Book Club with new releases, special offers, and other bits of news. As a special thanks to new members, please enjoy a handful of novellas and short stories from my many and sundry universes FOR FREE.

ALSO BY TAMMY SALYER

SPECTRAS ARISE SERIES

When all other options run out, never let go of your gun.

In a few hundred years, the Algol system becomes humanity's new home. The question is: Is it a better one?

THE SHACKLED VERITIES SERIES

In a Cosmos-wide war between celestials, humans are as expendable as pawns. Until Ulfric Aldinhuus, leader of the Knights Corporealis, uses the celestials' weapons to fight back.

OTHERWORLD OUTLAWS SERIES

A sawbones fae with a supernatural-sized grudge, a necromancer gnome obsessed with pixie dust, and a hoodoo cowgirl with a Sharps buffalo rifle and damn good aim—the Tuatha Dé Danann will never know what hit 'em.

COLLECTIONS

A Scorpion's Heart: Four Twisted Tales of Love and Lust

SHORT STORIES

Artificial Fate * Creepers * No Suede Soles in Hell

Visit my website to see all new releases.

www.tammysalyer.com

1

The smoky air of the battle between the fae witches, Brother Havóq the lich, the ghost town's resurrected dead, and the Otherworld's elemental werewolves lay stagnant across the churchyard like a mute witness to all that had occurred here. In opposition to the stillness, I was feeling rather spritely—particularly for someone who'd just returned from the limbo of death myself. Knowing now what I did about the puzzlingly impermanent afterlife, *limbo* seemed far more apropos than *death*.

Stepping out of the church alongside Hattie, with Lugh's golden spear clutched in one hand, I felt like an ancient conqueror, perhaps a Celtic warrior facing down the Romans with magic and might in equal measure and a bit of bloodlust to top it off. It might have been some kind of transference of the spear's innate nature. Then again, it might have just been the me I really was, deep down, who had decided not to be held back by the world's expectations any longer.

"Oh, this is lovely, I see you have already assembled a group to serve us," the spear said. It had a voice that set my teeth on edge. Simultaneously airy and screechy, the way a screaming butterfly might sound, wholly irritating to… not so much my ears, because I wasn't hearing it aloud, but to my mind itself.

"They're not servants, spear," I said openly. Hattie looked askance at me, and I turned to her. "This shouldn't surprise you, I would guess, but the spear speaks. I'm assuming you don't hear that?" I lifted my voice in hope with the question.

"All I hear is you sayin' someone's not your servant. And I'm pretty sure you're not crazy enough to be talkin' to yourself—not that I'd blame you after today—so it has to be you talkin' to that pig sticker." She leaned close and peered in my eyes, her nearly black irises not three inches from my own green ones. Her breath was warm against my lips, and I wondered at how loose-limbed it made me feel. "No, not crazy. Might be headstrong, but sane enough." She glanced at the churchyard. "Given the circumstances."

"Headstrong?" I asked, but she gave me a lopsided grin, teasing me. I grinned back. "I prefer *determined*."

"I'm sure you do." She reached up to adjust her hat farther back on her head and winced.

"How about you?" I asked, suddenly rethinking all she'd been through. First, possessed by the Feathered Serpent, then shot in the heart, then struck in the back of the head with a rock. "Your chest, your head?" *Your spirit,* I wondered, too, but didn't ask.

She reached delicately for the back of her head. Her eyes narrowed when her hand brushed the bump she had there. "I'll live, I guess."

My eyes fell on something then that I didn't expect but brought me unaccountable relief. "Your neck," I said.

"What about it?"

Instead of saying anything, I reached for her hand and guided her fingers to where I could see her pulse, once more beating as normal, on either side of her throat.

Her eyes widened. "Well now, isn't that fine as cream gravy. I'm back to bein' a livin', breathin', heart a'beatin' woman again."

"Truly a marvel," I agreed.

"And you?" she said, gesturing to my own neck. "You're back to... I can't say *normal* is the right word, but livin' and breathin' with no permanent damage?"

I toyed with the end of the kerchief presently hiding the gash from

Quetzalcoatl that had turned my throat into a waterfall and sent me into a Purgatory I felt confident no preacher had ever envisioned. I'd been what most would term dead, same as Hattie, yet here we both were, sitting and having a regular, in relative terms, conversation. Truly a wonder. "As far as I can tell," I confirmed.

"So that's what this was all fer," Toxicore butted in. "A shiny club with a pretty rock stuck in it."

"Tell the miniature troll not to speak of me thus, descendent of Lugh. Those who dare disdain my power and might in such insulting words often find them to be their last," said my newly acquired artifact.

I winced a bit, the spear's voice not only scratchy against my sensitive brain but also too loud. "Can you tone it down a bit, spear? I can hear you, you know. It's not as if there are noises to distract me from the sounds coming from within my own brain."

"My, rather sensitive, aren't you?" it responded. "I suppose this is what happens when the mighty Lugh failed to rear his descendant in the art of battle and crushing enemies."

"I really don't need to be condescended to by a golden stick... sorry, weapon."

"And I don't need to be wielded by a mere child of my master, but here we are."

"Why do you keep saying that? I'm a descendant of Lugh? I—" My attention was suddenly captured by the eyes of my friends. Everyone, from Leannan to Paddy, along with the other fae witches, Orville, and Tox, was staring at me with mixed expressions of concern and surprise. "Ah," I said to them. "The spear appears to be verbal and has its own, er, unique personality. And also, it keeps telling me I'm descended from Lugh, which must be some absurd jest, I'm sure. Odd for a weapon to have a sense of humor, I admit, but then..." I shrugged.

When I trailed off, Orville and Leannan exchanged a measured glance.

The Sídhe looked back to me. "It's as I thought. A Danannín."

I smiled haplessly, waiting for her to explain her statement. The term *Danannín* didn't automatically lend itself to any internal glossary or catalogue in my mind.

"So, the wards weren't forgotten. She was able to break through them on her own," Mathilda marveled.

My smile drooped as I inquired, "She? … Do you mean me?" I frowned. "No, no, I'm not… I don't… my father is Bran, a simple fae, as I understand it."

But when I looked back to Orville, his face was serious. "Doctor, I think it's probably time someone told you the truth."

Coming from him, a man who seemed on only very loose terms with the truth on the best of days, this was ironic, a joke even. Blinking in the smoke-laden air, I could only buttress myself for a punch line.

It was no joke.

"Bran is Lugh, you say?" I asked Orville through cold lips. "Lugh of the Tuatha Dé Danann, Lugh of the Long Arm, god of justice and craftsmanship." I'd done some homework. "The warrior who fought the Fomorians and killed King Balor. My dad is Lugh?"

Tox had taken a seat on the hardpacked earth next to Paddy and was rummaging through a pack he must have taken from someone. Orville was seated on the steps of the church beside me, Hattie on my other side. Leannan and the rest of the fae witches were wandering the yard, taking up trophies or other odds and ends from the dead, or so it seemed. I was too distracted to pay attention.

"Now that I t'ink on it, makes perfect sense," Tox said. "Lula, as in the child of Lugh—couldn't've been any plainer if she'd told me herself. Did you know, Stowe?"

"I swear upon every tree in the sacred groves of Wicklow that I had no idea at all." He scratched behind one ear. "Though, now that I hear it said aloud, I don't know how I missed it."

The two laid their eyes back on me, a sheen of wonder in them.

I found the entire idea wondrous also. But the sheen in my own eyes was not of awe. It was anger.

"You—" A sudden lump in my throat forced me to swallow. "You knew!" I accused Orville. "All this time you knew and you didn't tell me!"

Orville blinked and flinched a bit. "Now, Lula, I—"

"Don't you dare *Lula* me, Downs, and don't you dare begin your damn obfuscations and evasions. You tell me the truth right this instant or so help me... Look at me when I'm losing my decorum at you!"

His eyes had fallen to the steps, to my hand specifically, which was still wrapped around the spear lying next to me.

"Now calm down, please. I'm doing my best to come clean here, but it's going to be difficult if you impale me with that thing."

I looked down and saw the most unusual thing. The slight fae-ish aura enveloping the spear was now a fulminous orange, like firelight glancing off a clear lake, and spreading. "My, that is unique," I muttered.

The spear's shrill voice oozed through my mind. "Shall I slide through his guts, my lady, or into an eye socket perhaps? Cook his brain while I stir things around?"

"No! No, thank you. I'm sure Orville and I can handle this like adults." Thinking on the many adults who had recently battled in this churchyard and committed multiple murders, I added, "Without the bloodshed."

The spear's light dimmed a little. "Mmm, well, I shall thank you to remember that I serve a purpose, a very specific and definitive purpose."

"Somehow I don't think I'll be able to forget it." I returned my attention to Orville, who was staring at me wide-eyed.

"It's speaking to you, is it?" he asked, concerned.

"It's offering to do as you suggested. I've asked it to wait, for now." The flush of hot anger in my cheeks was not yet cooled. It would take a miracle for that to happen. "You were saying why you've *lied* to me about my father all this time."

"Now, *lied* isn't exactly the correct—"

"Orville," I warned.

He cleared his throat. "Yes, all right. I'm a druid. Our job is to practice and apply wisdom."

"You call withholding the truth 'wisdom'?"

He had the temerity to look chagrined. "As I've already stated, I've never been a very good druid. I did what I thought was least likely to result in danger—to you. I didn't know the spear could be so... forthcoming with information."

I had to agree. A talking spear was unusual.

"First off, I didn't tell you, for your own protection." I scowled, and he raised a hand to quiet the unladylike things I was close to shouting. "You see, Lugh has many, many enemies, and there are more than a few fae who can read the thoughts you think are your own. If you knew who your father was, you'd have been even more of a target than you are now.

"Second, as you can see," he continued, "there are quite a few, ehm, advantages to being the child of a god, a Danannín, as the fae call it. Not the least of which is immense power, along with access to a great many enchanted and mystical items that few others can wield. Weapons, for example." He glanced to the spear and subtly shifted further aside. "There's an innate and some might say an incalculable danger to having the strength of giants, the power of gods, and the skills first introduced to us mere mortals by ancient spirits—and *not* know how to use them. You see, in the timeless erudition of the fae, there is one law that supersedes all others: there is no stronger magic than the magic of belief."

"You're equivocating, and I'm losing patience."

"Am I? Trust me, I'm explaining everything in full, it just takes a moment."

"It shouldn't take long to explain why you lied," I countered. "How complicated can it be?" I was being headstrong, as Hattie had accused me, but I was angry.

Paddy spoke up. "Lula, my dear, I can see you're vexed, but this is the time to learn, not the time for lost tempers."

I nearly snapped at my uncle too, but the spear cut in first.

"We could speed this along if I were to tickle his toes a bit," it seethed. "I am well past due for a good stabbing."

I gripped it tighter and did not respond. I was impressed at its ability to be euphemistic, though. Fae weapons have some truly surprising properties. "Go on," I capitulated grudgingly.

Orville stroked his mustache, looking far away, as if the thing he was attempting to explain required some contemplation. "Belief in magic, you see, is easy if you're born with it and raised among others who wield it. But for those who come to it late in life, and especially come to it from a life of rejecting it as folly"—his glance into my eyes when he said this was filled with knowing, as though he could plainly see my twenty-seven years of strict adherence to rational explanation as a form of armor against anything that might be considered super-natural—"discovery has a certain level of inherent volatility."

"You're tryin' to tell the doc she might go off like a powder keg that someone threw a match into, aren't you, Downs?" Hattie said. I noted the impatience in her tone with a touch of justification.

"To put it bluntly," he agreed.

"Why put it otherwise?" she countered.

"Indeed. But what might be even worse is a false sense of security in your own abilities."

"I do not lack for confidence, Orville," I said.

"No, I can see that, but you haven't faced anything yet that was stronger or wiser than you."

"Such as?"

"Such as your fae kin, the Morrígan."

Tox chimed in. "Aye, she's a wily one, and mean as bad beans in a bubbly belly. But I'm not sure why ye're implyin' Lula is even a wee bit wise."

"In conclusion, Lula," Orville went on, ignoring Tox with the same facility I'd developed, "much as I feel it's not my place, I do have to say that you may have been better off not knowing this truth about yourself before you were ready to master your strength."

I pondered this a moment, but concluded: "What wasn't your place was withholding the truth, even if you don't like what it might lead to. When will you learn that you're not a gatekeeper to others' lives?"

He eyed me, careful to keep his face neutral, though I could see I'd gotten under his skin. "As you say, Doctor. But there's one final reason I played this hand close to my vest."

"Which is?"

"If your own mother chose to keep you in the dark, who was I to reveal your lineage?"

My jaw grew slack.

"He's sayin' yer mum lied to you, Looloo," Tox unhelpfully noted.

"Yes, I realize that," I snapped. I didn't know what else to say. Why had she hidden this fact from me? Was it because of what Orville was telling me, that I might become too much of a loose cannon now that I knew who my father truly was and what I may truly be capable of?

I stood and stepped onto the hardpan. "If you all would be so kind, I need a moment to myself," I said over my shoulder.

Hattie stood too. "You all right, Doc?"

"I'll be fine. I just… it's a lot to take in. I'll meet you all back at the boarding house."

As I began to walk toward Carter's horse, stepping around the dead bounty hunter's stiffening body, Paddy called to me, "Are you sure 'tis safe, Lula? The werewolves—"

"I'll be fine," I repeated, with more force. "I am well-armed, after all."

Looking to the spear shining like the glittering rays of the sun in my hand, I thought no words could be any truer.

2

I was halfway back to Denver before I realized I didn't know the way. Fortunately, the path was well-worn from the volume of travel of late, and my borrowed horse seemed to know his directions with or without guidance. If Havóq had believed himself well hidden, he was delusional. Then, anyone who chose to wear four-hundred-year-old armor over their equally aged dead body was an easy fit for the word.

Much as I wanted to be alone with my thoughts, one quality of my newfound artifact quickly became apparent. It was chatty. Annoyingly so.

"And where shall we find the nearest gateway to Tír Na nÓg, my lady?" the spear gabbed as we ambled across the hills. "I can see clearly that we're not on the right plane. Dirt everywhere. You'll note I'm made of gold. You have noted this, yes? Dirt is such a base element. It belongs nowhere near m—"

"I wonder," I cut in abruptly. "Is it possible for you to contain your thoughts, if that's the correct word, for a bit? I have quite a bit on my mind."

"Contain my thoughts? You ask this of me, when I've been asleep for so many seasons? Seasons upon seasons, I sense. I'll have you know that I have an agenda, and until I've seen it fulfilled, I wish to not be inhibited from speaking my mind and pursuing my goals."

"… Your mind…" I shook my head. Wasn't it just dandy that I'd found the most important key, the literal key, to freeing my father, and it thought itself to be some kind of living creature, with personal rights and independence? With a *mind*? With a self-pitying sigh, I said, "I suppose if you're, well, some*one* instead of some*thing*, I should at least name you. That is, if you don't have one already."

"Names are the trappings of flesh-and-blood creatures. I transcend these base components."

"Right. Well, I'm not just going to call you 'spear.' How about… Sleg? I could call you Assal, but that sounds too much like something else."

"I have no opinion on the matter," it griped. Why it was griping could only be guessed at.

"That's settled then. This agenda. Since you're planning to be"—*overbearingly irritating*—"persistent about it, would you mind telling me what it is?"

Sleg was silent a moment, and though it was the outcome I'd wished for, I sensed a condescending impatience in the pause. "I've told you, my lady. The Morrígan must be held to account for what she's done to me."

"She's the one who put you into this long sleep?"

"The very one. And caged the master."

"I'm under the impression that greater fae goddesses like her are unkillable." I startled a bit in my saddle, suddenly realizing this may apply to me too. I was half-goddess, or godling, apparently. But what did that mean? What was the full complement of magical endowments thrust onto me? When I'd been trapped in the phylactery, was I really dead? Did that word even have any meaning in relation to anything in my life anymore?

"Oh, they like to make people think so. But that doesn't preclude one from trying, does it?"

"Sounds to be more of a vendetta than an agenda," I commented, only half-interested in the rambling weapon's personal problems.

"A word quibbler, hmm? Aren't you the cheeky one? You must get that from your mother. So again, now that I've repeated the urgency of returning to Tír Na nÓg to deliver rightful justice, I repeat also the question: Where is the nearest gateway?"

"I honestly have no idea." Maybe Motherlode Mankiller's storage room was in the Otherworld, but I wasn't going to ask her if my family heirloom and I could pass through it. The troll turned my blood cold.

"No idea? Then where are we going?"

"I..." I fell silent. That was an easy question to answer in the short-term, but plans needed to be made. Now that I had the spear, I had all I needed to free Bran... Lugh. Sleg, I realized, had the right idea.

I gave my horse a pat on the withers. "Let's pick it up a bit, boy, if you can. There are things I must see to soon." I could feel sorry for myself and my unconventional family matters later. The goal remained the same for now. And odd as it seemed, Sleg's and my goals were partially aligned.

By suppertime, we'd reached the track that would widen into Wynkoop Street and lead me to downtown Denver, upon which time I realized something I'd overlooked. Carrying a six-foot-long golden spear with an apple-sized orange gem at its tip would be an excellent way of getting myself robbed. Frankly, that wasn't what worried me, though. I'd been through enough battles by this point to know it would take more than a gruff threat to disarm me and take my belongings. Sleg was said to have the power to kill on command, too. The weapon had made it clear it would not hesitate to do so if I asked, or if it felt threatened. But the last thing I needed was too much attention. Brigid's werewolves were likely wondering the streets, waiting for me.

It was time for an experiment. I had gradually become aware that having Sleg in hand felt a bit like gripping the throttle of a steam engine. It thrummed with a low vibration, and I sensed a great deal of energy pent up within the magical weapon. What kind of energy, I couldn't guess. But I wondered if it could be siphoned the same way I had to siphon a bit of the spirit energy of others to sustain my glamour. Without seeking Sleg's consent, I tested the theory, wetted my neckerchief with the canteen attached to the horse's pommel, and donned my glamour, disguising myself as a middle-aged man. A quick glance over my hands and clothing showed me it worked splendidly, and Sleg did not complain, if it even noticed. Well, that was one less worry, I supposed.

Sleg, upon being asked, told me it could not hide its true nature in such a way. After a bit of consideration, I dismounted and unsaddled my borrowed mustang and pulled off the saddle blanket to wrap the spear and keep it hidden. Riding bareback on the pegasi had given me the practice I needed to confidently complete the journey to one of Denver's liveries without the saddle. I could hide it in the brush and come back for it later.

"Now, just a moment!" Sleg complained before I'd barely begun wrapping it up. "That cloth is covered in hair and animal sweat. I can no more abide having that near me than I can abide being tossed in a mudhole!"

"What do you care? You're made of metal and rock."

"Would you like it if someone covered you with animal excretions?"

"Of course I'd mind, but that's different." I was having a hard time believing it was necessary to argue with an inanimate object about taking precautions for its own safety, but here I was.

"Oh, explain how. I'll wait."

"... Explain how? I-I'm a human being. You're a tool!" This was an obvious argument to me, but Sleg differed. Because of course it did.

"I am not a tool. I am a weapon. The finest in Tír Na nÓg. The greatest ever made by the Tuatha Dé Danann. The Long Arm of Lugh himself! Neither a tool nor a glorified tree branch, like that thing hanging from your belt."

"My shillelagh? It's easily as magical as you."

It scoffed. "Is it now? Can it do this?"

I had no time to suggest the weapon calm itself before it jerked from my hand and blazed to light so bright and so sudden that I had to fling a hand over my eyes to shield them. When I was confident I hadn't just been set ablaze, I lowered my hand and peeked through narrowed lids.

Before me, Sleg hovered a foot off the ground, suspended in the air all on its own. But it was no longer the spear I knew. It had transformed into a radiant galvanic streak of what could only be called lightning, but lightning that was contained in a six-foot span. The white-yellow streams of light comprising it were interwoven with a deep orange, the color of its embedded crystal orb.

My temper and patience were by this point in the day critically shortened. I was tired, hungry, sore, annoyed, and vexed about my future and all the unknowns it contained. I didn't want to be quarreling with a fae spear about getting a bit dirty, and was more frustrated with it than I might have been because I was filthy myself. The clothes I wore beneath my glamour were torn and stained with dirt and blood, not even fit for a rag bin at this point. I needed to bathe, have a cup of tea—or something stronger—and take a precious moment or two to think and could see that none of those things was coming soon enough.

After catching my breath at the surprising display, I said, "Fine, your point is made. My shillelagh can't do that. But it also doesn't complain. If you insist on showing off, and clearly don't need me to carry you, you may as well find your own way to my lodgings. It would be ideal if you refrained from murdering anyone on your way there."

Sleg's next words were delivered with an unexpected note of circumspection. "Are you releasing me from your service, my lady?"

I said nothing for several seconds. I hadn't known it was *in* my service, and I didn't know exactly what that meant. I had to be careful how I answered. "Not at this time, no, but I am asking you, politely, to consider how much easier it would be on us both if you would follow my lead and let us get this horse stabled so we can get somewhere safe."

"As you said, I can get there myself, and I shall. You lead, I shall follow."

This wasn't getting me anywhere. The thing was behaving worse than an untrained dog. At least a dog would appreciate you if you showed it kindness; I suspected that would not be the case with this lump of metal. The only thing that would be more prone to drawing unwanted attention than a golden spear was a golden spear that also floated through the air on its own like a will-o'-the-wisp made of lightning.

"I can be very covert if needs be," Sleg continued and then dimmed to a fluttery white-gold translucence before my eyes, like a heat shimmer on a dune.

Tired of fighting the thing, and just plain tired, I gave in. "Fine, do what you can not to be seen." I glanced toward the saddle I'd already concealed behind a dense cluster of creosote bushes, sighing. "I'll come back for that later. Come on."

I threw the saddle blanket back on the mustang and pulled myself atop him. He gave me a sympathetic nicker, and I ran my hands along his neck affectionately. "Thanks, boy. I'm glad to have one companion who isn't a giant ass."

The livery owner, a doughy, gap-toothed Scottish gent, recognized the mustang when I brought it in.

"Where's Carter?" he asked.

"Oh, well, she's been called to"—I cast about for a name of a city that could support a reasonable lie, still dreadful at making up stories on the spot—"Boston. Took this morning's train. She's asked me to bring her horse back to your establishment."

He scratched deep within one of his thick red muttonchops, excavation style. "That may be, but she's only paid up till Friday, now. When will she be back?"

"Friday," I blurted. "And if she's delayed, I'll be back to collect him myself." I patted the horse on the neck to show my earnestness.

The livery owner's eyes narrowed a bit, proving I was still as shoddy a liar as ever. "You know if you don't, it's my right to sell the beast and keep the cash as payment."

I pushed the reins into his hand and began to make my escape. "Of course, of course, as is only right. But I assure you! Either Miss Carter or I will return by Friday. Don't worry, sir, you'll not be taken advantage of." My back hit the livery door and I scooted out into the rapidly darkening twilight without letting him say another word.

With a deep breath to clear my head, I turned up the street and paced toward the alley I'd told Sleg to hide in until I got back. The street had its share of drinking establishments, and music and loud voices filled the air. It was barely seven in the evening, but frivolity knew no timetable.

I turned into the alley alongside the livery, aware of the darkness the way one is aware of cold rain on exposed skin. The odor of horse manure permeated the air, and a wheelbarrow and pitchfork leaned against the building midway along one side. I gazed into the dimness but could not see my family heirloom.

"Sleg," I whispered. "Spear, where are you?" I took a few steps into the dark alley. "Hello? Where did you go?"

Something behind me hooked my attention and I spun around, afraid of who or what might be sneaking up on me. Not Quetzalcoatl, surely? He was trapped in a green crystalline Purgatory.

In my sudden apprehension, the shadow I made out at the mouth of the alley looked like a low-set demon. But when it spoke, I nearly withered in relief.

"Lula-lee? 'Tis only me."

"Uncle, don't sneak up on me like that!" I rushed toward him and knelt to wrap my arms around his doggy shoulders. "How did you find me?"

He licked my cheek, again evoking the sensation of hot sandpaper against my tender skin. "I know you preferred some personal time, but I was worried, so I've been following you. I'm still your uncle, and I can't help looking after you, my dear."

I wasn't mad, even if I held my scowl for a moment to pretend so.

"I'm glad you're here, honestly. I was feeling a little, I don't know, on edge."

"Aye. Don't feel bad about that. Fighting monsters all day tends to make one so."

"You're probably right. But now, where did that thing go?" I turned and scanned the darkness, still looking for the troublesome weapon, describing it to Paddy as I searched. "The spear has a couple of remarkable capacities. One being the ability to move on its own. Another being that it's fastidious enough that I'm starting to wonder if it refused to hide in this alley because of the horse dung."

As I spoke, I stepped down the alley farther, peering into the dark. Hopefully, Uncle Paddy had better night vision than me.

"Oi."

The voice came from the mouth of the alley. Paddy and I both turned quickly and faced the speaker to discover that *he* was actually *three*. There was something off about them that I couldn't make out in the gloom, but it was their fae glow that held my attention. They all appeared human, or at least wore human glamours. Two were as squat and round as beer barrels, and the third was taller and unnaturally thin, gaunt even. There was enough light coming from gaslamps along the street for me to see that much.

"Yes?" I said cautiously. Paddy was alert beside me, ready for anything. I took comfort in knowing he was there.

"You the half-blood?" one of the squatter ones said, the same who'd called out initially. "The one what rubs elbows with that t'ievin' hobgoblin?"

"Wha—?" I looked at Paddy. How could they know who I was? I looked nothing like myself. "Why would you think that?" I equivocated.

The thin one spoke in a nasally voice just edging into a feminine vocal range. "Know many other fae wandering around Denver with a dragon hiding in a dog's coat, do you?" She took a step toward me, and the streetlamp flashed off her eyes. They were the color of a lizard's, brilliant yellow flecked with green. These were not the kind of eyes you'd find in a normal human, and I wondered who she was trying to fool with a glamour that failed to cover such an unlikely feature.

Paddy growled protectively, and the sound sent a shiver up even my spine. *I have nothing to fear,* I told myself. *Not with my uncle with me.*

"Now now, Dorkus, no need to menace the mädchen."

I knew that voice. Trolls are distinct in every way.

To confirm my suspicions, a bulky figure stepped into the alleyway. Taller than me by two feet, hunchbacked as Quasimodo, and wide as a barn—Motherlode Mankiller.

"Madam Mankiller, how unexpected to see you here," I said, trying to keep my voice steady. I thanked fate that she was at least in human guise, sparing us from the sight of her pocked flesh and wicked tusks. "Have you been looking for me?"

"Not you, but you vill do. That verdammt hob, Toxicore Darkheart, is who I seek. He is sehr *sehr* much in my debt now that he has taken vat vas not his to take. Und I prefer to have this debt paid in blood. You vill take this message to him for me, ja? He has till tomorrow to return mein schneekügel to me, along vis his apologies and one hand, and I vill decide to call it even."

She loomed, there's no other way to describe it. She didn't step closer or change her posture in any way, but suddenly the darkness limning her deepened and grew, like a sponge soaking up black water, making me feel as small as a mouse before a lion. "If he does not, mein freunden vill find him and I vill take more than a hand. You understand, mädchen?"

Now seemed like an inopportune time to tell her the snow globe had been destroyed. "Perhaps I can offer terms that many would find more reasonable. Toxicore may have taken the globe"—no use in denying it—"but he is very sorry, I assure you." He was definitely not. "He should pay for his mistake, but losing an entire hand just seems a bit more severe than necessary."

"You think to question vat I deem necessary? You, a tiny half-blood vis no more pixie dust to sell, hmm? If mein schneekügel is gone, what vill Darkheart offer to repay me for vat he has stolen? You know better than me vat its value is?"

"No, madam, not at all. I'm simply saying that I understand you're upset, and rightly so. It's just that a hand, you know, it's extreme."

"Now, yer backtalkin' Mankiller, half-blood, and we're not goin' to stand fer it." This was the other short figure. His voice, like his shape, nearly indistinguishable from his twin in the shadows. "You keep it up and I'll paint yer knickers yellow."

"You'll what? I'm sorry, I don't—"

"Don't go actin' like you don't know when ye're bein' threatened!"

"That was a threat?" I whispered to Paddy. "It sounded like a poorly worded offer by a witless clothier."

"I think the witless part is accurate," he responded via mental conveyance.

"Be silent, Knob," Motherlode commanded. "One day, that is all the time I vill allow Darkheart. Should he take longer to return vat is mein, I vill…"

Motherlode's eyes sparked in the lamplight as they shifted to something over my shoulder. I glanced back and was instantly relieved. Floating stealthily toward me was the missing spear, returned to its former solid-gold self. I heard Motherlode suck in a breath in surprise.

"Is it…" she began but faded out before completing her question.

I reached out to grasp the hovering spear, as if having an archaic weapon of war levitating at one's side was normal. That little shock that went through my palm and up my arm every time I took hold of it zipped into me.

"Is there some killing that needs to be done, my lady?" Sleg asked with so much hope that I almost felt bad for having to disappoint it.

Motherlode stared on, her mouth agape. I didn't like the gleam in her eye, one of either fear or greed, it was hard to tell. Neither boded well. A frightened troll was something I didn't need experience to tell me would be unpredictable. And greed has a long and storied history of making dangerous people out of those it affects.

"No, I don't think so," I told Sleg. "Not yet at least."

"Not *yet*? Then there is hope!"

"Vat vould you take for that weapon, mädchen?" Motherlode inquired.

"This? Oh, sorry, it isn't for sale. Family heirloom. Sentimental value, you know."

"For it, I vill forgive Darkheart's theft, ja? No hard feelings, as they say."

She drove a tempting bargain, but there was nothing in this world that could persuade me to part with the spear willingly. I didn't want to tell her that, though, to avoid introducing her to the temptation to find something to change my mind. "Toxicore will make amends, Madam Mankiller. But unfortunately, this spear can't be part of them." I kept my voice firm, hoping to quell any further mention of it.

"Family heirloom, hmm? Fine. You vill tell Darkheart vat's expected of him, ja? I vill see him tomorrow then."

With that, she spun about and paced into the evening's gloom, trailed by her three hobgoblin—I suspected—companions. I'd learned a valuable lesson tonight. As far as hobs went, Toxicore was not the worst I could be companions with. And here I'd thought I had already found the bottom of that barrel.

3

The encounter, though unexpected, did not leave me much shaken. By the time I made it back to Madam Sídhe's boarding house, I'd come up with no solution for Toxicore, but greater subjects occupied my thoughts more. The rest of the group who'd been to Havóq's church were seated for dinner, awaiting me.

The women who'd been left behind out of the fight were eager and relieved listeners to the tale of the encounter with the lich. Leannan sent the iron box containing the phylactery to be stored in her chambers, and we all sat at the formal dining table and discussed the event while eating.

When it came to containing the Serpent, Leannan made one thing indubitably clear: we had a problem.

The Sídhe had placed her keys on the table and absentmindedly ran her fingertips along their metal bodies as she spoke. "The snake god will not be held by the wards of my pishogue box for long. In due time, he'll interpret the runes and subvert them, and then everyone within his sphere of influence will be subject to his will. We've seen what a mere man with access to the phylactery can accomplish. Though we don't know what the Serpent's plans for it are, given his past actions we can only assume the worst."

"Might I propose," said the silver-haired Fiona, the most elfin of the coven, "we leave the gem in the hands of our Danannín. She should be capable of withstanding the Serpent's will—long enough to get him far from us, at least."

Across from me, I saw Orville wince at the idea, but I didn't need him to object. "No!" I blurted. "I mean, I am not sure I'm the right woman for such an important responsibility."

Tox, who sat beside me and whom I had not yet had a moment to speak to about his awaited fate, nodded and gave his opinion. "Till today, she didn't even know she could break a wee paralysis spell with her own power. Not the sharpest godling what e'er lived."

"Thank you for your support," I said flatly.

"Don't have to t'ank me for sayin' the obvious."

Leannan gave me a long look. "I agree, Lula is like the first bud of a new rosebush. Delicate and easily harmed, even though she is capable of greatness." I delighted in what I thought was a compliment, until she finished her statement. "She has yet to blossom, and the Serpent would have little trouble corrupting her."

Wanting to be credited with a bit more competence, I suggested, "Perhaps I know somewhere it would be safe. My mother's realm. It's well-hidden and even better defended." *That should do it,* I thought.

"Do you really want a dragon with the strength of a god, who breathes fires that would make the hanged god's nemesis Lucifer cower in his very own lake of fire, coming under the sway of the Serpent?" Leannan asked in her calmly disgusted way.

"… I see your point."

"Your mother is not of the Tuatha Dé Danann, daughter of Lugh. She's not even fae. You may as well give the phylactery to an angry child."

"I said, I get it," I grumbled and took an aggressive sip of my tea, holding Leannan's critical eyes with my narrowed ones.

"Good. It was your missteps that brought us to this point, so I do hope for some productive ideas from you eventually."

I became aware of the silence that had fallen over the rest of the room, all eyes pinging back and forth between the greater fae witch and I. The pigheaded, temperamental woman in me had several retorts bubbling at the back of my tongue. In particular, *Madam, you are aware that you're speaking to a demigod, aren't you?* The only thing stopping me was the warning Orville had given me. A god who didn't know their strength could use it poorly.

The thought evaporated when Hattie spoke up. "This pretty rock being so valuable leads me to think it might be worth somethin' to the one person we need somethin' from."

For a split second, I wondered if she was speaking of Motherlode—except she hadn't heard about my exchange with the troll yet.

"The Morrígan, I mean. Could we exchange it for Lula's pa?" She looked at me with raised eyebrows.

"Absolutely not!" said Leannan at the same moment Orville blurted, "Don't even speak of it!"

"Miss Dumas," the Sídhe continued in a softer tone, a tone, I had noted on several occasions, she only used with Hattie and Orville. Was I jealous, you might ask. I prefer not to say. "You see, if Lady Morrígan were to use the phylactery to pass through the gateways to this plane, she would be even more of a threat. Not just to Lula, but to all humans."

"Not if we capture her and use those last two mesmerism charms you collected from Havóq's dead bounty hunters to do away with her like we did him," Hattie urged.

This brought a hush to the room. Among the dead in the church-yard had been two more unidentified humans. Not ones who'd recently been pulled from their graves by Quetzalcoatl, but ruffians of the likes of Pygmy Bell and Sophia Carter. They'd presumably been part of Havóq's cabal of hired guns, as they'd worn charms like the monks and other bounty hunters had. The witches took them, and they were now kept with the phylactery.

Mathilda was the first to speak. "But we'd need five charms. The spell only works with five."

"You're the witches, and you're the ones with that old book on the craft. I'm sure you can figure something out," Hattie said. At this point, we'd shared each other's company long enough that I could hear her barely concealed impatience and... was she being smug? I had to hide a grin behind my teacup.

Leannan gave Hattie a scowl that could freeze water. I couldn't put a finger on what had made her angry, though.

"Lady Leannan, Miss Dumas, if I may," Fiona said placatingly. She looked to Hattie with a serenity I found nearly beatific. "Your idea has a great many merits. And all here understand why you would want to rid Lula of one of her greatest enemies. But we fae do take some exception to the idea of murdering members of our own kind. Enemy or not, the Tuatha Dé Danann are the greatest of the fae, and inviolable."

"They tell you this when they're tryin' to kill *you*, do they?" Hattie said.

I reached out and put my hand on hers, squeezing ever so slightly. Hattie was playing with a spark here that could easily become a bonfire.

To my surprise and admiration, Fiona's serenity was unmarred. "We cannot expect you to understand, not being our kind."

"No, I guess I don't." Hattie frowned, frustrated, but she settled.

I cleared my throat. "Leannan, if you don't mind me asking, how long do you think we have until Quetzalcoatl breaks the wards?"

"Weeks, maybe. Or days. His spirit is unfamiliar to me. I cannot judge how adept in Tuatha magic he might be. He has shown he is cunning, but cunning isn't wisdom."

"This phylactery," chimed in Sleg, who leaned against the wall next to the dining room doorway, "it reminds me of the divinity orb I carry."

"The what?" I asked aloud, and everyone looked at me. "Sorry," I said, blushing a bit. "Sleg, I mean, the spear is telling me something."

"Well don't sit there and carry on your one-sided conversation," Leannan chided. "Tell us what it's saying."

I couldn't very well refuse and be rude to my host (even if I felt like it). "It said something about the phylactery being like"—I turned around and looked at Sleg, self-conscious about talking to a piece of metal—"a what again?"

"My divinity orb." The gleaming orange sphere mounted inside the quad-bladed speartip glowed for a moment.

I repeated the message before asking, "What exactly is this divinity orb?"

"The divine quintessence of the master, of course."

I echoed Sleg while my brain tried to make sense of it. "Do you mean that this orb is a manifestation of that which makes my father Tuatha Dé Danann?"

"Thusly so."

Leannan rubbed a finger over her plump bottom lip. "It explains much," she commented. "This stripping of Lugh's divine power is what made him weak enough for the Morrígan to cage, and what made him capable of moving through the gateways. As merely a greater fae, he would not be confined to one plane or another."

Her tone was contemplative, but I was troubled by the mere concept. "How could anyone... divide themself in such a way? And why?"

"The why is a simple and ignominious matter," Sleg said. "He fell in love. His lady love was human. So he debased himself in order to join her as husband and wife."

"That isn't a very kind thing to say," I huffed without repeating his words to the others.

"I'm a weapon of war, my lady. I'm not created to be *kind*."

Through thinned lips, I told the others, "He says Bran, or Lugh I guess, separated his divine nature from his fae nature in order to be with my mother."

"Man's love is a man's life a part," Orville said philosophically, quoting Lord Byron. I was pleased, at least, that he stopped there without adding the next line: "'Tis a woman's whole existence." I was sure my mother would have her own thoughts on that, as did I.

"Crafty indeed," Leannan crooned, smiling to herself. She seemed overly impressed with my father's skills, and Orville's jealous glance showed he liked it as little as I did. "But"—she lowered her gaze at me —"that leads to an interesting question. Did Lord Lugh help to conceive you before or after he was so sundered?"

The room focused on me—as if I should know. "I... I haven't the faintest," I stammered.

"She was able to slip through the boardinghouse's wards," Paddy said. "Doesn't that prove it?"

"Hmm, it might. But then, even if Lord Lugh was diminished when he fathered her, enough of his divinity may have been retained to make her strong enough to subvert the wards," Leannan suggested.

"Is there a way to test?" Paddy asked.

"Test her divinity?" she said. "If she had the capability of demonstrating her own power, that could solve it. But since she is still a mere child, and ignorant of herself at that, she doesn't seem as though she can do much. Of course, there are other ways to test, though she might not survive it if she is just a common fae."

"I've lived this long in my ignorance," I said, disgruntled, "I don't see the harm in continuing so for now." Besides, all I had to do was secure my father's release and ask him myself. Or ask my mother the next time I saw her. Thinking about what she'd hidden from me made the spit in my mouth go sour.

"As you like," Leannan said. "Yet something does occur to me. Could we replace the divinity orb in Lugh's spear with the phylactery and therefore use it to better contain the Serpent?"

"I am not a jewelry box," objected Sleg.

"No," I said simply.

Leannan sighed. "Then we are no closer to a solution. But I am tired, the day was trying, and tomorrow may bring us clearer heads." She reached out toward Orville, who rose obediently and took her hand. With a tip of his chin to me, he followed her from the dining room.

It was the cue for the rest of the coven to clear away dishes with my and Hattie's help. Toxicore disappeared in his usual way the moment work began. The shirker.

Table cleared and dishes put away, I asked Hattie to join me in searching for him. We found him in the sitting room, tucking into a bottle of his preferred after-dinner, not to mention noon-to-pre-dinner, tipple.

He laid his one eye on me suspiciously as I sat in the chair across from the settee he occupied. "We need to talk, Tox."

"*We* don't, but I sense you do."

"Yes, well. I've had a visit from Motherlode Mankiller this evening, along with three rather odd companions of hers. You can guess what subject she wanted to discuss."

"The difference between freshly dead and aged corpses?"

"Don't be macabre. She wants her snow globe back. Along with, er, a bit of compensation for its theft."

"Can't imagine the look on the hag's face when you told her 'twas broken into bits." He grinned roguishly and took a long drink of his absinthe, straight from the bottle.

"You could fetch a glass from the kitchen, you know," I scolded. His manners were the bane of my existence.

"I could. But I'm not."

"Shall I spear him through the belly for his rudeness, my lady? Hobs do have the most appealing screams while they're deflating," asked my ever-willing-to-defend-me-from-derision murder stick.

I took a deep, long-suffering breath. "No. And, Sleg, in the future, I assure you that I will tell you when I'd like someone harmed. You really don't need to keep asking."

"But we've been acquainted for hours now, and you've yet to make a single request. You cannot blame me for thinking you need a bit of help making your wishes known."

"Yes, but I don't wish for... anyway, I've let you know my preference. Please do quit asking."

It fell silent, but it was a silence thick with antipathy.

"You sound crazy as me old aunt Knoot, carryin' on talkin' to thin air like that," Tox said. "She used to talk to the fishheads in her stewpot as she was cookin' them. And she always swore they were answerin'."

"The spear does speak to me."

He winked knowingly. "Just like me aunt's fishheads."

"In any case," Hattie cut in, to my bottomless gratitude. "What did you tell Motherlode, Doc?"

I shifted and crossed my legs, trying not to feel bad about the dirt, and other muck, I was getting on the fine velvet-covered Queen Anne chair. "I told her Tox would make it up to her, but I didn't say it was broken. I think Tox should be the one to tell her."

"I smashed it savin' yer life, you might recall," he said. "And speakin' of compensation, it brings to mind the notion o' debts, like the one I'm no longer in regardin' me'n Paddy and bein' yer guardian."

"I wasn't just my life you saved by breaking the globe—" I started, too used to arguing with the gnome, but then I realized what he'd said. "Paid up... ? My goodness, Tox, it's true! In fact, I've lost count of how many times you've come to my aid."

"Aid? I call it *rescue*. And pullin' you back from the veil should've been enough to call me'n Stowe square, but today did give me plenty o' opportunities to see just how incapable o' keepin' yerself out o' trouble you are, Looloo. I very much doubt you could get through a single day without ol' Toxicore." He took another drink of his absinthe and wiped his mouth with the back of his hand. I noticed with embarrassment at my disheveled state that his own outfit looked as fresh as when he'd donned it. Undoubtably, he kept spares in his pocket storage dimension.

"Does that mean," I said cautiously, "you're planning to leave us?"

"I'll be damned, maybe there is a god," Hattie proclaimed.

"Didn't you hear me, lass? I said you couldn't do a t'ing without me. Wouldn't be fair to you if I left you on yer own, now would it?"

My head spun. "Fair to me? What about fair to you?"

"Indeed, Master Darkheart," Paddy put in. He'd taken up residence on the other settee, six cats surrounding him and fawning on him as though he were the king of beasts. "You've made your feelings about the oath that bound you to Lula clear. You've wanted nothing so much as to be quit of her since you met. Why would you change your mind?"

"Please don't change your mind," said Hattie.

"Why? Naw, the question is: Why not? 'Tisn't as though I have elsewhere to be, and there's not much out there more amusin' than watchin' the half-blood fumble with her magic like a toothless rat tryin' to gnaw on hard cheese."

Hattie said flatly, "Mm-hmm. And you got plans to use us to distract Motherlode when she comes for you, don't you?"

Tox didn't answer and crossed his short legs, picking at something on his knee.

I needed a moment to fully consider what this meant. It sounded as if Toxicore was, as the saying went, hitching his wagon to ours. He'd been undeniably essential to me in countless ways since I'd met him, but did that make up for his abrasive, tactless, haranguing personality? I stared at him, and him at me, neither of us saying what both of us were thinking. It wasn't just me who needed him; he needed me, or perhaps us, too. It must have been lonely being so annoying.

"Well, then," I said. "Since we're a… a merry band of magic-makers"—Hattie let out a groan—"we'll figure out what to do about Motherlode together. She said you have until tomorrow to return the globe, an apology, and… well, and a hand, or she'll take action."

"What kind?" said Tox.

"What kind of action? I don't—"

"Naw. What kind o' hand?"

That was his reaction? Not shock and horror at being asked to sacrifice a limb. "She wasn't specific," I responded with a bit of fluster, "but I can't imagine a troll is that creative. She'll probably just shoot you once you tell her you've broken the globe."

"You need to put a little more effort into developin' yer imagination, girly-o. Here, this'll help." He held out his half-empty bottle.

"No. I couldn't. But thank you."

"So 'tis not much o' an issue anyhow," he went on. "We just get on out o' Denver afore the sunrise. She'll be none the wiser and have to somehow just live without her silly knickknack. 'Twasn't even magic, after all."

"Should you really cross someone with so many *real* magical artifacts at her disposal?"

"Eh? I *already* crossed her."

"Yes, but again?"

He shrugged nonchalantly, as if he'd merely eaten the last cookie from someone else's jar.

"If you're set on hangin' on to us like a tick on a pig, Darkheart, Motherlode chasin' you means she's chasin' us," Hattie said. "Why would you think we'd want to get in her crosshairs for you?"

Toxicore's voice was as casual as could be. "'Cause yer ma likes me."

"What have I told you about talkin' about my ma?"

"Arrah now, don't get a case o' the fantods. Miss Gitty and I go way back, you know, and she'n me've been useful to each other on many an occasion. Plus, who else do you know what can get her pixie dust whene'er she runs out? She likes that dust near as much as me and won't be too pleased if she knows you turned yer back on her best purveyor."

I snickered at the image that rose in my mind: Toxicore wearing a shopkeep's apron and standing before a store with a sign over his head that said "Darkheart's Dust – The Finest Dried Monster in Town."

"You think he's funny, huh?" Hattie said, not entirely affronted.

"Funny, at times. But more often, handy in a pinch," I said, growing serious again. "Even you have to admit it, Hattie."

"I don't have to do any such thing." But her tone said she knew it was true.

Inexplicably, Tox disappeared from sight, as was his most tiresome wont. A moment later, he was back. Clutched in his fingers were four pear-shaped dram glasses. He sat them on a side table and poured out four absinthes. After passing one to Hattie and me and setting the fourth in front of Uncle Paddy, he took up his own and said, "To the finest three fae this side o' the gateways and the sharpest shootin' witch in the West." He slammed back his drink and gave a long, satisfied belch.

Before sipping my own, I glanced to Hattie, wondering if she'd take the gesture of peace in the spirit it was meant.

"Shaman," she said.

"What now?" said Tox.

"If you're goin' to lay an appellation on me to do with magic, I prefer shaman."

"Sharpest shootin' shaman, then," the gnome said, and poured himself another belt.

Her lips pulled back in a slight grin, almost as if against her will, and she swallowed her glassful. Paddy somehow managed to lap his portion up from the dainty cup, and, with a relief I was not surprised to feel, I cautiously tasted my own. Absinthe tasted as foul as Toxi-core's manners, but I forced myself to swallow, smiling inwardly. If I'd been able to choose my companions through careful consideration instead of us having come together through danger and duress, I could still have picked none better.

4

I was awakened later that night by the softest of voices whispering in my ear, "Lula... Doctor, might I speak with you?"

I blinked awake and tried to see who'd spoken. The room was dim, but lights from the Row's gaslamps filtered through the window's lace curtains. Sitting up, I saw no one I shouldn't have. Next to me, Hattie lay on her side of our shared bed, facing the window and clutching Judgment, her Colt Peacemaker. On the floor, Uncle Paddy was sprawled on his back, his four paws lifted into the air. One was twitching.

I must have been dreaming, I thought and began to lie back.

"Lula, come out to the hallway. I don't wish to wake the others."

It was Orville's voice, smooth as fresh cream, but I could not see him at all. The door to the room was open, and as I peered that way, it widened just a few inches more as though someone had brushed it as they passed through.

What in the world?

Hattie and Paddy slept on, thus allaying my concerns. Perhaps I was hearing things; or perhaps the druid was playing some magic trick I didn't know. Whatever the case, I was awake now, so may as well assuage my curiosity.

Standing on the smooth pine floor, I reached for my borrowed robe —an elaborate maroon-and-sage-flowered brocade that only reached my knees—and donned it, then padded as quietly as I could into the hallway. At the top of the stairs stood Orville holding a candlestick. He saw me and beckoned me to follow him downstairs.

We reached the kitchen and he closed the door to allow us to speak privately. The clock sitting on the kitchen fireplace's mantel read just after one in the morning. I saw at once that Orville was fully dressed, and a packed rucksack leaned on the wall by the door to the alley.

"What's this about, Orville, and why couldn't I see you in the bedroom?"

"Just a little druid trick. The Shadowed Moon, a darkness spell to hide one in plain sight. The better to let Hattie and your uncle sleep on."

Clever, I thought, then looked to the rucksack once more. The sight of it caused anxiety to find footing among my nerves. "Going somewhere?"

"I am. But before I tell you where, I want to tell you why I woke you. I need you to give me your word that you won't go to Tír Na nÓg to search for your father until I've returned."

What a puzzling request. "And why not?"

"Because that is where I am going."

My anxiety bubbled over. "No, Orville, you can't go anywhere, least of all there. I need your help to find my father. I was going to ask you tomorrow. You know the way to get into and out of the Morrígan's court undetected, and you know where she's keeping him. You mustn't leave now, you simply mustn't." It did not concern me whether he'd want to help me or not. I would bind him with the vines of my shillelagh and drag him to the Otherworld if I had to. And if he tried to leave right now, I would tackle him to the floor and scream until Hattie and my uncle came to help me subdue him, I swore to myself.

"Calm down, Lula. I intend to do just that."

I was so surprised to hear this that I couldn't find the words to reply.

He flashed a coy smile, amused at my speechlessness. "Leannan and I may know a way to expel the Serpent from the phylactery—or we know where to look to find the way. So I must leave now for Tír Na nÓg. And when I get back, I will help you."

I sensed bottomless depths to what he wasn't telling me and wasn't about to let him play me for a fool. "When you get back from Tír Na nÓg, hmm? From where you stole Lugh's spear. Next you're going to tell me you're going to the Morrígan's court specifically, as if she isn't likely to have scouts on the lookout to prevent another such theft. She probably even knows it was you who took it."

"You are cleverer than you know. That is precisely where I'm going."

I slapped a palm to my forehead. "That's madness. I thought you were supposed to be wise! Orville, don't you understand that you are probably the only person in either world who can possibly help me with this?" A sudden thought burst through my roiling agitation. "How about a bargain? What would it take to buy your loyalty? Anything you want could be yours once we free my father. He is the great Lugh, remember. He can grant your deepest wish, whatever it is. I know he'll do it, but you have to take me to him."

"Please, give me a chance to explain everything."

He gestured to one of the chairs at the little kitchen table. I almost refused, too wound up to sit, but gave in. I'd achieve nothing with hysterics.

Taking his cigarettes from his shirt pocket as he sat across from me, he said, "There is a library at the Morrígan's fortress with books in it that contain all the knowledge from the fae realm. Leannan knows of one dedicated to the various techniques to both wield and contain power, going back to before even the Tuatha Dé Danann existed. Though the sorcery used to create phylacteries didn't come from the fae directly, this book will surely list ways to manipulate the inner workings of the one we have or the spirit housed within. Most magic has a common thread. I intend to collect the book Leannan told me about and bring it back here, not only to sort out the Serpent but also to help you reunite with Lugh."

"Reunite with Lugh? That's what I need *you* for."

"Yes, yes. But freeing him is only the start of this quest. I believe it is for everyone's benefit that he be reconciled with his divinity. A god divided upsets the balance of so many things that I shudder at the very thought."

"Why now?" I asked cynically, settling back in my seat.

"Why now, what?"

"Why are you suddenly concerned with this balance? It didn't seem to bother you all this time when you knew the spear was Lugh's."

"I knew that, but I promise you, I did not know what secret that orb it carries contained. But now that I do, so much makes sense that never did before."

"Such as?"

"Such as how the Morrígan managed to capture Lugh to begin with, him being weakened as he now is, and how the key works. You see, it's not as though you insert the spear into some elegantly bizarre keyhole. It's the orb. Reunite Lugh with his divine power, and the Morrígan's deepest, most secure dungeon will be no match for him."

He watched me through the rising smoke of his cigarette as I took this in. "I think I see what you're saying," I averred. "But something doesn't add up. If Lugh forged the spear and imbued it with magic that makes it always return to him, how was it separated from him to begin with?"

"I think I know. You remember it telling you the Morrígan put it to sleep?"

I nodded.

"It's a common enough type of spell, but one she must have adapted specifically for the spear. It couldn't return to Lugh because it was asleep." He took a deep drag, letting the smoke seep from his nose as he continued. "And, Lula, if you take that spear back to her domain, she'll just do it again. Danannín or not, you're no match for her. She is ageless, vicious, and worst of all, patient and wise. She'll have spies everywhere that will tell her the second the spear crosses back into Tír Na nÓg, and you'll get no farther than you can see before her henchmen will track you down."

"You really know how to discourage a girl, you know?"

"But fear not!" he said with dramatic Shakespearean elocution. "Just as all wards can be broken, all spells have counterspells. The book I seek may contain enough information to solve most, if not all, our known problems."

I chewed my lip for a second, ignoring the word *known*, and doing my best to rationally think through what I was about to propose. In the end, my mouth overrode my caution. "I can be ready to come with you by morning. Just give me a bit of time to pack." And awaken the others, who may or may not like what I was about to ask of them.

"Do you think it wise—" he began in a carefully neutral tone but cut himself off.

I followed his eyes to the kitchen doorway and saw why. Sleg had floated into the room, acting for all the world like a curious puppy.

"So we're to return to the master," it crooned. "And the time will soon come for me to have my revenge."

"We are, tomorrow," I confirmed, not as surprised as I could have been at the way Sleg tended to follow me.

"We are what?" said Orville.

"Returning to Tír Na nÓg," I explained.

One of his eyebrows rose in vexation. "Didn't you hear me? If you take the spear back without a way to overcome the Morrígan's spell…"

"Then all I'll have is a heavy, lethal spear instead of a heavy, lethal, *talking* spear. And once you find the book, that problem will be solved."

He smashed out his nub of a cigarette and leaned back, staring at the ceiling as if searching it for a way to quell my insistence. I gave him time, sure that he could not refuse. He'd already said he was going to help me. If that hadn't simply been a manipulative ruse to reduce my objections to him leaving, then there was no argument he could make for not taking me with him.

But, damn the druid, he found one anyway.

"Lula, have you considered the possibility that your father is no longer in the Morrígan's domain? That he may not even be in Tír Na nÓg?" Before I could reject his absurd claim, he went on. "It seems all too likely to me that once she discovered the key to her prized prisoner was lost, she would have found a deeper, darker hole to hide him in. The kind of pit that monsters even a powerful full-fae woman wouldn't want to face would be guarding him day and night. Do you really want to blithely fumble through a land you've never lived in, to the fortress of one of your worst enemies, with no more than hope and determination at your disposal on the off-chance that the Morrígan is only half as clever as she's already proven herself to be and you're twice as lucky as you've been in life thus far? Furthermore, do you want to bring your friends into that scenario, blindly and with no more of a map or a plan than a pig in a slaughterhouse?"

"... Um..."

"No, you do not. That's why you need to practice the two greatest gifts you'll ever have, fae or human, the two your war-loving fae sister definitely has. As I've said, patience and wisdom. Let me go alone, where I don't have to protect a fledgling fae like you, and find out where your father is and how to get both him and that spellbook. Upon my return, I give you my word that we'll get him back."

All but trembling with frustration and distress, I bit my tongue. He was right. I would fling myself from the tallest cliff in the Rockies if I thought it would get me closer to my father, but I could never ask that of Hattie or my uncle. Toxicore... well...

"H-how long will it take?" I half-whispered in defeat, then added defiantly, "And I don't need your protection."

Wisely, he didn't gloat over his victory. "Two weeks at most."

"Two—!"

"Shh, yes. It's a three-day hike to the nearest gateway. That's why there are so few fae here in Denver. Then two or three days to get to the Morrígan's. I'll need to stay low, move with care, keep in the shadows. That will take more time. The best-case scenario is that I'll find Lugh and the spellbook in a day or two. But when sneaking through the Morrígan's domain, best-case is barely more than a wish. I could be there for days before accomplishing my goals. Then there's the journey home."

"I don't like it, Orville. Not a bit."

"Not much to like." We fell silent, then resolutely he stood and began to gather his gear. "Wish me luck, my dear. I will see you soon."

He reached out a hand to shake. I took it, finding his palm smooth and warm in my cold one.

"Good luck." *Please don't make me regret this,* I added internally.

5

Hattie and I rose early the next morning, though I'd never been able to return to sleep. I'd lain awake until dawn, fretting over things I could not control, worrying about the future, and wondering what I was going to do for two weeks to keep myself from going crazy with fear and agitation during the wait for Orville's return.

Characteristically, Hattie grunted a good morning and nothing else before dressing and sitting down in the kitchen to a morning cup of coffee. I joined her glumly, and once the beverage gave her the perk she required, she noticed my state and asked me what was wrong.

I shared Orville's intentions with her. Pouring her second cup from the carafe on the table, she said mildly, "Two weeks should be plenty of time to get back home and take care of a few things at the ranch. Then we can come right back and be ready for Downs when he returns. I'm sure the ladies here'll be glad to have their home to themselves again."

Callie, the young witch from Texas, was cooking herself some eggs and overheard us. "It's been fine as a filly's whiskers to have you gals here, don't think it hasn't. You're welcome to stay as long as you like."

"That's kind of you to say," Hattie said. "I wouldn't blame you for wantin' the goblin out of your hair, though."

"Oh. Him. Well, I think even Mathilda might agree that him and y'all are no trouble," Callie added through an ornery grin. "She ain't workin' on a hex to turn Toxicore into a tadpole, not anymore at least."

"Too bad," Hattie mumbled, sipping her coffee.

As if on cue, Toxicore lurched in, all of his three and half feet looking like something a cat coughed up. His white bursts of hair stood up in thick, disheveled columns, leaving his long ears and the equally white tufts of hair emitting from them exposed. One side of his face was imprinted with deep wrinkles from the fabric of the pillow he'd slept on.

"Good morning, Toxicore," I said.

"It'll be good when we're sixty miles from Motherlode and I've had a good bowl o' conny wobble to fill me belly."

"Conny wobble?" I asked.

"Brandy'n eggs mixed up to drown the dog what bit me."

As my own belly gave a disgusted lurch, Hattie said, "Sounds like you need to lay off the green fairy and stick to sober water more often."

He gave her a shocked look. "Water? What d'you t'ink I am, a fish?"

"'Bout as pretty as one."

"Said like a true—"

"Why don't you take my chair, Tox, and I'll make us all some breakfast," I cut in before it was too late.

He plopped himself down, and Hattie's face settled into a deliberate scowl with her eyes focused on the middle distance. Toxicore slurped the rest of my coffee noisily, almost as if trying to provoke her.

As I sliced potatoes, I asked, "Has anyone seen Paddy?"

"He was still buried under a pile of cats when I came down," said Hattie.

"Hopefully he doesn't miss breakfast. He tends toward grumpy on an empty belly." This was true when he was human. In his dragon form, I'd noticed his grumpiness was the same when he was hungry, but now it manifested in a disturbing reddening of his eyes and a tendency to revert to a feral, skulking beast that seemed more likely to bite your hand than lick it. Paddy claimed to love his transition to dragon, but there was a new side to him that now and then gave me the willies. On top of that, if he wasn't careful about where he drooled, things tended to burn to a crisp upon saturation. Most likely a side effect of the Orb of Celestial Incandescence still residing in his belly... or whatever internal organ a dragon had for that sort of thing.

While I fried up the potatoes along with eggs and sausage, I filled Toxicore in on Orville's trip and Hattie's plan for us to return to Abilene until he returned. I half wondered if he'd still be willing to tag along with us, even though he'd professed his desire to do so the night before. I wouldn't call Tox's personality mercurial—as he was unerringly waspish—but he did have a habit of doing unexpected things. Changing his mind did not seem out of character for him.

Though, for all my doubts in him, warranted or not, his intentions to throw in with my quest remained firm. "There are too many ladies in Abilene what are missin' dear ol' Tex Darling, let me tell you. Couldn't disappoint them, could I?" he said.

At the table, we all began to eat. "That leaves the question of Motherlode," I said. "Do you think there's anything we—that is, you—could do to appease her until you can pay for or replace the property you stole from her?"

Tox used nearly half a shaker of salt on his already-salted sausage. "Appease her? Why would I do that? Do you t'ink she came about all that junk in her cave honestly and fairly?"

I thought back to the vast amount of "junk," though the word didn't feel right, that had filled the troll's storage cave. "She treated us squarely," I said. "I wouldn't have any reason to suspect she'd be different with others."

"Know many trolls, d'you?" he said.

"More than I'd like," I replied with utter sincerity.

"I'll save you the suspense and just tell you that none o' them is any more decent than a pile o' cow pellets 'neath the blazin' sun."

"That's rather unkind."

His response was to shove an entire egg into his mouth.

"Though, I will admit, when she saw my spear, her eyes took on an uncomfortable shine."

"Aye. They do like gold. And anyt'ing they can sell, steal, or trade fer their own advantage."

"Well, that sounds like about half the people I know."

"Do half the people you know also eat corpses?"

"… If you're using that as an example of how trolls may be a more formidable foe than your average miscreant, your point is well taken."

"'Course 'tis. And furthermore, 'tis all I should need to say to make you see that skippin' town now is better'n tryin' to *appease* her. She's not the first troll I've taken liberties with, and she won't be the last."

Hattie and I both hushed and stared at him.

"What? You ne'er took liberties with someone you'd sooner kick than chinwag with?"

Hattie let out a mocking chuckle, which I echoed after a moment. "We know what you meant, Tox," I said. "It's just the phrase you used. 'Taking liberties' means something different to most people."

His nose wrinkled in distaste. "Minds in the gutter, lasses. Like a couple o' hedge creepers, you are."

"I hate to say it," Hattie said. "But he's right. His crudeness seems to be rubbin' off on us. And if you so much as snicker about me sayin' 'rubbin' off,' Darkheart, there's not a spell in the universe that'll stop me from turnin' your hide into a handbag."

In what was clearly the same effort it might take a man to lift a mountain, Toxicore pressed his lips closed tight. To distract himself, he took a drink of his coffee, grimaced, and held it toward me. "'Tis cold," he said, intending this as a request that I warm it for him. Sighing, I obliged.

"I'm not one for runnin' out on my debts," Hattie said. "But this one ain't mine. If he wants to anger an eight-foot-tall cannibal with horns sticking out of her jaw, that's his business. I say we thank Madam Sídhe soon as she's up, pack our gear, and head out to the trail to whistle in Sings the Wind and Star Racer. Mama'll be glad to have me home, and she'll welcome you as well, Doc. Both of you, much as I hate to admit it," she finished, glancing at Toxicore.

"All right, then. I guess that's settled," I said, not altogether at ease with the plan. Motherlode did not strike me as the type of "person" you should cross.

An hour later, we were saying our goodbyes. The coven members wished us well and promised we would be welcome upon our return. Leannan called Hattie aside, and they spent a moment alone in the sitting room. I would have given the first knuckle of my ring finger to be a fly on the wall and listen to what was being said. I refused to admit that I was jealous of the attention the Sídhe gave Hattie, but I couldn't ignore that the greater fae had a certain effect on my friend. Hattie's rough edges smoothed around Leannan, making her not necessarily meek but certainly gentler. Whatever their familiarity was, I hated to be left out. Why exactly that was, I'd yet to examine.

As they emerged, Leannan approached me. Unlike Hattie, I tensed, at least inwardly, whenever the Sídhe and I interacted. She'd not treated me badly, but she hadn't shown me much fondness either.

Though she was only an inch or so shorter than I, it never failed to seem as though I had to look up at her when she spoke. "If we don't meet again, child of Lugh, let me leave you with one final bit of wisdom. Do what you wish with it, as I know you will. Keep that spear safe, and never let it out of your sight. Lugh's magic is known only to him, and none of us can guess what the divinity orb might be capable of. We don't even know if he was its craftsman. It could be wonderful or it could be terrible if it fell in another's hands. We are lucky Havóq was so simpleminded, as zealots tend to be, but there are many who are much cannier and whose ends are much less commonplace."

Calling Havóq's plans to kill all the world's witches and druids *commonplace* had exactly the effect on me she wanted. If that intent was mild, then I could hardly imagine how truly horrific others' ends might be. Fortunately, so far Sleg had shown an unnerving devotion to me and always remained close by my side, even when I hadn't requested it. It would make it a bit easier to heed her warning.

"Thank you, Madam, and again, thank you for the aid and comfort you offered us all. We'd have been far—"

"Safe travels," she cut in, spun around, and drifted in her unearthly way to the sitting room.

Gruffly shouldering my rucksack and taking Sleg in hand, I turned toward the door and followed Hattie out. My last act before leaving was to borrow some money from Tox—who never seemed to run out —and give it to Callie to care for Carter's mustang. He was a fine horse, and I felt the coven would take care if him. Sleg was now wrapped in a silk cloth Fiona had given me, having refused something so common as a modified burlap flour sack. The weapon would still be a target for the curious kind of thief, but at least its golden length was hidden.

Noon found us a mile from the last building on the edge of Denver. The summer sun warmed us through our clothes, and I was glad when Hattie said we'd gone far enough. We had packed light, only bringing a day's worth of food and water. After reuniting with the two pegasi, we'd probably spend one night out on the prairie and get to Abilene late Thursday evening. So much had happened since last we'd been there, but I noticed a certain anticipation sink into me, even an unexpected fondness for the small town, especially Ghitaine's ranch.

We found a shaded cottonwood glade near a stream to sit and wait. Upon using her magic whistle to signal to the pegasi that they were awaited, Hattie dropped her gear and stretched out in the grass. I sat beside her as she pulled out her old pipe and packed it with tobacco. Saving her favored exotic cigarettes for special occasions, I assumed. Paddy fell asleep beside me, and after a minute, I shut my own eyes. The sound of the creek, the rustle of a soft breeze in the dry cottonwood leaves, and the kinks and knots leaving my muscles after yesterday's battle had the most soporific effect. I barely heard Toxicore comment that he was going to have a look around as I drifted off.

Toxicore's yelling—or more accurately, his enraged and highly descriptive cursing—woke me. Startled nearly out of my skin, I leaped to my feet. Paddy stood already, his full dragon form on display, teeth bared and wings half spread to take off at a moment's notice.

Hattie had Judgment drawn and was staring in the same direction my uncle was. The grove of cottonwoods was both old and thick, making it impossible to spot Toxicore, though he didn't sound far. We'd find him without trouble as long as he kept up the racket.

"Feckin' hob bastards! You come any closer and I'll have yer eyes with my teeth! Come on, you dung-colored weasels!"

"What's happened?" I asked Hattie, keeping my voice low. I had a hard time believing Tox could be in serious trouble, given the strength of his voice. How could someone not even four feet tall make so much noise?

"Don't know, but I'll confess I'm not in a hurry to go find out. He's trouble on two feet and probably deserves whatever he's into."

"Hattie..."

"I'll go see. You two sit tight," my uncle said.

"Just get a view from above, Uncle. See if you can tell what he's carrying on about," I suggested.

"I shall endeavor to do so." He leaped upward and spiraled in tight circles toward the sky.

"Come on," I said to Hattie and began creeping toward Tox's yammering. I'd drawn my shillelagh and stayed close to the stream, ready to dip in a toe and summon the water for aid if needed. It didn't occur to me to ready the spear. I would hardly have known how to properly hold it much less throw it if necessary.

We hadn't gone more than ten yards when Paddy returned and landed. Projecting his mental voice so both Hattie and I could hear, he said, "Toxicore is hanging in a tree by one foot from some kind of a wire."

"What?" was all I could think to say.

"Hunter's snare?" asked Hattie.

"I don't believe so." Paddy was emphatic. "Lula, those three figures from the alley last night, you remember them? Motherlode's companions? They have him surrounded."

So, the troll sent someone to keep track of Tox. We should have known better than to think he could make a clean getaway.

"Is Mankiller there?" Hattie asked.

"I haven't spotted her."

At her size, she'd be hard to miss. But even if she wasn't visible now, I'd learned from Orville's clever Shadowed Moon trick that it didn't mean she wasn't here.

"You two, follow my lead," said Hattie. "We'll move up on 'em quiet like. Don't wanna have to start throwing lead plums around if we don't need to."

Careful to follow in Hattie's footsteps with exactitude, I surprised myself with my own ability to prowl in near silence. Shortly, we crouched behind the ample trunk of a fallen tree and were rewarded with a sight I'd not soon forget. Not because it was all that terrible, but because it was rare to see people display such an absurdly high level of incompetence that it bordered on outright farce.

"Ach, that hurts!" shouted one of the short, stout men. Indeed, I quickly recognized their forms, if not their specific features, from last night's encounter. He'd grasped the links of a chain that was wrapped around the trunk of a cottonwood, then promptly dropped it as though it had burned him.

His twin laughed at him cruelly. "That's what happens when you wrap yer fingers around iron, you dumb hob." He proceeded to lean over and grab the chain in much the same fashion, and like the first, sucked in a pained breath and flung it back down. "Hot! Hot!"

"The two o' you still aren't winnin' any medals fer brain size, are you?" Tox jeered.

Now that I was seeing the two figures in daylight, my suspicion that Motherlode's three minions were hobgoblins was confirmed. Toxicore had called them "hob bastards," and that was the only thing that could explain their bizarre appearance—the hob part, not the latter. They appeared vaguely manlike, if they were men who'd been drawn by a half-blind clown. Their shapes were mostly correct, with four limbs, a head, torso, and facial features that matched those found on humans. But their proportions were completely wrong. They were short because their legs were barely longer than my thighs alone, and not much thicker, leaving their longer-than-normal arms to dangle far enough that their knuckles nearly touched the ground. Their eyes were much too big to be humans', making them appear owl-like, but not in the least wise. And their ears and noses resembled Toxicore's in his natural state, the noses bulbous and lumpy, the ears with long, dangling lobes and slightly pointy helixes. One wore a derby that was barely perched on the cone-shaped crest of his head, much too small to fit over it. The other had lost his hat, if he'd ever had one, and his pate was as hairless as a newborn's bottom. Overall, the effect was so weird and befuddling that I couldn't tell if they were in their natural hobgoblin state or were simply very bad at conjuring a glamour that would make them look like men.

"Whose idea was it to use a feckin' iron trap to catch him?" yelled the one who'd just burned himself: Derby.

"Yers, Knob. I told you we should've used rope," said the first: Baldy.

"And how were we goin' to catch a hob with a rope?"

"… First make him drink a sleeping potion?"

"And how were we goin' to get him to drink it?"

"…"

Before Baldy could hurt himself trying to come up with a response, the one called Knob chided, "Motherlode doesn't have time fer yer dumb ideas, and nor do I." Then, inexplicably, he reached for the chain again. Before he could repeat his previous mistake, he was caught short by another voice.

"Leave it be! And shut up, both of you. How did you get the trap set to begin with?"

"Bob wore gloves," said Knob.

"Well, put them back on, you eejits!"

This was the final figure, the tall, gangly one. I'd missed her to begin with, as she was standing in the shade of a nearby tree. She was indeed as thin as she'd looked last night, nearly flat as a board from neck to feet, front and back, but her features were more like a person's should be. The proportions, in any case. Her eyes still shone golden green, bright as a candle flame in the daytime. She wore a Mexican-style poncho over a flax-colored sacklike dress that was frayed at the hem, and her hair was the color of bright summer moss, braided in one long plait down her back the way Hattie often wore hers.

"Motherlode's on her way," she continued. "She'll get him down when she comes. Unless she has other plans..." she added with a sinister edge.

Toxicore was, as Paddy had said, dangling by one foot from a branch ten feet over the ground. He appeared to have a wire around his leg, snared like a rabbit. Though thin, the wire was attached to the much more formidable iron chain, which neither of the shorter hobgoblins was apparently intellectual enough to remember not to touch. The wire itself must have had iron in it too. Otherwise, Tox would have had no trouble escaping with his usual disappear-reappear talent.

He'd been startled out of his glamour, and his face was beet red from hanging upside down. "You tell Motherlode I'll get her a new globe soon as I—"

"Save it, Darkheart," said the tall one. "We'll no sooner let you go than we'll turn into pixies and fly off in the winds."

"Speakin' o' flies, Dorkus, it boggles one's mind wonderin' why you're still with these two dung lovers," Tox goaded.

"Says the hobgoblin currently spinning in the air like a wingless insect."

This one, Dorkus, was brighter than the other two, prompting me to turn to Hattie and whisper, "We'd better intervene before it's too late. If we can free him before Motherlode gets here, she's unlikely to be able to send these three to track us once we've taken off on the pegasi."

"I'd agree with you," she whispered back, "even though I'm enjoying this more than I should. But I think we're too late."

She pointed toward the tall one, who'd turned her back to us and was staring at a point in space that had suddenly taken on a strange luminance, like a blue heat shimmer in midair.

From inside that shimmer emerged first a foot wearing a woman's boot, except its size was ten times greater than any woman's shoe I'd ever seen; then a thick lower leg; and finally Motherlode herself. She wore the same dress she'd had on when I first met her, a burgundy damask set of skirts and matching bodice that looked sized for a rhino.

I had to blink to believe what I was seeing, the way she appeared from thin air. It was obviously a magical portal of some kind. The question that came to mind was whether it was a magic innate to trollkind, this ability to transport from place to place without abiding the laws of physics, or if it was achieved through some occult treasure she had squirrelled away in her troll cave. I thought back to the masses of items in it, and the arcane symbols covering the walls. This was a creature who collected and hoarded magical and all other manner of artifacts the way squirrels hoarded nuts. It wasn't too surprising she'd have something with this kind of power.

"Vell, vell, vell. Toxicore Darkheart," Motherlode intoned as she paced toward him. "If I'd known who you vere ven ve first met, I'd have paid closer attention to you, little toadstool."

Was it wrong of me to feel an unmannerly iota of satisfaction that I wasn't the only one who thought Tox resembled a large fungus? No answer required.

"Motherlode, I don't know how you came to know me so familiarly, but I can tell you this: you don't know who ye're messin' with!"

She laughed at him, revealing teeth as ivory as her tusks and nearly as big. "You are a funny little hob, Darkheart. Do you really think you can intimidate me? I've taken bigger squats than you."

"That must have been the mother o' all loads. But how about this. If you let me out o' this feckin' iron rabbit gallows, I can get yer snow globe back plus a whole heap more pixie dust. You just name the amount."

"You already tried to run off vith mein property and you ask me to let you go now vith nothing but a promise to compensate me. Vat is that saying, again? Oh, yes—do you think I am as dumb as a hob?" Her eyes shifted to the two shorter of her companions, who were presently both attempting to don sets of gloves. One appeared to have two right-hand gloves, and the other two left, and neither seemed to understand the reason they weren't fitting correctly.

"That's not a saying," said Tox, clearly affronted.

"No? Vell, it should be. Now, if your half-blood friend did as I asked, she told you vat I vant. Mein schneekügel, und a hand." She withdrew a positively medieval-looking dagger from a sheath belted around her midsection.

"A hand?! I got hands aplenty in me pocket. Just let me down and I'll get them."

"Did I say 'a' hand? My mistake. I vill have *your* hand." She raised the dagger, now less than a yard between them.

"Oh dear," I whispered. Motherlode was not simply trying to frighten Toxicore. She was really going to slice his hand off right here, before our eyes. I couldn't stomach the thought and sprang to my feet. "Wait!"

All three of the hobgoblins startled, but Motherlode turned toward me languorously, not in the least concerned.

"I vondered ven you vould show yourself, mädchen."

A mere twenty feet of cottonwood grove spread between the three of us and the five of them, but it felt like no more than twenty inches. Next to a dragon, a troll is truly the most intimidating creature I'd yet crossed paths with, and that included the lich, the werewolf, and the cannibal serpent god. It stood to reason Motherlode would have guessed I had accompanied Toxicore, and she was likely to have prepared some kind of magical protection because of it. If I was going to persuade her to let him go, reason, not magic, would have to be my argument.

"Motherlode," I implored, "Toxicore broke your snow globe, but you have to believe me that none of us would be standing here now if he hadn't. It was for a good cause, possibly the greatest, and it saved many lives. It was terribly wrong of him to take it to begin with; I completely agree with you there. But I know he is sorry for his mistake, just as I know that he will be more than willing to make it up to you if you give him the chance."

Hattie had risen as well and now stood beside me, her elbows crooked ninety degrees and pinned to her ribcage on either side, anchoring her brandished six-gun and now her rifle as well. From the corner of my eye, I thought she looked as relaxed as a cat in a sunbeam, but I knew she was as deadly as a rattlesnake about to strike.

"Broke it, you say? Tsk, tsk, half-blood. You should have told me that before. It vould have saved us the trouble of capturing Darkheart. Instead, I vould have just cursed him to melt like a spoonful of butter the next time the sun rose."

"This troll sure is fond of her knickknacks," Hattie whispered.

"Um, yes, well," I blustered. "Be that as it may, Toxicore can fix this. Right, Toxicore?"

"That doodad is layin' on the ground in two hundred pieces," Tox said. "Me fixin' it is about as likely as that spear behind you turnin' into Lugh himself."

"Spear behind…" I spun, realizing what Tox meant.

"Apologies for my late appearance, my lady. You might be surprised to learn just how difficult it is to escape a silken cocoon. I have a new appreciation for butterflies, I must say," said Sleg. It hovered a foot behind me. Any closer and it might have tickled me.

"What are you doing here?" I whispered.

"Seeking to spill blood, of course. Same as you."

"No, not the same. We're just trying to get Toxicore out of this pickle he's gotten himself into."

"By stabbing the four creatures who hold him captive, yes?"

"No! Please, just stay there and be quiet." I turned back to the group before us. The three hobgoblins and troll were all staring keenly at me. "Excuse me, I, uh, didn't mean for everyone to overhear that."

"'Tisn't the everyday fae what speaks to themselves when others are listenin'," said the hob called Knob, who now wore two right-hand gloves, both on his left hand.

"I wasn't talking to my—never mind," I said, realizing this was not the time or place to explain Sleg's unique verbal properties. By the sly look Motherlode was giving me, she understood better than the others.

"I vould still grant forgiveness to this pilz of a hobgoblin in exchange for that weapon. Und I vould even let him keep his hand," Motherlode said magnanimously.

It was the opening to reaching a bargain that I needed. Now I just had to find out what I might exchange for Tox's freedom instead. "The spear isn't up for trade, but Tox wasn't lying. We know where a massive flock of pixies is." The thought of them made me shiver. "We could have another several bagfuls for you in two weeks. Less if you wouldn't mind taking them fresh and do the drying yourself."

"Pah, nein. Pixie dust is no better than dirt compared to this debt."

"How would you like to have the power to raise the dead?" Hattie said, jolting me. "Tox can teach you how it's done."

"Should we make that kind of offer?" I whispered, but I needn't have worried.

"Vy vould I vant to reanimate humans?" Motherlode said. "They are much tastier after they have fermented a bit."

My stomach turned over lazily. "Is there anything you would accept, Motherlode? We are willing to bargain with you, but your, um, tastes are somewhat difficult to predict."

"I have told you vat I vill agree to. If that is not negotiable, then there is no bargain. I shall have my hand, and with it a—"

She'd taken the last step, closing the gap to Tox, who now bucked madly from his wire snare, trying to get away from her. His face had gone an alarming shade of red, and his single green eye resembled a grape about to pop. Hattie stiffened, ready to open fire.

"What about a phylactery?!" I blurted. It wasn't mine to offer, I knew, but the idea went from the tip of my mind to spilling from my mouth before I could stop it.

Motherlode cocked her head at me, her ropey conjoined eyebrows wriggling in a way that suggested it was ruled by its own ignited curiosity. "Vat did you say?"

I glanced at Hattie from the corner of an eye, and she was staring back quizzically. I needed no other hint that I may have said the wrong thing.

"A..." I had to clear my throat. "A phylactery. It's currently occupied, but once it's empty again, would it suffice as compensation for your lost curio?"

"Lula-lee, this may not have been a good idea," Paddy warned, but resignedly. It was already too late to better examine the idea.

Motherlode took a step back and turned toward me fully. She tapped her bouldery chin with the giant dagger, nodding her head. "This is something I can use. But you say it is not available. Vy, then, should I take this bargain?"

"Because it is made in good faith by someone you can trust. You've only known me a few days, but I think I've shown you I can be relied upon."

"It would cost you nothing if I were to kill them all," Sleg suggested.

"Shh!" I whispered.

"But you are friends vith this thieving arsch. That nullifies any trust I might have given you."

I looked frantically between Hattie and my uncle, hoping for any suggestions.

Motherlode, however, relented. In retrospect, I should have seen the manipulation for what it was, but I was too desperate in the moment. "Vould you make a pledge—one sealed vith a sigil—to give me this phylactery if I release Darkheart?"

I looked to Paddy. "Should I agree?"

"If you seal a promise with magic, there is no taking it back. Whatever terms you agree to will enforce themselves," he warned. "Think hard about it before you say yes."

"Can either of you think of another way to get him out of that snare?"

"I can think of a number of reasons not to," said Hattie. "But that's as far as my imagination goes."

The three odd-looking hob-humans watched me curiously. Motherlode was picking her pointed teeth with the tip of her dagger, as nonchalant and unhurried as you could please. The burden was heavy upon my shoulders to save Tox after all the times he'd come to my aid. Whether he'd done it out of the goodness of his heart, whatever form that might take, or simply out of obligation did not change my own sense of obligation to him.

"Yes, I'll swear." My voice needed a bit of coercion to speak up. "What are your terms?" And why was I always getting into these quid pro quos with supernatural beings?

"The phylactery in exchange for the hobgoblin. If you do not get it for me, the spear is mein."

"The spear isn't—"

"No more stalling, half-blood. My portal vill soon close. If you don't like these terms, then it is Darkheart who is mine." She brandished the dagger at Tox's face. "Choose now."

"Fine! Yes, all right. But I need one month."

"That vas not part of the deal."

"I'm making it part of the deal. I have some business to attend to in Abilene first, and I need one month to get you the phylactery. What difference will it make if you have to wait a bit? You didn't even know it existed until now."

She scowled at me, then gave one curt nod. "One month from today will be Lughnasa, the first day of August. I shall vait only that long. Now." She hunkered down into a squat, and it was like watching a mountain slowly crumble in on itself. After brushing away leaf detritus and clearing a patch of earth, she drew a symbol comprising lines and arrows like the ones adorning my shillelagh with the dagger. When she was done, she beckoned to me. "Vell?"

Hesitantly, I approached, unsure what came next. She waved me closer to her until I knelt on the opposite side of the sigil.

Speaking in Old Irish, she closed her eyes while I listened. When she was done with whatever she was saying, her eyes popped open, and she held her hand out, as if to shake mine, then said in English, "You swear by the spear you deemed a family heirloom that you vill meet Motherlode on Lughnasa, 1880, and give her a phylactery, a promise made in exchange for the life of the hobgoblin known as Toxicore Darkheart. The phylactery or the spear, one month from today."

Her massive hand with its thick yellowed nails waited, and I reached out to grab it. "I agree, er, swear."

Instead of shaking it, she angled her dagger toward me. Realizing what she was about to do, I withdrew my hand.

"This vill not vork without a drop of your blood to seal the pact," she warned.

"That's fine. I just prefer to use my own knife." If I'd learned nothing else over the course of the last few weeks, I knew better than to let anyone else near my blood. It was a much-sought-after commodity these days. Even a drop on Mankiller's knife was more than I was willing to risk. "Hattie," I said, turning toward her. "Mind if I use yours?"

She unsheathed the hunting knife she carried and passed it over. I drew a fine cut across my palm, and Mankiller did the same to her own. I'm proud to say I didn't even flinch. The two of us waited until our blood (hers was an alarming shade of yellow that would have opened entirely new avenues in medical science under different circumstances) dripped onto the sigil. The moment it did, the sigil's indentation in the earth bloomed with dozens of bright green clovers. They sprang from the dirt instantly, growing from nothing but magically conjured spores to full size in an eyeblink.

"The promise now has a life of its own," Motherlode said. "Breaking the promise kills it, along vith the one who broke it."

"Wait, I didn't agree to that!" I yelled, leaping to my feet.

She looked genuinely surprised, much to my dismay. "Vat did you think the consequences vould be? A lecture on honesty?"

I looked at Paddy helplessly. The dragon scales around his eyes crinkled in a look of sympathy, but he offered no reassurance.

"Fine then. I have no intention of breaking my promise anyway." I tried to sound brave and unconcerned, but an unintended squeak punctuated my words nonetheless. "Now can you cut him down before he turns into an eggplant?"

Toxicore had gone a deep purple by this point and had all but quit fidgeting in his snare, on the verge of passing out.

Motherlode's dagger slid through the thin wire with no more difficulty than a fillet knife through fish guts, and he thunked to the ground. I jumped to his side, patting him gently on the cheeks until his eye came into focus.

"Are you going to be all right?" I asked.

He sat up and reached into his jacket, withdrawing a bottle of something. After several deep drinks, which had a revivifying effect, he put it back and replaced it with a set of thick cowskin gloves. After donning one, he loosened and then removed the wire snare, his face scrunched into a hostile scowl the whole time.

When it was off, he tossed the wire in the direction of Knob and Bob. "Take yer damn string, you bubble-faced gowls! Next time I see you, 'twill be yer necks 'tis wrapped round. And learn how to cast a proper glamour, for the love o' Brigid's britches! You look like somet'ing me ma would have skewered through the heart with a pitchfork."

The two jumped clear before the wire touched them. "Tough talk from a hob what can't even get back to yer own lands. You'll ne'er catch us on the other side o' the gateways," said the one called Bob.

Toxicore stood, brushed off his clothes, and gruffed, "We aren't on the other side, nitwit."

The two odd hobs exchanged sheepish glances, like children who'd been caught putting tacks on their teacher's chair. Bob opened his mouth to speak, but Dorkus broke in. "Quit while ye're ahead, Bobbelek. Or at least not so far behind that ye're chasing yer own buttocks."

The woman hob was apparently the brains of the trio. I didn't find this surprising.

Motherlode had stepped back to the wavering blue opening in the air. "I vill see you next month, half-blood. Auf Weidersehen." This was said in a girlish trill that was somehow horrifying.

As she passed into nothing, the three hobs chased after her and were gone.

I looked at Hattie. "I hope your mother has something strong to drink waiting for us in Abilene. I'm going to need it."

6

"**B**ob, Knob, and Dorkus, my three least favorite hobs," Toxicore mused from his seat upon Sings the Wind's back behind me. "I'd hoped ne'er to see those twats again after me bein' kicked out o' Tír Na nÓg, but no luck. Bein' cursed 'tisn't fer the faint o' heart, especially thanks to a blighted feathery gallnipper god. But I'm preachin' to the converted, aren't I? You know what bein' cursed is like."

"I'll agree I've had my share of unfortunate run-ins with the Serpent. But I've been lucky enough to avoid a curse thus far."

"What do you mean, you avoided it? Ye're as cursed as me, girly-o, in a different way though, o' course."

I turned my head to get a look at his face. It was arranged in a look of frank surprise. "Are you referring to the magic spell my father cast on my blood? I guess it's a curse, but frankly I don't think he meant it to be. Does the intent of one's spell matter?"

He cleared his throat. "Sure, that, the t'ing what turned yer blood into a lodestone what pointed to Lord Dagda's cauldron. 'Tisn't a surprise you'd t'ink of that as yer curse and the reason ye're in all this trouble to begin with, right? But I couldn't see it, 'cause ye're right, 'twas ne'er meant to be a curse. I'm speakin' o' the other curse, the one what Lord Dagda cast on you. Clear as the nose on me face."

He did have a particularly prominent nose, but that wasn't the part of his statement that held my attention. "You can see curses?"

"All hobs can. The way a fae can see a fae, a hob can see a curse, the bearers o' which we normally avoid. Keeps us from gettin' mired in others' drama. Most especially you mortals and yer many woes." He performed such a beset eye-roll that you'd have thought the drama was all his.

"And yet here you are," I quipped, then added more seriously, "But when we spoke in Deadwood, you only theorized Dagda had cursed me, you didn't say it was certain."

"Longer someone's cursed, the more it shows up," he said simply. "Curses sink in, one might say, and settle, like maggots in the dead."

Rather than maggots—thankfully—a chill settled just beneath my skin that had nothing to do with the cool air blowing against us atop Sings the Wind's back. "I see," I murmured. The question of *why* Dagda would lay a curse on me died on my lips. I knew why, didn't I? He'd spoken this wicked enchantment under his breath when he'd left my hotel room in Deadwood after learning that Uncle Paddy had permanently taken over the body of Dagda's former dragonlet pet. That day, he'd said, "But you've still taken more from me than me from you. I shall make it a fair trade." He'd cursed me out of spite—as if I'd had any say in the matter of whose body belonged to whom.

Now, of course, the question had to be asked: "And what is the curse exactly?"

"Oh, now, that we can't see. Just that the cursed one bears it."

He waxed laconic, a trait he and Hattie shared, though I doubted either would appreciate hearing it pointed out. Reflexively, I nodded but wasn't sure if his demeanor seemed more shifty than usual. Continuing to hold my stare on him from the corner of my eye, I asked, "Is that true, you don't know?"

"I'm not a soothsayer, Looloo... or a cursesayer." He studiously scanned the earth far below us, refusing to meet my eyes.

"If I find out you're not telling me something, Tox, you can... you can expect to drink cold coffee for the rest of your days." The sharpness of my piddly threat was not because of him, though. It was simply because now I had yet another mystery, one that by its very nature portended unpleasantness, with no easy resolution. I didn't *feel* cursed, but how would I know what that felt like to begin with? And how would I learn what the curse was and how to break it? Something told me being the target of a lord of the Tuatha Dé Danann's ire would not be an easy mantle to shirk.

We fell into silence for a while, watching as the flat fields of eastern Colorado spread out below us. Paddy flew alongside the pegasi, his dragon lips pulled back in a rictus of pure delight. His tongue dangled, and for the first time I noticed it was black as coal. The wind occasionally caught it and gave it a slight flap, which only enhanced the vision of pure joy that was his reptilian, yet doggish, face. The day was nearly magically perfect, the breeze at this height mild and relaxing. Paddy's delight made utter sense to me. I could have flown on the back of a pegasus forever, if my life had been less complicated. I wondered how Hattie could bring herself to live a more mundane life running her livery when these amazing creatures were always nearby. The freedom she could enjoy if she wanted to...

"You're a creature of true majesty, Sings the Wind. But you know that, I'm sure," I said as I patted the noble steed on his withers. He nickered and tossed his head proudly, and I settled into the ride once more.

We were somewhere in the middle of the territory by the time Hattie led us to ground near a wide blue river. The sun was setting behind us, the air cooling, and we were all quite hungry.

While Toxicore made a fire, I set about arranging our small camp. Hattie went off to fetch us some rabbits for our dinner, and Paddy did the same for his own. As we ate, all of us settled into our own thoughts. Of course, I pondered the one time I'd slept out on the prairie like this before. No more than three short weeks ago, though it felt like a lifetime. We'd had the captive—Henry Ryan, a werewolf working for Lady Brigid whose past life as a murderous scoundrel was likely as morbid as the life he'd assumed by consenting to be Brigid's lycanthrope lackey. Now that he was dead, his life snuffed out with the very revolver Orville had given me, I was a fugitive in the eyes of the law. I would have to remember to keep my glamour well entrenched while in Abilene.

With these unsettling thoughts weighing on my mind, I double-checked the magical bracelet Tox had made me, which had saved me from the wiles of Brigid last time I'd slept on these plains, and fell into a fitful sleep.

The next day was much the same as the previous one, minus the disturbing clash with the three questionably capable hobgoblins and Motherlode Mankiller. I had decided not to fret one iota about the bargain she and I had struck until I'd reunited with Orville or saved my father. In two weeks, one or both—I hoped both with all my might —was going to occur.

Toxicore and I chatted a bit, and he explained his comment from yesterday regarding wishing to never meet the three hobs again. They were known to him through long association back in Tír Na nÓg, the trio being notorious helpmeets to anyone who was willing to pay them their going rate. I'd seen the two stockier ones bumbling about enough to wonder how they could be in any kind of demand but didn't spare it much thought. Who could say what types of tasks the citizens of the Otherworld would pay for, or what was considered fair payment.

I knew so little about the world that I belonged to, at least in part, and was becoming more and more rattled at the thought. In retrospect, I think deep down I knew I'd go there someday. Even Mrs. Dumas had as much as told me so when she'd "read the bones" for me. But did I belong there or here? This world, the one with natural laws and predictable rules was the world I knew, a world of logical causes and effects and, most comforting of all, reliable physics. But knowing my father's homeland was as distant and seemingly unattainable to me as heaven was to most who called themselves Christians made me feel lost in a way I never had before. In my bones, I felt untethered, a drifter between worlds. Deep questions had begun to bubble out of newly struck cracks that snaked through my certainties about life: Who was I really? What was my true purpose, not only in career choices but in life in general? Would I ever be able to settle down, have my own family, my own dinner table and spouse with whom I exchanged tales of the day with in the evenings? Was that what I still wanted, after all this? Was it what I'd ever wanted? Hattie seemed more than content with her life as a spinster, and I admired that. I could even see that for myself. But so many unknowns now rained on me daily that I no longer even knew how to imagine a future...

By the time the herd of horses that lived on the ranch Hattie's mother owned came into sight below us, I had spun myself into quite a solemn state of dissonance between what I'd left behind and what I might have lying ahead. As we settled in among the herd, I resolved to focus on one thing and only one thing for now. I had to find and free my father, and I would not allow myself to get distracted by my mundane "personal problems," as I chose to categorize them.

After dismounting Sings the Wind and attempting to conceal it as I rubbed my aching backside, I enjoyed the pleasant distraction of the herd of thirty or so beautiful steeds that surrounded us. They exchanged many soft nickers and gentle bumping of noses with the two pegasi, welcoming them home. Hattie was likewise treated to a few playful headbutts, and her smile beamed with affection.

"It's always good to be home," she said to no one in particular, deep satisfaction in her voice.

I caught her eye and shared a smile. But inside I wondered: Did she feel the same dissonance I did? A woman from two worlds nearly as unlike each other as my own? I would ask her when the time was right. I was thinking then and have thought ever since that this shared state of being two parts of a whole was one of the things that drew us to each other.

"C'mon, you three. Jimmy will be hanging out of the barn with a rifle on us till we get close enough he can make us out. Let's not leave him in suspense. Though, I'm sure Mama already knows we're here."

Toxicore lightly tossed something up in one hand and caught it again. "Sure'n she'll be happy for the gift I've brought her."

Hattie and I eyed his palm, which held a leather bag about the size of a crabapple.

"Is that what I think it is, Tox?" I asked.

"Finest and freshest pixie dust there is. Miss Gitty does have a taste for the best."

"I hardly know to whom I'm speaking," I teased. "Toxicore Darkheart? Bearing a gift for someone he doesn't owe it to? Has the world suddenly turned inside out?"

"You keep flappin' that wiggly tongue and you'll ne'er be the getter of me gifts."

"I can only hope I'm so lucky." I winked at him. After deciding whether to sulk or not, he winked back. An odd-looking expression for a "man" with only one eye.

"Is your mum any more fond of dogs than she is of cats, Miss Dumas?" asked Paddy.

"She loves 'em. But I bet you she'll like a dragon even better."

His lips did that stretch again that looked impossibly like a grin. "Splendid."

As we neared the barn, Hattie stopped and waved to the hayloft, whose door was slightly ajar. Dusk was already beginning to settle, and I couldn't see anything but blackness through the crevice, but as soon as Hattie waved, it swung all the way open. Jimmy stepped into view, holding a rifle with the barrel turned down, just as Hattie had predicted.

"Welcome home, Sis! Mama's been cookin' since two o'clock. I hope you're hungry."

7

Jimmy and Hattie shared a hug as he deluged her with questions about all that had become of us since being chased across the prairie three weeks prior, pursued by US Marshals. Hattie had sent a telegram from Deadwood letting her mother and brother know we'd made it there safely so they wouldn't worry. But a brief telegram could hardly be sufficient to express all we'd seen and done in the intervening weeks. Before Hattie could launch into a description, Jimmy stepped over to me and pulled off his hat.

"Dr. Cullen, it's mighty good to see you again."

"The pleasure is all mine, Jimmy," I said, smiling. The red that bloomed in his dark cheeks was as ardent as coal embers.

The two chatted solidly as we approached the family's rambling Second Empire home. Before we got to the back porch, Mrs. Ghitaine Dumas opened the door and stepped out.

She wore an orange and navy-blue tignon and a simple dress of navy-blue to match. Yet for the dress's plainness, the cut was precise enough that it seemed to be part of her, and the cloth was a high-end wool. The woman was Hattie's height and carried herself like a queen. I mentally compared her to Leannan Sídhe for a moment and concluded that there likely wasn't a building or home in the country that could accommodate the two of them at once. Ghitaine's nobility was different from the fae's, but her humanness in no way diminished her.

"Chil', I have been waiting for you to get home. Always runnin' off after trouble, girl," she said as Hattie ascended the steps to the porch.

"I'm home now, Mama," she said, embracing Ghitaine.

"Yes you are." Ghitaine embraced her back, then stiffened and took a backward step. Her nostrils flared as she scowled. "You got the stench of somethin' mighty unusual to you. I saw it in de bones, but I couldn't tell what it was. What exactly have you been up to, Henrietta?"

"I will tell you all about it, Mama. But I smell something that's makin' my mouth water like the Arkansas. Could we discuss it at dinner?"

She gave a quick dip of her chin. "Get inside and wash up."

Hattie crossed the threshold into the house. Toxicore crooned and clucked at Ghitaine, going so far as to kiss her hand, and she ushered him inside with all the flirtatiousness of a school girl toward her crush. I found their relationship as unconventionally weird as the first time, but at least I was prepared for it now. As I climbed the steps, Ghitaine was waiting for me.

I stopped, not quite certain I was prepared for what might come. I'd been the reason for her daughter being in rather a lot of danger of late, and I had seen myself that she had ways of knowing things that went beyond a good guess. "Mrs. Dumas," I said, "thank you for having me at your home once again." Shifting the silk-wrapped spear to my left hand, I held my right out to shake hers in greeting. "I know I was a bit of an inconvenience last time, and I hope to make amends."

Her dark eyes, the same unreadable void as Hattie's, held me in stillness for a beat. "A woman who thinks of fate as trouble is bound to live a life of it," she said cryptically. "You look different, chil'." She sniffed the air. "Smell different too. You met your mère, your mama, I see."

My eyes widened. Indeed, this was beyond a guess.

She looked pointedly at Sleg. "And your père, as well. Now isn't dat a turn of events dat bears a telling. Come in. Soup's on."

"Yes, thank you, Mrs. Dumas. First, I should like to introduce you to… er"—no reason to cloud the truth—"Patrick Stowe, my uncle."

Paddy stepped up onto the porch and sat like a very good boy. He wore his bullmastiff glamour still, for Ghitaine's benefit.

She didn't even blink. "Not your uncle but your guardian, I would say. And not a dog at all. Show yourself, creature."

With a shimmer of air, he appeared in all his scaly, toothy glory.

"Ah, me, what a sight to behold. I think we have met before, but your name was something different den."

"Yes, Madam Dumas. I was previously borrowing the physique of a black cat," said Paddy.

"No." She shook her head. "Dat's not what I mean. You were a petite dragon by another name, part of a thunder of four, yes?"

It was my first shock of the day, but I'd grown used to being shocked by now and it hardly jolted me. "Mrs. Dumas, do you mean you've met Lord Dagda and his four dragonlets?"

She eyed me and gave me a smirk that was so much like Hattie's that they could have been twins. "Come inside, Lula Cullen. Tell me your stories."

She turned and paced through the doorway, leaving Paddy and I to share a curious glance before following her.

Dinner was a lavish affair, and I was happy to find myself eating more than speaking as Hattie described our many exploits. Her family listened with subdued surprise, but Ghitaine had let the cat out of the bag when she'd recognized Paddy as one of Dagda's pets: she was no stranger to the fae realm. The fact that she'd never told any of what she knew to her children was the most surprising of revelations, at least to me.

Sleg had shed its silken wrapper and joined us in the dining room. As Hattie described what we knew about the artifact's magical origins, Ghitaine eyed it appreciatively.

Hattie wrapped up our many exploits just as I pushed away the remains of my delicious dinner and asked, "Mrs. Dumas, what became of the marshals who were after us? Did they come back to harass you at all?"

She took a sip of her tea and said, "Yes, of course. It is der way to try to take advantage of someone dey think of as an old woman. But dey left here believin' dey had it all wrong. My daughter would never get involved wid de likes of a dangerous fugitive."

I was not liking what I was hearing at all—other than the part where it appeared Hattie's name was in the clear. At least that was one less set of her troubles that I was responsible for. "So I'm still as wanted as before," I mumbled.

"Dere is only so much I can influence a white man's mind, chil'. Dey is stubborn and thick as granite. It's hard enough to get through to dem using reason. De magic of my homelands is not so powerful dat it can hammer through stone. Not wid'out de ancestors' and maybe even de gods' help."

"Of course. I'm just relieved Hattie and you and Jimmy won't be any more put out by misinformed lawmen."

"I wouldn't go so far as dat, but not about dis matter at least. You will still have to use caution when you're in town."

I nodded. I'd learned a thing or two about situational awareness over the last weeks, and using my glamour was becoming second nature.

After dinner stewed chicken and tomatoes with a zesty spiciness, hominy grits, corn in cream sauce, and a sour apple pie with more sugar in it than I normally eat in a year—I was full as a tick. I picked up that delightful aphorism from Jimmy, who only managed to stop blushing every time he looked at me after Hattie retrieved a bottle of whiskey and poured us all a hefty serving. Ghitaine declined, though I'd noted, she had two slices of the pie. I couldn't imagine where the lean woman put it all. She and Toxicore disappeared together into another room in the house for a short while. The beautiful, stately woman seemed to have a new glow upon returning, likely the effects of Toxicore's pixie dust. They imbibed in it the way some men took snuff. Faintly curious at the relaxed and magnanimous effect it had on Ghitaine, I almost considered asking to try it myself until its origins flooded back into my mind. If I never see another of those grotesque, many-limbed, beady-eyed monstrosities, I'll nevertheless still feel the urge to retch each time I think of them.

After dinner, I settled on the back porch with Hattie as she smoked her pipe. The earth-scented night air was as calm as could be, and the slightly sweet scent of my half-drunk glass of whiskey and musty, warm odor of Hattie's pipe smoke created a tranquil cocoon of stillness around us.

"Pretty soon, I need to get down to the livery and see what kind of mess Jimmy has made of things," Hattie said kindly. Her brother was two years her junior, though their obvious affection for each other was as strong as if they were twins.

"He's quite the gentleman. I'm surprised he hasn't settled down with someone and started his own homestead."

She chuckled in the back of her throat. "Not a lot of folks like him and I around here, you might have noticed."

"Oh... yes." I fell silent, embarrassed once again by my myopia. Indians living off the reservation and Black people were a rarity in the territory, and the intermixing of either with white people was heavily frowned on. "Has he considered moving back to the Dakotas?" I finally ventured.

She took a deep draw of her pipe and let her next statement ride out of her lungs on the pungent smoke. "We're not gonna be run out of the country for the convenience of anyone. We'll stay right where we are until *we* decide it's time to go."

Trying to lighten the mood, I said, "You're nearly as stubborn as me. Must be why you haven't gotten tired of my company yet."

She looked aside at me and gave me her cheeky half-grin. "You're about the least boring woman I ever met, Doc. That ain't no lie."

I beamed back. "Same to you, Miss Dumas." We smiled into each other's eyes for a moment, then I said, "And fortunately for us, it doesn't seem as if our adventuring-together days will be coming to an end anytime soon." *And if I have my way, they never will,* my mind added out of nowhere. It startled me. Did I really relish this constant upheaval and danger so much? Or was there something else that made me want it to continue…

This line of conversation somehow led to me thinking about yesterday morning.

"Hattie, I hope you don't mind me asking, because it's certainly none of my business, but I'm curious what you and Leannan discussed before we left the boarding house."

She gave a wistful grin that was not directed at me. My mood curdled a tiny bit at that.

"She keeps tryin' to talk me into stayin' with the coven," she said matter-of-factly. "But truth be told, I don't think Madam Leannan likes me just 'cause I have a bit of magic in my blood."

"What do you mean?"

She gave me a keen look, like she was measuring how I might react, before answering. "She may be married to a gent, but that doesn't mean she doesn't have wider interests."

"Wider interests? You mean, oh…" My eyebrows rose when I realized what she was implying.

"Yeah." She nodded. "The romantic kind."

I had to think that over a moment, as it was both such an unusual preference and so infrequently discussed, especially among the urbane and mannered. But the moment passed, and curiously, I found I could dredge up no objections. Being flip, I said, "Well, Miss Dumas, I'm honestly not a bit surprised. A woman like you must have to fight off suitors of all kinds."

Hattie took the bait with a chuckle. "All shapes and sizes, it's true. Long as they ain't shaped like that damn hob, I'm not too fussed by it."

The back door opened behind us and that damn hob came out, bedecked in his glamour and a finely pressed suit. "Miss Gitty is pokin' around with her fancy bones, and I'm not intendin' to waste this dust. I need a horse so I can go and see what kind o' life Abilene has left in it."

We were both accustomed to his particular habit of making

requests sound like demands, and I responded mildly, "We've only been gone three weeks, Tox. I'm sure it hasn't changed that much." Abilene had been rowdy enough on my first visit, what with an unlimited number of saloons, ruffians who tried to steal from defenseless women (or so they thought), and the occasional werewolf to liven things up.

He sniffed. "You been there? After Denver, this wee town is barely more'n a charnel house where the bodies still fire off a few rounds o' lead now'n again."

"That doesn't sound dull to me."

"Nor me," Hattie said. "Hope that dust makes you spry, goblin, 'cause you're not takin' one of my horses."

Jimmy stepped out to join us. "It's all right. I've got to get back to the livery anyway. Toxicore can come with me."

Hattie eyed him, two streams of smoke coming from her nostrils. "You leave the Snelling boy to watch things while you're home?"

Jimmy nodded. "Albert takes good care of the horses, even wants to start learnin' how to tame them."

"He's a fine kid, I always thought. I'll be comin' to town in a couple of days after I see what needs doin' on the ranch," she said.

He nodded again, not apparently bothered by having his older sister checking up on his management of things, then gestured to Tox. Shortly, the two set off under a moonless July sky. I didn't expect to see Toxicore again that night.

"Do you plan to get back to work tomorrow?" I asked.

"With forty acres here to look after, I'll be workin' all right. There's always some things that could use fixin' up here and there. You're welcome to help out. If nothin' else, keepin' up with a ranch and a stable will make two weeks pass like lightning. Downs will be back before your first blister even starts to heal."

"You make being a rancher sound appealing," I joked.

"Probably not as hard as bein' a surgeon, but at least you get outside some and don't get covered in sick people's muck. Just horses', chickens', and the occasional goat's."

I laughed and stretched my legs out. "It would do me good to do something useful while I'm here. You just point me in the right direction and I'll be roping horses and chewing tobacco in no time."

"Don't get ahead of yourself, city girl," she said, chuckling.

8

We'd arrived on a Thursday, and by five days later, even my blisters had blisters. I ached in muscles I didn't even know I had, and I was pretty sure I'd learned them all during my attendance at the Boston University School of Medicine. My career path had done nothing at all to prepare me for the hardships—and, dare I admit, satisfactions—of living life on a frontier horse ranch. The clean alfalfa-rich air filling my lungs with each breath alone made me wonder how I'd ever managed so long in the odiferous, teeming density of Boston's streets.

We spent the days doing everything conceivable in keeping up a ranch's property, and many not so: mending barbed wire fences; digging new fence post holes; chucking hay bales; patching the house's roof where shingles had gone missing or split; patching the mortar of a short brick wall surrounding Ghitaine's kitchen garden; cleaning horse stalls in the massive barn; checking and mending leather tack; picking fruit from their numerous pear and apple trees; canning the surplus, along with the vegetables from the garden; and sundry small building projects to fix or improve furniture, cabinets, doors, and window frames for the house. I received more of an education in rural domesticity in that short week than I'd had in my previous twenty-seven years combined.

I was so busy that, as Hattie had known, I barely had time to worry about Orville and what luck, or unluck, he might be having in Tír Na nÓg.

But with the two of us, and Jimmy's help part of the time, we soon ran out of pressing tasks. By Wednesday I'd decided to join Hattie on a trip to Abilene, a two-mile ride along a dirt track through midsummer fields of bright yellow goldenrod, blueish-purple bellflower, white and blue larkspur, and other varieties of prairie flowers. The tapestry was alive with color and butterflies, the mellifluous beauty making me wonder if I'd somehow already slipped into the Otherworld.

Jimmy greeted us as we rode our horses into the livery. I was fortunate enough to have found an old friend at the ranch: the appaloosa named Brushy, a mare Hattie had rented to me when I first came to Abilene and was shepherded from town by Toxicore. Hattie rode her favored noble stallion, Paint.

"I can watch the shop for the day, Jimmy," Hattie said as she unsaddled Paint. She looked over her shoulder at me and smirked mischievously. "The doc said she's eager to learn a few things about taking care of horses."

"Did I now?" I asked.

"I don't mind helping out, if you need me," Jimmy said.

"It's all right. Mama gave me a shopping list, and I'm givin' it to you."

After she passed over a crumpled sheet of paper, Jimmy donned his wide-brimmed hat and filled her in on what the various customers' horses were in need of. He stepped into the heat of the day, and the sunlight coming through the barn door illuminated the interior brightly. It was hard to believe a man—who was really so much more than a man—had died on the hard dirt floor not a month ago, right before me, put there by a bullet I had fired. There had been enough stains and straw ground into the barn's floor since then to wipe out any trace of Ryan's demise, but I would always know what had happened.

"Come with me, tenderfoot," Hattie said, pulling me from my reflections as she beckoned toward the tack room.

And thus I was given an introduction to the crafts of a farrier, groomer, and equine veterinarian, turning what I'd thought would be an afternoon of much-needed relaxation into an entirely new kind of labor. I wouldn't have traded it for anything.

When evening rolled in, Jimmy returned with the shopping, and Hattie suggested she and I get some dinner in town before heading back to the ranch. Neither of us was dressed for the upscale restaurant La Belle, where I'd taken all my meals upon first arriving in Abilene, but Hattie knew a smaller, rough-and-tumble establishment that catered to Abilene's working class. Though I had no trouble looking like I belonged at the Bucking Stallion saloon in my male glamour, I had to clip the wings some on my manners to ensure I stayed indistinguishable among the cowtown rabble. I'd learned that passivity and anything beyond the most basic level of politeness toward the hoi polloi tended to rile them, as if my innate gentility were mocking them. Yet the very same manners were expected of me in my natural state. Humans, it turns out, are as strange as some of the fae. I did note, however, that despite Hattie being the same gender as I, she had no such trouble with anyone whether she was polite or not. I believe people were a touch afraid of her. Or in awe.

The establishment was merely a dressed-up saloon that happened to serve a few items of food. Regardless, Paddy remained on the boardwalk outside, ever vigilant. His beyond-typical hearing would alert him if his aid was needed inside, and there wasn't a door in the country, at least not an unwarded one, that could keep him out if he wanted through it. I'd heeded the Sídhe's directions to keep Sleg with me at all times... somewhat. I couldn't very well walk around town carrying the spear, so I'd told it to remain in the livery with Jimmy. It grumbled about being misunderstood and misused, which I took as a backhanded complaint that I'd not allowed it to commit mass murder, but did as told.

Among the twenty or so tables inside the saloon, all but four were used for varying types of games for gamblers: faro and poker, which I recognized; and others called brag, three-card monte, and a dice game named, for no clear reason, chuck a luck. As the sky faded into darkness, Hattie identified each for me, and we basked in the loud but jovial setting, enjoying our surprisingly well-cooked steaks and less palatable beers.

Until I spotted some faces I was not expecting.

"Hattie, over there—don't look!—at the farthest faro table. Do those three, um, individuals look familiar?"

Still wearing her hat, she tilted her head back just enough to see beneath the brim without anyone being able to follow her gaze. She chewed her mouthful contemplatively as she got an eyeful, swallowed, then said, "I reckon they do. What were their names again? Stop, Drop, and Roll? No... Snap, Crackle, and Pop?"

"I think they're called Bob, Knob, and Dorkus. And I am entirely uncertain if I want to know why they are here in Abilene."

It was undoubtably the same three hobgoblins. The one called Knob wore the same beat-up brown derby on his conical cranium, and his twin, Bob, had the same bald head. Dorkus, whose back was to us, wore the same dress she'd had on in Denver, but her hair had shifted from green to a hue that was more dirty blonde, and more unremarkable. I wondered if she'd toned down her eyes to better fit a human's as well. As for the twins, their proportions had evened out some, though they both still had their extremely jug-like ears with dangling, though not as long, earlobes and the bulbous noses of long-time pugilists. I couldn't see their legs, so it wasn't clear if they'd grown any taller.

Hattie went on. "You and I both know it's not for anything on the up-and-up. I'd bet Darkheart's other eye they're here after that spear. You and I both saw how much Mankiller wanted it, and it wouldn't surprise me at all if she's the type of, uh, woman to hedge her bets on you makin' good on your deal."

"I resent that anyone would think they had reason to have such limited trust in me." I lost my appetite and pushed the remainder of my steak away.

"You do hang out with a low-brow, cunnivin' goblin who stole from her."

"… You have a point, just as she did. Still, what do you think we should do?"

Hattie swallowed a drink of her cloudy beer and ran her finger over the rim of the glass upon setting it back on the table. "They can see you're an Otherworlder, even if they don't know you in that get-up. But since they got a good look at me back in Denver, I don't see much reason to try to hide. May as well go find out what they want."

"Yes, we… what?"

She'd forked her last bite into her mouth and stood up before I realized what she meant.

She was already pacing toward the three badly disguised hobgoblins when I whisper-shouted, "Hattie…!" But I was speaking to myself. Reluctantly, I rose and followed.

The three hobs were the only guests at the faro table, and the dealer, a man in a black vest and cravat over a starched white shirt, was grimly dealing out a hand with a look that said he wanted to be elsewhere. Hattie obliged him

"Daly," she said, tapping him on the shoulder. When he glanced up, she gave him an agreeable nod. "I'm thinkin' you could do with a break while I chat with my friends here. Tell Smitty at the bar your next round is on me."

He didn't need to be asked twice. The suit of cards he'd begun laying out were swept back up in a flash, and he rose to his feet, tucking the deck back into his vest pocket. "Obliged."

The three hobgoblins watched carefully as Hattie leaned over from behind the dealer's seat and placed her palms flat on the table. "Hello again, gents and… lady. Now imagine this. I'm sittin' over in the corner eatin' my dinner and looked across the room to find the three of you here, in my town, tryin' your hand at faro. And I couldn't help but wonder just what brought you to Abilene." She looked all three in the face, one by one. "Who wants to go first?"

"Dark Princess Lady, we don't owe you any kind of—" Knob began.

For the shortest slice of a second, Hattie's normal steeliness was fractured in confusion by the title "Dark Princess Lady," but she quickly recovered and cut him off. "Now that's where you're wrong, buddy. Near as I can tell, you don't belong here, and I ain't just talkin' about Abilene. If you're here to mess with my friend the doc, I'm just doin' you a kindness and lettin' you know that you should take yourselves right back where you belong—and I ain't talking about Denver—before I make you. Which I'll do just because, frankly, I don't like your faces."

I knew my friend to be a fan of Shakespeare and quite well read, but she had a habit of letting herself dip into much more "rustic" language when she was angry and had a point to make. The effect usually seemed to be exactly as she wished it to be, but the hobs were a different sort from our usual encounters.

Bob leaped to his feet and faced off against Hattie, nose to... well, he didn't quite come up that far on her. To avoid being vulgar, I'll just say his eyes were level with somewhere between her chin and stomach. It might have been a tense moment had it not been for the comical difference in height and the way Hattie's downward stare at the creature confronting her held nearly as much mirth as it did sincere menace.

"You don't scare us with your threats, Lady of Dubnos. We'll cut yer grass shorter'n worm knees afore you can pencil your gun."

Hattie didn't even try to hide her snort of amusement. "Pencil my gun? You mean draw it? If you weren't already on my last nerve, I'd say that's actually pretty funny."

"What? What's funny?"

Now that I'd had a moment, I could see that the proportions of Bob's glamour had not cleaned up as nicely as he'd apparently tried. His legs were longer, he had crafted that right, but bowed so badly that the effect was to make him no taller than before and even more odd looking. Tox had said these three were notorious everything-for-hires in Tír Na nÓg, and it was becoming obvious that they were not used to being outside the fae realm, still learning what passed for normal among humankind. Their so-called threats alone showed their grasp on how to intimidate humans was as weak as their grasp of what passed for typical physiques.

"You're tellin' me you don't know?" said Hattie. "And no, that ain't a threat. I'm just tellin' you what'll happen if you cross me or the doc. And more than that, I'm tellin' you you're in a town where you're not wanted. Most folks without a fixed address are smart enough to get while the gettin's good, hearin' a thing like that. So are you?"

The other two watched her and Bob, Knob with a penetrating gaze that showed he was listening closely, Dorkus with an expression of such practiced neutrality that it almost seemed as if her face was frozen. Her eyes had been toned down to a much more humanlike dull brown. As for Bob, he was looking from side to side, his brow fixed in a look of deep concentration.

"It's not a hard question," Hattie said. As we waited for his response, I noted that all the nearby tables had grown still and were watching us. Not a few hands had disappeared under tables or dropped to their waists, where six-guns and knives hung.

I cleared my throat. "Hattie, we might want to take this outside."

Before we could, Dorkus spoke up. Her voice was reedy and thin, much like her physique. "She's asking you if you're smart enough to know when you're not welcome, Bob." Looking to Hattie, she finished, "But I think the answer is obvious."

Hattie had far less trouble knowing which way the winds of the conversation were blowing than the thick-headed Bob. "Looks like you're the one I should be talkin' to. Dorkus, right?"

Dorkus pushed back from the table and reached for something at her side. Hattie's Peacemaker was in her fist too fast to detect so much as a tensing of her shoulder. "Careful, Miss," she warned, so calmly that she could have been commenting on the mediocre quality of beer in this establishment.

I looked around the restaurant, keenly aware of the attention we'd drawn. Several people had stood and their weapons were now in hand rather than within reach. Others were leaving through the front door. This quickness to arms, more than the presence of the hobs, increased my nervousness, and I had a moment to wish Toxicore were with us rather than off in some who-knows-what kind of mischief in town. He'd be a much better ambassador among folks of his own ilk.... On second thought, perhaps not.

The gangly hobgoblin slipped her hand into a fold of her dress, not in the least worried about Hattie's this-time very real threat. "I have a note here from Mankiller," Dorkus said. "Now where did I..." She rummaged in her dress pocket for a bit, seeming to my eye to be exaggerating her search. As she sought the note, Bob looked back and forth between Hattie and his twin, seemed confused about what to do next, and sat back down. Hattie acted as if he'd simply ceased to exist, keeping her Peacemaker aimed like it was an extension of her arm.

Dorkus pulled her hand free of her dress, holding nothing more than a clump of what appeared to be lint. "Hmm, I may have misplaced the missive." She shook her hand and let the pocket fluff fall to the floor. As it landed beneath the table, I thought I caught it moving from the corner of my eye. Not in the way dust and lint waft about on an air current, but in an insectile, leggy way, as though purposefully. When I shifted my head for a better look, the clump was gone completely, presumably farther beneath the table and out of sight. *Odd*, I thought. *You're not one for seeing things, usually.* I dismissed it as a figment of my imagination, given the dim and smoky nature of the saloon's interior and the heightened tension of the exchange.

I stepped in. "What does Mankiller want, Miss Dorkus? We have already come to a perfectly reasonable agreement. She surely can't be attempting to change the bargain at this point. There are significant stakes for doing so," I reminded them.

Dorkus's eyes narrowed at me. "Ah, the half-blood. I thought that was you. Cullen, isn't it?"

I shrugged internally at my amateurish disclosure of my identity. I was so very bad at cloak-and-dagger. Then it occurred to me—I could not recall ever telling Mankiller my name, nor had Toxicore. She was clearly a troll of resources and probably had contacts and informants far and wide. But if she knew who I was, chances were better than excellent that she knew I was the target of the queens of the Tuatha Dé Danann. A wave of fear washed over me, leaving me weak-kneed.

Were these three here to abduct me? Had Mankiller made a deal with the Morrígan or Brigid—me for some coveted reward?

Oblivious to my sudden onset of paranoia, Dorkus went on as though I'd concurred. "No, no, you're right. Absolutely correct. Mankiller just wanted to send along a message to remind you of your bargain, but it seems she had no need to. You're so obviously completely trustworthy, yes, yes. We are just here to keep track of the... of you... to ensure all agreements are fulfilled to everyone's satisfaction. Yes?"

"Uh-huh," Hattie said flatly. "You can turn tail and go right on back to Denver now and tell Mankiller she needs to keep her dogs on a leash. The doc's no more of a cheat than your boss, and she and especially me don't appreciate bein' called liars, implied or otherwise. Not from someone who ain't willin' to say it to our faces. *Yes?*" She slapped her hand hard and suddenly against the tabletop, making more than the hobs jump in surprise. "On your way now. Don't let me see your" —she paused, seemingly at a loss for words—"downright weird faces again. I mean, Darkheart is right. You boys need to work on yourselves some."

Bob and Knob began to shimmer in that certain way Toxicore did when he was about to either disappear or shift into his glamoured self, and I had a second to wonder how the rest of the saloon's patrons would react to such a thing, but Dorkus reached out and grabbed them both by a shoulder. Their shimmering halted, only just.

"Come with me, lads," Dorkus seethed. "We know when we're not wanted."

The three started for the door. Hattie remain rooted in her stance, forcing them to walk around us. As the pointy-headed Knob passed me, the crown of his derby barely reaching my eyebrows, he murmured, "T'ink ye're tough now, do you, you plum-sniffin' librarian? We'll see how tough you are soon enough. Yes, we will."

"What did you call me?" My instinct was to be insulted, but the slander he'd used was too confusing to be angry about.

He huffed, not looking back, and the three left.

I turned to Hattie. "Plum-sniffing librarian? I do like plums, and libraries, but..."

"Don't let them get to you, Doc. They're just no-consequence toadies, and I do mean that in the amphibious sense. Let's get back to the ranch. They weren't just here to remind you of your bargain, and I think we'd better get used to bein' cautious again."

"Hattie, they know who I am. Which means, they might—"

"Yeah, I heard them use your real name. What've I told you about worryin'? You're right, they might be here to sell you out, but not if they don't catch you first. We'll be safe at the ranch."

Her certainty soothed my ragged nerves a touch. "Never a dull moment being a friend of mine, is there?"

She snorted. "It beats knockin' sense into rowdy cowhands at least."

9

On the way to the ranch, we pondered how Mankiller could have known we'd come to Abilene. I worried—despite Hattie's admonishments not to—that someone at the coven, or even Orville, had gone turncoat and given away not only my name but also my whereabouts. Then, I remembered making a comment about the town near the end of our encounter with the troll and her minions outside Denver. It didn't explain how she knew who I was, but Havóq had found out thanks to Quetzalcoatl, so it should have come as no surprise that Mankiller, obviously resourceful, had found out too. After some minutes of fruitless agitation, I persuaded myself to take Hattie's advice and quit worrying. I needed to focus on the here and now and keeping my head down. I figured it wouldn't be too hard to avoid the brick-short-of-a-load hobgoblin twins, though Dorkus would need to be afforded a bit more caution.

And if, by some chance, Mankiller wasn't just another bounty hunter, of a sort, working for one or both my enemies, the question remained of why she felt she needed to send spies to keep track of me, given that I'd be under the penalty of our magical bargain if I reneged. No doubt Hattie was right; there was more afoot than simple surveillance.

We made it back to the ranch without mishap. Even Sleg was cooperative, tucked away in its silk wrap. For only the first or second time since we'd been in town, Toxicore had made his way back to the ranch for the evening. He and Ghitaine—I couldn't bring myself to call her Gitty, the name simply didn't carry the weight her regal bearing demanded—had retired to her study, and their lively discussion, whatever it was about, carried throughout the downstairs.

"Those are two of the unlikeliest fellows I've ever seen," I remarked as Hattie and I took off our boots and hats in the foyer.

"Mama is the most tolerant sort you'll ever meet, so long as you don't cross her." Hattie unbuttoned her brown oiled-canvas duster and hung it.

Now that I had a moment to think, a crack in my confidence that I'd been assiduously plugging widened. "Speaking of crossing people, you don't think Orville—"

"Don't even give it a thought, Doc." She turned to face me, her staid countenance always reassuring. "I'm an ace at readin' people, and I'm tellin' you now—Downs may be a lot of things, but he's no double-crosser." She looked thoughtful for a moment, then added, "Not for personal gain anyway."

I sighed. "Yes, I know you're right. But we're down to under a week until he's due to return, and not hearing a word, good or bad, about what he may be doing or what may have happened to him is wearing on me."

"And is there anything you can do about not knowing?"

"Well, nothing I can think of."

She put a hand on my shoulder. "Listen to me, Doc. What he's doin' is tryin' to help you save your pa. That's all you need to think about. Thinkin' about anything else isn't gonna help him, or you, right? You keep your eyes on the goal and don't let doubt make you weak."

"Miss Dumas is right." Paddy, undisguised, loped up the outer steps and nudged open the cracked door. He'd veered away from us during our return home—to watch our tracks, he'd claimed—and now had a slick of what was undoubtably blood lining his jaws.

"Uncle, please tell me that blood is just rabbit or some other prairie creature."

He licked his serpentine lips. "Oh, dear me. I didn't realize I'd been so messy. Not to worry, Lula-lee, just dinner. Of the four-legged variety," he quickly added. He'd been hunting. The dragon may have become a vessel for a man, but the man was a servant of the dragon's nature as well. "As I was saying," he continued, "we don't want to put worry ahead of common sense. But we should begin to prepare for what we're going to do should Orville fail to return or Mankiller's hobgoblin aide-de-camps add to the troubles you're facing."

I glanced between the two of them. "It might be rude of me to say, but you're both quite adept at doing almost nothing to mitigate my fears."

Sleg, which I'd leaned against the wall, levitated swiftly, as though it was about to offer its thoughts.

"Don't say it," I blurted before the weapon could speak. "I know what you're, um, thinking, and that's not what we're going to do."

"Fine," it snarked. "But three fewer hobgoblins in the world could improve the quality of your sleep thrice-fold."

Hattie heaved a world-weary sigh. "All right, then, I agree. We got plans to make."

"Talkin' about that druid, are you?" Toxicore wandered into the hallway connecting the foyer to the study, smoking a pipe with a curious purplish smoke emitting from its, by most pipe standards, truly cavernous bowl. "Sure he's probably been snatched by the Morrígan and is hangin' by his toes o'er a river o' bloodthirsty eels right now. Worryin' isn't goin' to change that, but the druid made his choice to put himself right in the middle o' the last place in the world, either one o' them, he should've been."

Hattie scoffed. "And you said we're adept at stokin' your worries, Doc. What does that make him?"

"A marvel of unease," I mumbled. "Tox, why would you say such a thing?"

He had the nerve to look confused. "Why wouldn't I say it? 'Tis merely the obvious."

"Does Mama know you're smokin' that in here?" Hattie asked.

"Aye. She gave it to me." He waved the carved meerschaum at her by the stem, and I could make out strange, supernatural creatures of a kind I didn't recognize carved in the ivory bowl. "Want to try?"

"I don't want anthing that's been in your mouth near mine," Hattie said.

"Looloo?"

"Thank you, no." Heavens only knew what the concoction was, and I was happy to stay ignorant. The green of his eye had taken quite a shine to it, his pupil as wide as a saucer. I hoped whatever the pipe's effect was, it would not make the gnome erratic... *more* erratic.

"Suit yerselves." He took a deep draw, then blew out a plume of purple smoke nearly as big as he was.

"Let's have a sit down and talk about what comes next," Hattie said, abandoning the imbibing gnome for the kitchen.

I expected Toxicore to wander off, but he followed the three of us. Apparently his statement a few nights ago in Denver had been the truth. He was having more "fun" being my chaperone than was typical. Given the weight of troubles in front and behind me, that was more than enough reason to have grave doubts about Toxicore's sagacity, but who was I to judge another's choices? Live and let the necromancer gnome keep us that way, I told myself.

As the four of us settled around the kitchen table, Hattie filling three glasses with a room-temperature dark ale that I favored, Ghitaine came in. The tignon she wore this evening had a deep maroon-and-black pattern, and her dress too was black. It lent her a somber depth that foreshadowed the discussion we were about to have: what to do should Orville fail to return?

"Dere are important considerations to be had tonight, and you'll need de wisdom of your elders to see you through it," she stated without preamble. "Stowe an' I will do our best to cool your young fires wid de winds of de wise."

Toxicore snickered unbecomingly. "Winds o' the wise. Me gramps had some wise old winds o' his own, he did."

"And dat is why I consider you still a chil', ma chère," she sniped back, wearing a smile so sharp it could have sheared Toxicore off at the neck if he'd stood a bit taller. "You are welcome to go outside an' build dirt castles while de grown-ups talk if you're so inclined."

Hattie leaned in and whispered to me, "See what I mean about crossin' her? I don't have to warn you, but she's not fond of crude humor either."

"And who can blame her," I said, doing my best not to snicker at Tox's comeuppance.

"I'll have you know I was dancin' through the forests o' Hibernia eight hundred years before yer grandmot—"

"Tox!" I cut in. "Perhaps you should be reminded that you are a guest of Mrs. Dumas, and she is very unlikely to let that arrangement continue if you say anything untoward about any members of her family."

As he fought to hold in whatever unseemly retort was bubbling behind his lips, his face wrinkled so badly that he appeared to be shriveling like a raisin. Finally, he blew out a forced breath and mumbled something that sounded very much like, "Then she'd prob-ably not like knowin' some o' the t'ings I've said about her daughter."

"What was dat?"

"Sorry, Miss Gitty," he said. "Sorry, fer bein' a—"

"Twat," Ghitaine said, and Hattie gasped audibly.

Toxicore squinted at the elder Dumas, and Ghitaine held his stare soberly. Yet even I could detect a wrinkle of humor in her face. A moment ago, I wouldn't have been surprised if Ghitaine had asked Hattie to toss Toxicore out on his backside. But in the next second, both she and Toxicore were laughing into each other's faces like friends enjoying a day at the carnival. I'd said it before, their strange affinity for each other was one of life's great mysteries. Perhaps it had something to do with whatever was used to make the unusual purple smoke in Toxicore's pipe.

Hattie's voice held a tinge of exasperation as she said, "If you two don't mind, we need to get down to business."

Once the air had settled, along with the six of us around the table, I jumped directly into the subject. "We are due to return to Denver in a week. If Orville doesn't arrive there as planned, I shall have to go to Tír Na nÓg with my father's spear and find Bran, or Lugh, myself."

Hattie sucked air through her teeth. "Not by yourself, you know that. But have you given any thought about how we're gonna do it?"

She said it like we'd already decided to go and were merely discussing when. "I'll ask Leannan, or possibly Fiona if the Sídhe is obstinate, for directions to the Morrígan's court and any information they may have about my father's circumstances. Between my ability to disguise myself with a glamour and whatever spells or enchantments Toxicore, Uncle Paddy, and the witches can help me gather to aid in any way, I'll simply begin searching for him clandestinely."

"You do make it sound simple, chil'," said Ghitaine.

"Mrs. Dumas," I said respectfully. "I know I'm young and no one would call me a warrior or sage even in jest, but nor am I entirely without my wiles. I will be prepared for the worst, but this is a risk I have to take, with or without Orville. And I have a few... I'll call them *resources* at hand I've not yet tested." I was speaking, of course, of the elixir from Dagda's cauldron that would ensure Toxicore would never again have to summon my spirit back from the dead. I still had no desire to imbibe in it. Yet, if no other option presented itself, I would. But that wasn't my only advantage—Lugh's spear was a weapon that could make its wielder nearly undefeatable at the mere suggestion that it attack one's enemies. I didn't know if I could make Sleg follow my commands, but it had shown more than once that it was ready, willing, and able to shed blood at my request. Even without a request, if it could get away with it.

"You're thinkin' about that sunbeam javelin, aren't you?" Hattie said, reading my mind, which she was getting better and better at the more time we spent together. Another advantage, and by far my most prized.

"Indeed. I know having it will get me in more trouble than otherwise with the Morrígan, but she'd have to catch me first."

"She knows how to disarm it, is the one problem I see. And it's hard to say what good my Sharps and Peacemaker will do in another world. Rules that we take for granted here may not apply there."

Toxicore gave a derisive chuckle but remained silent.

I gathered myself with a deep breath. "Like I said, it's a risk. But I'm not about to live the rest of my days knowing I could have tried to free my father and didn't have the courage."

"That what ye're callin' walkin' into the fortress of the most dangerous livin' Tuatha Dé Danann, what by the way, has her mind set on drip-dryin' you the moment she catches you? 'Tis courage, is it?" said Tox.

I narrowed my eyes at him. "More courageous than running away and doing nothing. What would you call it?"

"Oh, I have me words, but I'm just goin' to keep them to meself."

"For once," Hattie sniped. "Don't you worry, Darkheart, we're not forcin' you to come with us. Doc and I, and Stowe if he's willin', will be fine on our own if you're too yellow."

"Pff." He tossed the now-cooling pipe on the table. "That'll be the way 'tis. If ye're plannin' to do t'ings all arsy-varsy and go where I'm highly suggestin' you don't, you'll be doin' it without the help o' the smartest fae in the room."

Despite Hattie's taunt, I couldn't quite grasp why he'd refuse to come, after all his talk of being bored and the pleasure he took in watching me risk my life. "I hate to ask it, Toxicore, but is Hattie right? Are you actually afraid?"

He looked at me flatly with that sparkling green eye. "I seen you get lucky at the gamblin' table, Looloo, but are you sure ye're playin' with a full deck? Fear's got nothin' to do with it. I *can't* go to Tír Na nÓg. I'm banished, good and proper and utterly. The second I step through a gateway without dispensation by a member of the Tuatha, I'll become just another stone statue for the Lady Brigid's garden. And the Lady Morrígan is probably lookin' fer me now as hard as she's lookin' fer you after I gave her a useless map and then scarpered."

I nearly slapped myself in the forehead for having forgotten such a crucial bit of information. It did nothing for my confidence to realize I was forgetting such important things, or that I'd have one less ally in the foreign world of the fae if it came to it. Uncle Paddy had spent decades, perhaps centuries, there and would be able to lead and advise me to a great degree. But no guide could be as valuable to this endeavor as someone for whom Tír Na nÓg was, or at one time had been, home.

I sighed. "That is—"

"Great news," Hattie said.

"—terribly unfortunate," I finished.

"Spells are only as strong as de one who casts dem," Ghitaine said. "And dey can be uncast by someone stronger."

We all looked to her. "Do you know someone stronger than Lady Brigid?" I asked.

"De one you call Dagda, he owes me a favor."

Our looks were much longer, and much more wide-eyed, this time.

Finally, Hattie said, "But he's in Deadwood. And besides, Mama, do you really want to waste a favor like that on this goblin?"

Ghitaine smiled darkly at Toxicore. "Not for nothing, I won't. But if ma chère Darkheart wants to be freed to return to where he came from, he and I can discuss de price another time."

"No. Really," Hattie said. "We can do this on our own."

"No. You can't," Ghitaine said, her unyielding tone brooking no disagreement.

"But—"

"Chil', I been in dis world and others longer dan you. Did you forget how to listen to your mama?"

Hattie visibly strangled the temper rising up in her. "I know you're tryin' to keep me'n the doc out of trouble, Ma, and I know—now— that you've done and seen a lot more than you ever told me and Jimmy. And I swear it's not just 'cause my feelin's about Darkheart aren't the most charitable, but a thing like a favor from that burly ol' boy we met up in the Dakotas—even I know a thing like that has some value. It's not a poker chip you can just trade in lightly."

"My girl." This time Ghitaine's smile was ageless in her over-whelming affection, no, her love for her daughter. "Dere is nothing in life or death dat's more valuable to me dan knowin' my Veiled Moon is safe. As safe as she'll allow herself to be, anyway."

This was maybe the only thing that could have staunched Hattie's anger, and she sat back in her seat looking not defeated but oddly vulnerable.

Giving her a moment of privacy, I looked to Toxicore, who wore an expression of cautious glee. Not one to let a sweet moment go unspoiled, he blurted, "Let's not fooster about, then. What's the fastest way to get ol' Lord Red Eye to break this curse on me head?"

10

I was dreaming late that night, and I knew it to be a dream because I was lying in my own bed on the second story of my tidy home in Boston, three doors down from my uncle and aunt's bedroom. My old room's mint-green damask drapes in the pattern of blossoming mums were parted just slightly, letting in watery light from the street's gaslamps as the fog from the harbor washed through the quiet city streets.

Home. It was peaceful, more peaceful than I remembered it ever to be, in fact, and that more than anything told me it was a dream.

Something was tickling my ear in the dream, and I brushed at it, feeling the loose lace at my nightgown's sleeve flit over my cheek as I reached up. But instead of the smooth skin of my ear, my fingers happened upon something both fuzzy and wiry, like a little ball of yarn filled with unseen needles.

I yanked my hand away and sat up quickly, blinking myself fully awake. The starlight coming through the curtainless window was disorienting, as was my sudden awakening. The contrast of my old room in my dream and the guest room at Hattie's left me off-balance, confused and still groggy. I had never been prone to night terrors, nor to sudden wakefulness. Perhaps the stress of the past few weeks was starting to get to me.

Still, the memory of that strange sensation at the tips of my fingers caused me to rub my ear, then the other, just to remedy myself of the dream's lingering sense of malevolence. As I lowered my hand back to the coverlet, preparing to try to get back to sleep, I thought I saw a small, round shadow no bigger than an apricot slink off the side of the bed and into the puddle of darkness beneath it.

I froze, peering over the edge of the bed to the floor, then chided myself. A dream, it was just the dream. I was spooking at shadows like a child. How old was I?

Flinging myself determinedly back, I nestled my head in my pillow and tried willing myself back to sleep, but was startled again by an unknown noise, loud and distant, but not distant enough to be merely a mirage. My eyes opened as wide as they could without letting the orbs slip free of their sockets, and I listened with my whole body. I hadn't been dreaming this time. No, this time something was truly wrong.

The thump of feet in the bedroom beside mine, Hattie's, and subsequent scuffling about told me she'd heard it too. Jimmy, who'd left the livery in charge of their hired boy, was moving about farther down the hall as well. Then it came again, the high-pitched whinny of troubled horses. Was there something after the herd?

My door swung open, and Hattie's shaped was limned by the light of the candle she held. "I'm goin' to see what's out there."

"Should I come?" I asked, but my feet had already found the floor and my hand had already slid my shirt from the bedpost.

"Do as you like, but you best come armed if you do. I swear if those damn goblins are out there…"

Her *if* was left unstated, but I knew exactly what she'd do. I stood, about to pull on my shirt, when an itching-stabbing spike of pain shot through my leg, just above my ankle. Falling to a seat on the bed, I leaned down and grasped the area, worried that I'd been bitten by something. Were there snakes in Kansas? Pulling my legs back onto the bed, I quickly lit the lantern on the bedside table, then leaned down and cautiously peered beneath the mattress. I could see nothing on the floor but a few lint balls. It made sense; this room had been used for storage before.

I swung the lantern around the room but found it just as devoid of anything that could have caused my distress. Holding the lantern down by the affected ankle, I saw an angry red welt, which was warm to the touch at the edges. Close inspection revealed two tiny punctures. A spider bite?

As I gingerly placed my feet on the floor, something from beneath the bed scuttled past them, hurtling for the cracked-open window far too fast to have been a puff of lint. I screeched windily and retracted my legs. With the lantern raised, I saw whatever it was scrabble up the wall and outside with all the speed of a fleeing rat. But it wasn't a rat, and with astonished dread, I realized the fluffy dark-gray *thing* was familiar. The hobgoblin Dorkus had pulled something that looked exactly like it from her pocket earlier in the evening at the Bucking Stallion saloon. Not pocket lint after all, but something else, something grotesque and alive, which had just bitten me. I shuddered, realizing my earlier nightmare had been real. It had been crawling over me as I slept.

It was gone now, though. I'd never find it in the darkness. Distressed, I considered what I could do, but the whinnying of the Dumas's horses and the slam of the back door pulled me from my own thoughts. We had more immediate problems right now than a biting spider that may or may not belong to Mankiller's hired hobgoblins. (*Please, let it just have been a spider.*)

Dressing as quickly as possible, I rushed downstairs to the back door. The rifle I'd "collected" from the dead troll outside Deadwood leaned against the doorway, and I swung it up to my shoulder as I stepped out of the dark house. Of course, I'd hung the shillelagh from my belt from a special loop of leather created just for this purpose as well.

Paddy stood on the porch already, awaiting me in dragon form. "Uncle, can you be our eyes in the sky to see what might be out there?" I asked.

"I shall," he said.

Hattie and Jimmy had already slipped into the night. Toxicore, who tended to sleep on the downstairs couch when he was here, was nowhere to be seen. Naturally.

Paddy launched skyward, and I did my best to follow the Dumas's as they moved toward the braying herd west of the house. I caught two silhouettes some distance ahead and rushed after them, but it was like trying to follow shadows through a cave, and in moments I could no longer see anything but the vague outlines of still prairie grass. The barn and stable loomed to my right like a behemoth, but I could see nothing else at all.

Coming to a standstill a few yards past the barn, I contemplated what to do. Give me a surgical gown and brightly lit table, a container of carbolic acid and my instruments, a patient, and possibly some ether, and I'd have known my next steps instinctively. But standing in the dark, holding nothing but a rifle and a handful of extra shells in my gunbelt, I was as lost as a kitten in a wolf's den. I couldn't even bring my elemental water magic to bear on the situation in the dryness of the plains. And, much to my bitter aggravation, I realized trying to follow Hattie and Jimmy might lead to more harm than good. If I fired my rifle into the night, I could just as easily hit them as I could whoever or whatever else was out there. Plus, my bitten ankle itched.

Just as the thought occurred to me that even if I might be an amateur when it came to combat, I had a magical weapon of war that very likely had the power to discern friend from foe, a series of shots rang out from far off in the field, followed by shouts of men. I caught the tiniest flicker of light from the weapons being fired. Closer to me, they came from ground level, and farther out on the plains, they came from higher up, as if someone was shooting from horseback. Without thinking, I launched into a full sprint toward them. Over the thunderous thump of my heart in my ears, another thumping sound pierced my panicked brain—the beat of several horses' hooves against the earth. Through my widened eyes, I saw a gout of golden flame burst out of seemingly nowhere thirty feet up in the sky, spraying forward with only the slightest downward angle. At the edge of the flames, I caught the silhouette of running horses, possibly with riders upon their backs. They were fleeing north at an all-out gallop. I kept running toward where I'd seen the flashes of gunfire on the ground. That had to be Hattie and Jimmy, and they had to be all right. They just had to be.

I nearly tripped over them before I realized I'd found them.

"Hattie!" I gushed, coming to a stop.

She was kneeling next to Jimmy, who sat on the ground holding his left arm with his right. There was only the light of the stars and waxing gibbous moon, but I could clearly see the angular contours of pain on his face.

I dropped to my knees as well. "Jimmy? Have you been hit?"

"Just a scratch," he said through gritted teeth, and I nearly wilted with relief. He might have been wrong about the damage, and who better to judge that than me, but at least he was not so badly hurt that he'd fallen into shock. Not yet, in any case.

"You see to him, Doc." Hattie rose to her feet, her Peacemaker held at the ready. "I'm about to get some payback."

She began pacing forward, and I realized one of the pegasi was ahead. The way he shone like a beacon of white light meant it could only be Star Racer. The chuffing sounds coming from his wide, deep chest could be mistaken for nothing else: the stallion was angry, and the way he kept rearing up and flailing his forelegs while staring at something on the ground indicated that whatever had angered him was still present.

Hattie stopped next to the pegasus and put her free hand on his back. "It's all right, boy. I'll take care of this."

She raised Judgment as if to shoot, and I said quickly to Jimmy, "Stay here. I'll be right back." I rushed over to see whom she was about to get payback from. Was Hattie really prepared to kill one of the hobs? And if it was one of the weird three, why weren't they disappearing the way Toxicore was so adept at?

The answer was mundane. Literally. A regular white man, nothing remarkable about him besides the fact that he was lying face-up on the ground with a solid stream of blood coming from his temple. He was moaning something—*flying… flying in the sky like an angel… a horse angel*—and his eyes were fluttering. The gleam of a six-shooter in the grass came from nearby. He must have lost his grip when he'd been wounded. In his current condition, he was no threat.

"Hattie, don't shoot him. He's harmless."

"Rustlers. Lowest form of life in the country. Next to land thieves."

"Rustler? Do you think he was trying to steal the horses?"

She patted Star Racer once more. "I got this, boy. You did good. Go check on the rest of the herd, make sure no one got nicked in the crossfire."

Star Racer pranced away. At the same moment, Paddy thunked down next to me. He saw the man on the ground and quickly shifted into his dog form. "I believe my display of dragonfire will require more than one of those hooligans to need a new pair of britches."

"That most assuredly gave them the fright of their lives," I agreed. "You didn't hit anyone, did you?"

"I didn't want to risk starting the grass alight or harming one of their horses. 'Twas more of a warning exhibition."

"Good thinking." My attention fell back to the wounded man.

Hattie had knelt next to him. His eyes squinted as he tried to focus on her. She grabbed him by the jaw to make him settle. "Who are you?"

The man just stared at her, so she shook his head. He let out a sharp yelp, followed by a drawn-out groan.

"I ain't gonna ask twice… Wait." She reached into her shirt pocket and pulled out a pack of Lucifer's matches and lit one. Holding it near his face, she peered at him. "Damn, boy, didn't I already shoot you once before for tryin' to steal my herd? I swear, white men are gettin' dumber every year."

"What-what are you gonna do to me?" the man rasped out.

Hattie called over her shoulder. "Swift Bear, you gonna live?"

Jimmy rose and came toward us. His gait was hesitant but steady, indicating he wasn't losing too much blood. "I reckon my arm's broken, but I'll be fine."

She shook out the match and looked back down. "You're a lucky son-of-a-bitch. I've a mind to make sure you don't come back this way again, but I happen to know that Sheriff Dickey has a special little hole in the ground for rustlers that won't treat you much better than the grave I have half a mind to put you in. He doesn't like dirty horse thieves any more'n I do."

With a relieved breath—I had no taste for killing when alternatives were present—I reversed my steps and met Jimmy a few steps away. "Let me take a look, Jimmy. Damn, I wish there was more light."

And like that, Toxicore was beside me, holding up a swirling ball of blue light, one of his little tricks.

"Nice of you to help," I said, choking back the sarcasm as much as I could.

"I need Jimmy in full health," Tox said. "'Tisn't as though I can saddle one o' the horses on me own. Unless I'm all mannified, and I don't like walkin' around in another's skin more'n I have to."

As I gently began feeling Jimmy's lower arm, his sleeve soaked through with blood, I mumbled, "Remind me not to take altruism lessons from a gnome."

"Taught you magic, though, didn't I?" Tox shot back.

"Just bring the light closer." I endeavored to pull Jimmy's sleeve away as he endeavored to hide how much it pained him. To keep his mind off it, I rambled a bit. "Swift Bear? Is that your Native name?"

He nodded, teeth gritted.

"It's rather a beautiful one. How does it feel when I touch here?"

He winced as I touched around the spot a bullet had entered. "Honestly, not so good."

"As I thought. We need to get you back to the house right away, before infection sets in. I don't want to be poking and prodding you out here. You're able to walk all right?"

"Yes'm, Doc."

"Hattie." I turned to face her. "What do you propose to do with that man? By the looks of his head, he's not walking anywhere on his own."

"Suppose I'll have one of the horses drag him to the barn and tie him up for the night. We can take him in to the sheriff's in the mornin'."

"No—don't! I can walk." The rustler rolled to his side and began pushing himself to his feet, but he could achieve little more than a pitiful moan and subsequent collapse to one shoulder, his hand rising to grasp his bleeding head.

He clearly had no capacity for a forced march to the barn, nor even to get to his feet on his own. The temptation to let Hattie tie him to a horse and drag him was there, I'll not deny it, but I cringed at the thought of further injuring him. He might be a criminal, but he wasn't dangerous now. "Can we put him on one of the horses and carry him back instead?" I suggested. "I'll help."

"Doc, you're tough enough, but you and I aren't gonna lift this dead weight."

"I can lend a hand," Jimmy offered.

"No, you'll do no such thing until I've seen to that arm," I said. "Doctor's orders. Tox? Can you help?"

"Put him out o' his misery?"

"No, get him on a horse."

"I'm not a man."

"Yes, I know that. But you're able-bodied and stronger than you look."

"No, Looloo, you don't seem to be catchin' on. The words 'manual labor' got a man in them. Which I'm not."

"You're impossible."

"Draggin' him it is," Hattie said with finality and whistled a sharp note, calling in one of her horses.

As a few of the herd members wandered over, the rustler valiantly dragged himself to his feet. Without doubt he was suffering from a severe concussion, though whether from a bullet graze or possibly a strike by a horse hoof was less certain. Just in time to save himself from toppling head first back to the earth, he managed to grab the mane of the nearest horse and keep his feet. Unfortunately, he doubled over and heaved messily into the grass.

"Christ on a railcar, maybe I shoulda just shot you after all." Hattie grabbed the back of his collar and kept the now-swaying man from going bum over teakettle, then with my help and what bit he could offer, we dragged him none-too-gently atop the horse. Straddling the mare, he leaned over her neck, grasping her mane for dear life.

"You spew on my horse, boy, and you can kiss your chances of havin' this matter resolved by the law goodbye," Hattie warned. "Jimmy, you want us to help you up on one of them too?"

He shook his head. "I can walk."

Clucking her tongue, Hattie started toward the barn, the mare following her lead. I walked beside Jimmy, keeping my hand lightly on his shoulder in case he stumbled.

The day had been long, the night longer, but I was consoled somewhat that the problem with the rustlers was new and not Motherlode's hobgoblins causing more trouble. Their intentions were as murky as their attempts at emulating humans, but at least they weren't attacking us. Unless you counted sending a grotesque spider that looked for all the world as though it were made of matted hair to bite me as an attack. And maybe I was just muzzy-headed from the poor quality of sleep and all the excitement; surely it had just been a *normal* spider.

After the energy it took to see to Jimmy's arm, using all the fae healing powers innate to me, I was too exhausted to worry further about the thing that had bitten me. It hadn't killed me and had scuttled off anyway. So I dropped into sleep for the final time not too long before dawn, counting down the days to Orville's return. A new worry tried instilling itself in my thoughts: if Ghitaine's ranch was being endangered by thieves, would Hattie still want to come with me to meet him in Denver? And would it even be reasonable of me to accept her help if she offered it, especially with her brother wounded and unable to protect the ranch on his own? Leave it to licentious humans to complicate my new fairy-tale life.

11

The rustler was looking the worse for wear in the morning, but he would survive. He lay in a pile of straw, his arms and legs both tightly bound, and his head wound sloppily bandaged. Hattie had seen to him herself, over my objections. I imagined that by this point, the rustler regretted nothing so much as the decisions he'd made in life that had resulted in the last twelve hours of painful discomfort—deserved though they were.

When Hattie and I arrived in the barn, Ghitaine was standing over the man, speaking to him, but I couldn't make out what she was saying. Whatever it was, he didn't like it. Based on the things she held in her hands—a bag of dried bits of plants, which she sprinkled over him, and a rattle of sorts made from a gourd, which she shook at specific points during her sermon—I took it to be a hex or incantation. Ghitaine's magic was unusual to me, but then, so was all magic, though it was becoming less and less so. One thing seemed certain; this man's thieving days had come to an end, even if he didn't go to jail. At least so far as the Dumas ranch was concerned. I figured he could count himself lucky if Ghitaine's chant only resulted in his inability to trouble her again and not any of a myriad of worse things. I had no doubt she was capable of all kinds of worse.

"Don't worry about him, Mama," Hattie said as she began picking up tack to saddle the horses we'd need to get to town. "Sheriff Dickey'll have him out of our hair for good this time. He's the one I shot last year, and the county court convicted him. Don't know how he got out of the hoosegaw, and I sure as hell don't know why he thought it would be wise to come back and mess with us again, but if he gets the same judge for last night's misdeeds, he'll likely be facing the noose this time. Will, if I have my way."

Ghitaine, picture perfect in a yellow and red tignon and a red dress to match, looked unconcerned. "He'll never come back to dis ranch, regardless of what Dickey does."

The cold certainty in her voice confirmed my suspicions. As Ghitaine left the barn, she stopped and addressed me. "You have a bit of a limp, chil'. Did you stumble during last night's excitement?"

"No, ma'am. I was bitten by a... spider, right on the ankle. It's fine though." But it hadn't healed yet, not the way my wounds usually did. For instance, the cut I'd given myself when sealing the agreement with Motherlode was completely gone, only a faint pink scar, right on top of the one Hattie had given me outside Deadwood. I had no others. Even scars from past injuries had always faded to nothing within a few weeks. Something about those created by blood pacts remained, despite my fae qualities.

"It must have been a terrible spider to ache so." She wasn't letting me avoid the topic that easily.

"Just a little bump, I assure you," I said. Despite the bite's lingering acuteness, in the light of day, the strange lintlike visitor of last night seemed less ominous and perhaps nothing more than a frazzled and overactive imagination's embellishment of a more typical spider. Hattie had told me enough times not to worry about things I had no control over, and I believe it had finally begun to sink in. I figured that with the ankle-biter far and gone, I'd let my concerns with it go too.

Her eyes narrowed for a moment. "When you get back from town today, I need to speak wid you about something." Then she continued out the barn door, brushing past Jimmy on the way in, and leaving me with a keen curiosity in her wake.

"Jimmy, what are you doin' here?" Hattie said. "I told you I'd watch the livery today."

Jimmy was dressed, but the buttons on his shirt were mismatched with the buttonholes. I'd bandaged his arm firmly and created a serviceable sling from old bedclothes. Doing up his shirt one-handed must have been as awkward as could be. "It's fine," he said. "You need to go see the sheriff, so I'll ask Albert to stay on and help out at the livery. He'll be happy for the extra pay."

I felt it my duty as a doctor to dissuade him. "I know it doesn't feel like it, Jimmy, but you're very lucky. It looks like you were hit by a Milie ball, and it went all the way through. I do think it may have nicked your ulna, but just barely and the break isn't bad. If it had hit…" I paused, thinking on some of the old soldiers I'd seen in the hospital and the ghastliness of their wartime disfigurements. "Well, suffice it to say, if this had been a direct hit to any bone in your arm, you'd have nothing but splinters left in there. You'd likely lose it completely. This should heal up in a few weeks"—I put a hand on his shoulder and made my voice firm—"as long as you *follow your doctor's orders* and don't use it. You'll follow your doctor's orders, won't you?"

"I promise, Doc, I won't use it till it's good as new. But I'm not gonna sit around here and help Mama can peaches and apples for the next few weeks, either."

"Not that you ever got the hang of it, anyway," Hattie said. She'd come to his side and helped him straighten out his shirt buttons.

"Hattie, don't encourage your brother. He could lose full mobility if he—"

"Don't worry," the two of them said together. Jimmy continued, "I told you I promise, and a promise is a promise. Now let's get this thief outta here before he stinks up our barn."

This stubborn streak ran in the whole family, and though it was exasperating, I wasn't one to complain about it. I was no different.

Hattie and I saddled up two horses for ourselves and were about to saddle a third and fourth when Jimmy said he'd ride with the rustler, the easier to keep an eye on him. I tried to protest, but Jimmy swore that if the thief gave him any trouble or couldn't manage to stay mounted, Jimmy would just let him fall off the horse without trying to catch him and inadvertently use his bad arm.

Feeling oddly nostalgic for my old profession, where so many of my patients refused to listen to their doctor—and learned their lessons the hard way—I gave up. Leaving Toxicore with Ghitaine, we set out for town.

After we left Jimmy and the horses at the livery, we walked the rustler just a few buildings down. It was a testament to how familiar Abilene had become to me that I already knew where the sheriff's office was. At ten in the morning, the town was bustling, but no one so much as glanced toward the stumbling, obviously wounded man. The folks here had seen it all. Or they thought they had.

"Hattie Dumas, how are ya, young lady?" The stocky, practically dressed Sheriff Dickey sat with his legs up on a weathered wooden desk, tipped back in his seat. He was middle-aged and softening in the middle, but that took nothing from his muscular build. The weathering around his eyes and redness of his knuckles told me he'd been a hardworking man before becoming sheriff, possibly one of the cowpunchers who'd once driven herds up from Texas, like so many of the men in town. Through deep crows feet, his warm brown eyes were neither cruel nor placid. I could see why Hattie trusted him.

Inside the low-roofed building were chairs for at least two more deputies, though they didn't have desks of their own. Hattie pushed the rustler toward the nearest, probably just in time to keep him from sprawling out on the room's floor. Dickey straightened in his seat and narrowed his eyes.

"This damn idiot and at least five others were at my ranch last night, Sheriff," said Hattie. "Shot my brother and tried to steal my herd. Yellow-bellies took off when we came for 'em and left him behind. I brought him to you, against my better judgment I'll add."

"How's your brother doing?" His voice had the roughness of someone who'd breathed their share of campfire smoke.

"He'll be all right, bullet went clean through his arm. Me'n the do —my friend here, stitched him back together. But he's not gonna be much use for a spell." Wisely, Hattie kept my profession out of the discussion. I was still wanted for Ryan's murder, and it was widely known I was a surgeon. A simple drifter, or better yet, a cowboy, was easily dismissed and forgotten.

Dickey looked me up and down, and I noticed how he paid close attention. He would remember me, I had no doubt of that, despite Hattie's omission of specific details. Then his eyes landed on the rustler. He rose and pulled a drawer open in his desk, retrieving some handcuffs. "I'm glad Jimmy's not too bad off. This feller doesn't look like much though. Did you shoot him or hit him?"

As he manacled the rustler's hands, receiving not even a voiced complaint in protest, Hattie said, "Neither. I'm pretty sure he got clobbered by one of my horses, and it serves him right. He look familiar to you?"

"Familiar?" He hunkered down and looked closer into his prisoner's eyes. "I'll be, this is the same guy you shot last year, isn't it?"

"The very one. I believe he's called Kern van Cleef. I'm hoping the judge up in Topeka decides to give him the noose this time."

Dickey straightened and rubbed his chin. "He could at that. You said there were five or so others? Did they get any of your stock?"

"No, Sheriff. Not for lack of trying. But Jimmy and I scared 'em off."

Dickey looked down at van Cleef. "Boy, you tell the judge who the others in your gang are, and you might live to see '81. You think about that while you're waitin' for your trial."

The thunk of boots on the boardwalk outside announced the arrival of someone new. We all looked toward the oak door and saw the outline of a tall man through the threadbare curtains on the window before the door opened.

The man who came in was city through and through. His suit was a pressed gray herringbone tweed tailored for his tall frame. I detected no dust on it and little on his more local-looking riding boots. He had to remove his felted-wool tophat to slide through the doorway.

This all registered quickly, and van Cleef's sharp indrawn breath was followed by, "Boss."

The stranger ignored him and spoke to Dickey. "Sheriff Dickey, I presume," he said, holding out a hand.

Dickey took it and shook. "That's me. You know this feller, Mister...?"

"Truman Radamus Knox, Sheriff. And yes I do. I heard from some of my other employees that there was a commotion last night east of town, and Mr. van Cleef here got a bit caught up in it."

"You call stealin' someone's horses a commotion?" Hattie said, her voice icy.

"Stealing horses?" Knox looked confused. "Whose horses are you accusing this man of stealing?"

Hattie scowled. "Mine and my mother's."

Knox pursed his lips, as though he'd smelled something distasteful. "Oh, do you own some horses, Miss? What is your brand, if I might ask?"

"We don't have a brand. Don't need one."

He blinked. "Don't need one? Well, then, if these horses that live east of town aren't branded, how can you possibly claim they're yours? What proof do you have?"

Hattie had grown very still, almost like a statue, but the smoldering blaze in her eyes was making the room twenty degrees hotter. Oddly, though, Knox wasn't sweating, as any sane man who'd become the focus of that red-hot glare should be. I decided I should say something before things got out of hand.

"Mr. Knox, there's no law requiring the owner of a horse to brand it." I didn't know if this was true, but it felt like a useful diversion. He looked like a city man and might not know either. "The herd in question is on Mrs. Ghitaine Dumas's land, which makes them hers. This is Hattie Dumas, Mrs. Dumas's daughter."

Hattie added, "Your man and those other boys weren't just stealin' horses, they were trespassin'."

Knox contemplated this silently for a moment. When he spoke again, his words hit us like bullets. "Well, I don't know how you can make these kinds of accusations or declarations, when in fact, I have a deed right here from the Kansas Land Office that says the forty acres in question belong to me." He pulled a folded paper from his inner jacket pocket. "My men were merely out on *my* land last night taking an inventory of a herd of wild horses reported to be roaming there. Sheriff?" He held the deed out toward Dickey.

Dickey took it wordlessly, a ladder of wrinkles from his deep scowl climbing his forehead to his salt-and-pepper hair. He unfolded it and began to look it over. A moment later, he shot a pensive glance to Hattie, who'd not yet released Knox from her ire-filled stare.

"Hattie, I gotta say, this paper looks legitimate."

She snatched it from his hand too fast for him to protest. "Let me see that."

While she was reading it over, Knox said placidly, "Sheriff, did you know there's a massive dog sitting outside on your stoop? It actually growled at me as I walked in. You may want to see to strays. I find it's better to shoot them than to let them wander and spread their diseases."

"That's my dog," I chimed in. "And he only growls at those who deserve it." Yes, I'll admit, I was feeling spiteful. The arrogance washing off this city boy—and who was I to be calling someone a *city boy?*—was getting under my skin.

"I never caught your name, son?"

This was Dickey speaking, but it took me a moment to realize he was addressing me. "Oh, I'm just an out-of-town friend of the Dumas's," I sputtered.

"Did your mother name you, or do you just go by 'friend'?"

"Apologies, Sheriff. It's, uh, Sargent. Thomas Sargent."

Knox eyed me. "Thomas Sargent? You mean the gentleman who's been missing since June?"

I realized too late how far I'd wedged my boot up my own... you know. "Missing, you say? As you can see, I'm right here, Mr. Knox. Hardly someone who can't be found."

Knox's gaze was skeptical. "Well... Mr. Sargent, you may want to contact your family. I'm on the board of the New Bedford Orphan's Home with your father, who very much believes you are missing. Has word of the reward for information about your whereabouts not reached Abilene?"

Every speck of moisture in my mouth had dried to dust, and, dumbly, all I could manage was: "You know John?" Thomas's father, a dour man who'd been as opposed to his son's marriage to a woman with her own profession as my Aunt Ada was to me having a profession.

"Yes, I'm well acquainted with Mr. Sargent." Knox's skepticism relented a fraction but turned to a new confusion. "You seem a bit pale, Thomas. Do you need to sit down?"

"What? No, I'm fine. I'll... I'll send my father a telegram forthwith."

With a final narrowing of his eyes at me, Knox returned his focus to the sheriff. "So, then, Sheriff, as you can see, my land is apparently being squatted upon by this Dumas family, and I'd like them off it by the end of the week. And anything they can't prove they own should not be taken along with them. Can I rely upon your office to get the job done, or should I call in help of my own?"

"Now, Mr. Knox, that's not the way this works," the sheriff said. I wanted to take some relief in his vexed tone, but the look on Hattie's face wouldn't let me. "I'll need to contact the Land Office and verify that this deed is in fact real. Shouldn't take more'n a week or two. The Dumas's have been livin' out here for quite some time, since before I took office as a matter of fact. Don't seem likely you could get a title for land that's already been granted. So, I'm tellin' you now, Mr. Knox, you're to stay away from that property until we can get this ruled on by the Land Office and make things official." His attention shifted to Hattie. "You'll want to bring your mother's deed down as soon as possible, Hattie. Maybe we can get this all taken care of faster."

He seemed confident that the matter was one simple step from being resolved. Without a word, Hattie shoved the deed back into Dickey's hands and began striding for the door.

12

"That deed's about as real as my eleventh finger," Hattie seethed. "I've half a mind to put an arrow straight through that man's forehead."

She was pacing in front of the dining room table back at the house. Ghitaine sat at the head, slowly shredding the dried root of an unknown plant with her fingers. She didn't seem to be discomfited by her daughter's temper, which put me somewhat at ease.

I said, "It's clearly some kind of misunderstanding or shenanigans that can be quickly righted by simply showing Sheriff Dickey your own title, Mrs. Dumas."

Ghitaine flicked me an unreadable look, which Hattie noticed.

"It's fine, Mama. Dickey's seen enough land certificates. He'll know this Knox no-account's is a forgery."

Ghitaine gathered the shredded bits of plant into a small pyramid. "Well now, dere's a problem, Henrietta. I don't have a land certificate."

Hattie stopped pacing. "... What do you mean?"

Ghitaine's face wrinkled up in disgust. "Land certificate, pah! All dat paperwork, it's all just de white man's grift. That's how dey stole de land of your père's people, you know. Paperwork and doublemeanin' words. Where I come from, agreements are settled with trade and a handshake, and anyone who breaks der word ends up bedridden with sores big enough and swollen enough dat der own wives can't stand de sight nor smell of dem."

Hattie's face had gone crimson, and her teeth were clamped over her bottom lip hard enough that it looked as if she was worried it might get loose and fly away. Finally she managed to regain some of the composure I'd only ever seen her lose with her mother. It reminded me of how I had argued with Aunt Ada when I was still a girl and she'd been the only female parental figure in my life. We'd fought till we were both blue in the face. But eventually, I'd lost interest in it, in *her*, and dismissed her completely. She was not my real mother, and any chance of forming a bond had withered the more I resented that fact. She had been strict, but now I wondered if I had been cruel to reject her so completely. I recognized the hollow feeling our lack of a relationship left in me.

But Hattie and Ghitaine still had that bond. It was both a blessing and curse, in that knowing its invulnerability, they were both willing to test it to the extremes. I envied that, odd as it seemed.

Hattie fumed, "Be that as it may, Mama, that white man's grift is gonna take your land too if we don't get some proof that you own this ranch."

"But dat's what I'm tellin' you, chil'. Dere is no proof. Ain't you been listenin' to me? Nul. Pass du tout."

"But... then how have you held on to the land for these last fifteen years?"

Ghitaine went back to shredding the root, having selected another one. "It's why we stayed here instead of going back to Nuhleans, mon chèrie. I have a cousin in de Land Office in Topeka, Cousin Jean-Louise. Anyone who applied for dis platte through de Homestead Act, Jean-Louise denied dem."

I looked to Hattie urgently, deeply worried that she might erupt. But to my surprise, her face had grown pensive.

"So that means, I'm right," she said.

"Right about what?" I asked.

"Soon as I touched Knox's certificate, I knew it was fake. If Mama's cousin is disappearin' all applications, Knox's never made it to Washington either."

I'd been near enough to her to see the document over her shoulder. "It looked real enough to me," I said, "though I admit I haven't seen, well, *any* land certificates. What did you see that makes you think so?"

She tapped her forehead. "It isn't what I saw, it's what I felt. Like I told you, Doc, I can 'see' things most can't, like your fae shine. And falseness stands out to me, not to my eyes, but to *me*."

Toxicore took this moment to wander into the dining room. He was gnawing on a chicken leg. "'Cause she's a witch," he remarked.

I shot him my most strenuous *would you please?* look, but he appeared not to notice.

Hattie pulled a chair from the dining room table and sat. She was thinking aloud as she spoke. "So we need to get down to the Land Office in Topeka, talk to your cousin, and see what he can do about this. Probably nothin', short of falsifyin' a deed for us, but I don't know how that'll work. Mama"—she spoke louder, bringing us into the planning—"why didn't you just get a fake one to begin with? Or better yet, a real one?"

Ghitaine sniffed. "Like I told you, white man's lies are just as black on paper as dey are in air."

Hattie shook her head. "White man or not, Knox is gonna take this land if we don't think of somethin'."

"We could shoot him," Toxicore offered.

I tutted, glowering at him.

"Why are you lookin' at me like that, Looloo?"

"Oh, I don't know. You suddenly took on the properties of a certain golden spear."

"So you're sayin' I'm fetchingly brilliant and worth a heap o' money?"

Hattie saved me from this utterly pointless, and also absurdly inaccurate, line of discussion. "Naw, we can't outright kill Knox, at least not if it looks like a killin'. That would point directly to us as the most likely culprits. An accident maybe…"

"I propose we look for more direct and less felonious options to start with," I said. "Besides, even with him dead, there's still the issue of this land not legally belonging to your family. If we can right that oversight, that could get us much closer to a resolution than a murder would."

"Oh, it wouldn't be one murder. I wouldn't stop until I did away with all the cretins workin' for that lout," Hattie promised. I knew her to be thoroughly redoubtable, with an internal streak of justice that would brook no trampling, but this was a new side I hadn't seen. It was dark, showing me just how far she would go to protect what was hers. Frightening, even.

"We could turn him into a toad and turn his gang into flies and roaches. Then we'll put them all in a jar and watch as he slurps them up," Toxicore suggested, now sucking on the thoroughly picked-clean chicken leg bone. We all looked at him. "And we could bet on which bug would last the longest. 'Twould at least be entertaining to watch."

Ghitaine chuckled with delight at this idea.

"That is deeply disturbing, Toxicore," I chided.

"Ach! That's yer opinion. 'Twouldn't be near as dull as using the Fíne Fergusoni Ink o' Influence to write yer own deed."

"The what?" I asked.

He eyed the chicken bone, shrugged, and popped the whole thing into his mouth, crunching on it contentedly. Through his mouthful of bone splinters, he said, "Ink o' Influence."

"Yes, I heard that, but what is it?"

He stopped chewing and looked sidelong at me. "It's an ink what influences t'ings, Looloo."

"Let me see if I can be of help," Paddy said. He'd been sitting quietly beneath the table, listening and occasionally eyeing Tox's chicken leg for the chance of being offered some. Predictably, Tox did not offer him some. "I've heard of this ink. The fae sorcerer Fíne Fergusoni created it many hundreds of years ago. If used with precise intention and the proper incantation, it will create a document that is not a perfect approximation of whatever document you wish; it is the authentic document itself."

"Wonderful!" I nearly shouted. "Where do we find it?"

Tox and Paddy exchanged a look, and I knew with a sinking heart what it meant.

"It belongs to either Brigid or the Morrígan, doesn't it?" I groaned.

"'Tis one o' the many things Lady Morrígan collected and keeps in her vaults," Tox concurred. "Bit o' a packrat, the dark queen is."

Coming from the gnome, whose pocket dimension held untold objects—such as, at one time, a pointlessly pilfered and what most would have assumed to be completely useless snow globe—this was a laughably ironic thing to say.

"Well, what about this Fergusoni fellow?" I said, grasping at options. "Can we perhaps find him and offer him something to show us how to create the ink?"

Tox shook his head. "Naw, been dead many a year."

Still grasping, now desperately, I said, "Then can you resurrect him? You are a, um, *great* necromancer, are you not?"

"Resurrect what? Looloo, I am many t'ings, but I'm not a gnome what can resurrect soup."

"… Soup?"

"Fergusoni was known to have a bit o' a gamblin' problem, and an even worse problem payin' off his debts. He tried to skip out on payin' a giant what he owed a tidy sum to, nigh on, oh, two, three hundred years ago. Got stomped into soup fer his troubles. The giant ne'er got paid, either. Giants aren't known fer their brilliance, I probably don't need to add." He side-eyed me again. "On, second thought, maybe I do."

My spirits, which had teetered on ill-advised hope for just a moment, fell.

Hattie, to her credit, did not succumb to my gloominess. Thoughtfully, she said, "… A disappearance…" With effort, I pulled my attention back to her. "Mama, can you and Jimmy take the wagon to Topeka tomorrow? Go and see what Cousin Jean-Louise might be able to whip up for you, a real deed or something to stand in for one. I don't trust this Knox and his gang to leave us alone, despite what Dickey told him, and I want you off the ranch for the time being. With Star

Racer and Sings the Wind here, the horses can look after themselves. While you're doing that—Doc," she said, leveling her keen eyes on me, "I know you're gettin' antsy waitin' on Downs. What do you say we go and find him?"

"Find him?" My spirits, no matter how I advised them otherwise, began to lift again.

"Hold on." She rose and hurried from the room. Her boots clunked up the stairway and down the hall to her bedroom. Within moments, she was back. In her hand was a smallish knife, the kind a hunter or fisherman might use to skin a hide or gut a bass. It looked vaguely familiar. A black crust had stained the blade nearly up to the hilt. Upon seeing this, I realized why it was familiar.

Hattie put the knife on the table. "That's the knife that Serpent pain in the ass stuck Downs with. He left it in the kitchen, and I took it—just in case. I've learned quite a bit about magic since meeting you and your gnome sidekick—"

"I'm not the sidekick here," Toxicore cut in, oddly vehement about it.

Hattie paid him no mind. "And the main one is, blood has power. You never know when it'll come in handy."

I put a finger on the knife hilt thoughtfully, a nearly uncontainable giddiness rising up in me. I was growing all-too-fond of danger, I told myself, which was quite unseemly for a lady of my practical, proper nature. And I damned well didn't care. "Finding Orville will show us the way to the Morrígan's court. Or if he's already on his way back, finding him will give us the chance to learn what he's discovered."

Hattie nodded. "And save us a trip to Denver, to boot."

Not a single doubt had a chance to make itself heard in my thoughts. "I'm in. No question."

"Good." She wrapped the knife in a napkin. "But first things first. Today, we get together everything we think we'll need for a trip to the Otherworld. Tomorrow morning, we head out right after we kidnap Knox. We'll keep him bound and gagged on the other side while we're busy. Grab him on the way back once we have this Ink of Influence.

With him out of the way, his gang will lay low, wonderin' where he might have gone and waitin' on his orders."

I'd slipped into pondering the monumental undertaking a trip to Tír Na nÓg would be and at first thought I'd misheard her. "Kidnap... what?"

"That's right, Doc, we can't leave him here. He doesn't deserve to be peacefully slumberin' in Abilene while he's scheming to take my family's land. I can't kill him without drawing suspicion, but if there's no dead body, there's no crime to be suspicious about. Darkheart, you remember that stuff you gave Ryan to keep him still? We'll use that to keep Knox from causin' trouble, and we'll stash him somewhere on the other side of the gateway while we're there. Keep me from worryin' about the land, and keep him from doin' anything' else that ensures I'll *have* to kill him."

Tox was nodding along, as though discussing not only kidnapping human beings but also taking them to foreign worlds was something he'd done plenty of times before. For all I knew, he had. "I'll go you one better, Dumas," he said. "You know the spell o' Eternal Youth?"

"We don't need the fountain of youth right now, Darkheart," she gruffed. "'Sides, Doc's already got that."

"Naw, naw. This isn't like what comes from Lord Dagda's tub. Well, this *is* like that, sure, but it keeps you young by sort o' puttin' you to sleep and freezin' you whole, mind, body, and spirit, till ye're awakened. Works like that fairy tale, you know the one? *Briar Rose*. Those Grimm boys did love makin' money off the stories the fae told them. Smart lads."

Hattie was staring at him doubtfully.

"'Tis like..." He looked around the room, scratching under his eyepatch. "Haven't you e'er seen a brain in a jar o' formaldehyde? Can't do any t'inkin', but it stays fresh all the livelong day."

"So this spell, you're sayin' it won't kill him outright?" asked Hattie.

"Sounds like suspended animation," I said vacantly. My words were coming to my ears from far away, sounding perfectly reasonable and relaxed, as though I discussed the kidnapping and enchanting of people every day. A more rational part of my brain was horrified into silence at the mere pondering of such reprobate practices. I preferred its silence, as I did not wish to go to war against my own sound reasoning. Because one thing was quite true: I liked Hattie's plan, and I was going to help carry it out. Knox had irritated me with his arrogance and scoundrelly behavior. I agreed with Hattie. There was no reason he should be at peace when he'd brought this conflict to her doorstep.

Resolved, I looked up and said, "Well, then. We'd best prepare for our journey. However long it may take."

13

Hattie and I got to work gathering the materials and equipment we'd need, and I studiously avoided the facts: we were about to abduct a man and then travel across a mythical barrier into an even more mythical world to confront dangers of, well, mythic proportions.

We discussed whether to take Earth-born horses there, but Paddy had suggested that they would be sheep in a wolves den among the unfamiliar creatures of Tír Na nÓg. This declaration did nothing to calm my nervousness, which was now beating a positively martial tattoo against the barriers of my mind. Hattie took this information in stride and commented simply, "Well, if the place is loaded with critters, we shouldn't have much trouble huntin' for our vittles instead of havin' the horses carry it." Practical as ever.

Toward evening, Paddy's ancient wisdom in the magical and arcane came in useful. As he directed Hattie on how to make a kind of ink from the scrapings of Orville's blood from the knife that had been lodged in his throat, I made for my room to gather the last small bits and baubles I'd need for the journey.

The light tap of a shoe in the doorway caused me to turn. "Mrs. Dumas?" I said.

She held a packet of something in her hand and came in without needing my invitation. She was staring at me pointedly as she said, "Do you know who you are, chil'?"

The question was so odd that it triggered my natural habit when confronted by things I didn't understand: a polite grin. "I'm sorry? If you mean have I finally learned who my parents are—"

"Not that. Do you know your name?"

I blinked in confusion. "Lula Maeve Cullen?" I don't know why I framed it like a question, but her tone had implied that I did not, somehow, know my own name. The implied lack was so strong that I believed it myself for a moment.

Then she confirmed that I knew as little as she was suggesting. "Not the simple name a girl is given by her père and mère. Your *name*, de truth of you, the name of power dat marks your very *soul*."

My polite grin had flattened, and my lips chilled. "Mrs. Dumas, I do not know what you mean."

She nodded sagaciously. "Dat's what I thought. You're going into de unknown, and you don't even know yourself. You are playin' a very dangerous game, girl. Very dangerous. And de longer you stay in de dark, the darker it will become."

Her habit of speaking in the way I'd observed fake occultists at their seance tables back in Boston speak, all vagaries and profound but ultimately meaningless pronunciations, should have amused me. But the look in her dark eyes was not amusing, and her tone even less so. I opted to do the wise thing and believe her, even if I didn't know what it was she was asking me to believe.

Besides, there was an undeniable ominousness to how similar what she'd just said was to something Orville had told me too. He had spoken of the danger of not knowing my strength, and she of not knowing myself. If recent company were to be believed, I knew very little at all. "And," I said, somewhat uncertainly, "how would I go about knowing myself better?"

"You can't." She said it with such finality that I half expected her to simply walk out and leave me with this gaping hole of knowledge for the rest of eternity. But when she added more, it was not the comfort it should have been. "You were cursed by Dagda to be ignorant of your soul name."

My soul name? I asked the question aloud.

"Your true name, a mark on your soul—or spirit, or essential nature, whatever de term is in your own people's way of thinkin'. It's *who you are*, deep down, *the truth* of your being. Whoever knows your soul name, outside of yourself, has power over you. Most people, 'specially white people, don't know der truth, but when others learn it, it can spell der doom."

The spark of a memory lit my thoughts. My first foray into the world of magic had been to try a ritual I found in Uncle Paddy's journal. I called upon the Morrígan through a magic mirror. When she'd looked at me through the mirror, the first thing she'd done was ask—no, command: "First you must tell me your name." I remember cringing internally with an uneasiness that went far beyond the matter of performing a magic trick. But, still such a novice to all I was about to encounter, I'd told her I was Lula Cullen. A mistake, of course, but perhaps not as bad as it could have been. If I had another name, a *soul* name, I hadn't told her, because apparently, I hadn't known it. And still didn't.

The concept alone was too farfetched and out of my reach, though it sounded like some kind of encyclopedia of my *self*. Being the avid scholar I was, this had a great deal of appeal, but I could do nothing but shrug internally after a moment's consideration. Toxicore had already told me Dagda had cursed me, and now Ghitaine had confirmed it. The means to "know myself" had been taken from me by the vindictive and, truth be told, somewhat childish member of the Tuatha Dé Danann. And anyway, it was hard to miss something I'd never known I had. So I asked the unimportant but no less curious question: "How did you know I was cursed?"

"Oh, de Dagda and I spoke when I asked him to remove de gnome's curse. He was surprised I asked for dat and not for yours."

I too was surprised, but then, why would she have asked for such a thing on my behalf? She and Toxicore had a history, as dubious and murky as it was, and I was still more a stranger than a friend. In the end, really, I needed Toxicore in Tír Na nÓg much more than I needed to know my soul name. I hoped.

"So what does that mean, Mrs. Dumas? How does not knowing this endanger me? More importantly, how does it endanger Hattie?"

I could have been mistaken, but it appeared that the hardness of her face slackened some at my question. "My girl can look after herself, and I think she'll do a fine job of looking after you, too. But you should know your limits. And don't be surprised when de things you want don't come easily to you."

When have they ever? I thought. "Thank you for the warning." There were more questions that needed asking, such as how she could speak to Dagda, who was an entire set of territories distant, but we were interrupted.

"Gitty," Toxicore called from down the hall, "night's wearin' on and we have but this wee bag o' dust left to smoke. Let's to it!"

Mrs. Dumas grinned girlishly. "I'll be right dere, mon ami." She turned back to me and handed me the packet she'd been holding: a sachet of herbs. "Take a pinch of dese in your palm, spit on it and make it pasty. Den rub dat on dat bite on your ankle. Should be healed in no time."

I took the small linen bag. "Thank you. What is the... salve composed of, if I may ask?"

She had a glint in her eye when she said, "I'll tell you when you get back. An evening with my du bon temps gnome awaits."

"Mrs. Dumas, I don't mean to be rude, but there's something that I just have to ask. You and Toxicore... you, oh, how do I put it? You do dote on him so. It may sound arrogant of me to say this, but you're so much more respectable, even noble, than he is. I'm just wondering, what is it you see in him?"

She seemed to take this lightly. "You don't think he's handsome?" She must have seen the startlement in my eyes. "When he's wearin' de glamour, I mean."

"He can be less than hideous, I suppose. But that isn't who he truly is."

She pursed her lips. "Chil', don't you know dat everyone wears a glamour of one kind or another? Have you ever met anyone who is exactly who dey show you dey are?"

I thought about it and gave a tiny, uncomfortable shrug. I wasn't sure where she was going with this, or if I was going to like it.

She went on, warming to her topic. "For instance, Henrietta tells me you were engaged to be married to an haute monde gent before all dis began, but you say dat you never loved him. Dat true?"

Before I could respond, she continued, not needing my confirmation at all. "See, you walked around pretendin' you loved a man you had no true feelin's for. Weren't you wearin' a glamour, tryin' to be someone you weren't for de sake of everyone else? Maybe even for de sake of your own ideas of who you were told you were?"

She didn't say for the sake of my own ideas of who *I was*, rather for the sake who I *was told* I was. She was looking into my very deepest self. The exchange underpinned our talk from moments ago about me not knowing my true self. It seemed almost as though she knew me better than I ever would. And I didn't know how to feel about that.

"I know you hide yourself," she said, "still, even after all you been through. I seen how you look at my chil' when you don't know others can see it."

I smiled and softly protested, "Jimmy is a lovely man, but I have no designs on him... in that way."

"Oh girl, I'm not talkin' about Jimmy."

The blush that overtook me started at my toenails and roared through my body to the roots of the hair on my head. I didn't know what to say. Mrs. Dumas went on, assuring me that I didn't know Toxicore the way she did and that he was a perfectly lovely gnome on the inside, if a bit lonely, but the last thing I really heard was "I seen how you look at my chil'" and could think of nothing until dawn except Hattie.

14

Toxicore was making himself useful, for once, yet nonetheless, I wasn't terribly comfortable with what he was doing.

We'd locked up the ranch and left at dawn, Jimmy and Mrs. Dumas taking their wagon to Topeka after dropping Uncle Paddy, Tox, Hattie, and I off near the stagecoach depot in Abilene. We'd guessed Mr. Truman Radamus Knox would be staying at La Belle Hotel, as it was the nicest in town, and the four of us made our way there as furtively as we could. For all I knew, Knox was now sleeping in the same room I'd previously occupied.

Toxicore had confirmed this five minutes later upon meeting the three of us where we awaited him, with Knox firmly "in tow." He was useful, yes, but I would never accuse the hobgoblin of having other's best interests at heart.

Let me elaborate. On my first visit to Abilene, when Toxicore had shown me his true form—back when I was still as green and naive as the newest and tenderest sapling in the forest—I'd fainted from shock. Somehow, he'd gotten me to my hotel room on his own, without either of us being seen. This morning on the way to town, we'd cast about for the best way to abduct Knox, and my previous experience with Tox had come to mind.

Upon asking Tox how he'd transported me so inconspicuously, he'd explained that while I was unconscious, he'd stuffed me away in his pocket dimension and then hurried unseen to the hotel in his remarkable, magical way. It hadn't taken long, the hotel being close to where I'd fainted and Tox being uncannily speedy. I had to harangue him ruthlessly before he'd divulged this next part: his pocket had no air to breathe. While this hadn't been problematic when Tox had used it to get me to my hotel, this time, I was concerned. The graveyard containing the gateway tree to Tír Na nÓg, where we needed to take Knox, was about a mile from the hotel.

Tox had made clear he was quite willing to risk Knox's life by keeping him "pocketed" until we reached the graveyard, but I'd demanded he meet us at one of the cattle pens on the edge of town and release Knox long enough to catch his breath.

Paddy went ahead to the pen, and Hattie and I got there within a few minutes. It was more of a catastrophe than I'd anticipated.

Knox was lying flat on his back, wide awake. He was indeed finding it hard to breathe, but not for the reasons expected.

"Toxicore! Why didn't you put him to sleep or at least tie him up!" I whisper-shouted from the haze created by the dust hovering in the air from hundreds of panicking cattle. It wasn't us people that had upset them, but the miniature dragon now standing firmly upon Knox's chest, breathing sulfuric steam menacingly into the terrified man's face. Knox must have tried to escape when Toxicore pulled him from the pocket dimension, and Paddy had cut short his attempt through sheer intimidation.

"I'm not a stray, sir, and even if I were, I find your unkindness towards animals to be unconscionable and obscene," Paddy said, his telepathic voice projected for all, including Knox, to hear. "In fact, your comments to the sheriff about killing unhomed animals made me quite angry."

Knox did his best to manage his fear, but his trousers were ruined nonetheless.

"I'm not puttin' him back in me pocket like that," Toxicore declared.

"It's fine," said Hattie. "We can walk it from here. Give him some time to dry out."

"Wha-what in the name of heaven...?" Poor Knox couldn't seem to find a solid direction to take that question in.

"Don't worry, Mr. Knox," I said placidly, a saccharine calmness in my voice that I hoped wasn't doing as much to soothe him as I was pretending to try. "If things go the way we hope, you'll forget all about this and be returned to your charlatan life as happy as you were."

Hattie gave me a raised eyebrow, and I amended, "Well, having learned some lessons about trying to swindle innocent people, that is. Some *firm* lessons." I patted my uncle's back. "I'm sure it would be fine to step off him now, Uncle."

Paddy curled his lip menacingly, revealing several dozen stilletto-like teeth, before retreating—but only by a foot or so.

"Get up, Knox. We have some business to finish," Hattie commanded.

The man lay still for a moment, panting, but soon caught his breath. He sat up and checked his pockets meticulously. He was fully dressed, even wearing his top hat, as though Tox had caught him moments before he was to step out for an early breakfast. I was strangely insulted that he'd think we'd robbed him on top of kidnapping him.

Until he said, "You may have stolen my deed and my wallet, but there's another copy on file with the Land Office. I have no idea how you've bewitched me into seeing things that can't possibly be real, such as this scaly dog and that go-by-the-ground manlike child with a nose like a misshapen mushroom—"

"Now, wind in yer neck there, you do-lally buckeen. No call fer insults. I could've let you suffocate in me pocket if I'd've known you'd be all hostile like."

Knox stared at the obviously disgruntled hobgoblin for a few moments, blinked, then decided to return to speaking with someone he recognized as his own kind. "But don't think, Miss Dumas, that you can bully me into retreating from the land I own, according to the papers our government holds."

I eyed Hattie, worried about what she might do. She took a step forward, and I tensed. Instead of retaliating, she put a hand down and scratched Paddy's scales between his horns. "Knox, it ain't *our* government, it's yours. And I ain't tryin' to bully you. I'm kidnapping you. And if you give me too much trouble, I'm gonna feed you to my friend's pet."

I didn't know it then, but Hattie's words had the ring of prophecy to them, much to my future horror.

She turned to Tox and I. "Let's git before too many folks're about."

But first: "Tox," I said, staring down the gnome, "give the man back his wallet."

Without a shred of shame on his face, he casually flicked the leather accessory to Knox.

"Now give him back the money from inside."

"Ach, fine," Tox grumbled. "Won't need it where we're goin' anyway."

Forty minutes later, we stood before the giant gnarled sycamore looming inside a ring of its smaller cousins in the Abilene cemetery. Knox's unease must have caught up with him when we arrived at the sacred plot of land, as he began to squirm against the restraints Hattie had tied around his wrists.

"Don't worry, we're not goin' to bury you. Today," Hattie told him.

"Then what, pray tell, are we doing here?" Knox said.

"You'll see in a sec," she said.

I had stepped a few feet off to the side to confer with Sleg. As I unwrapped it from the silken cloth, the weapon thrummed with a heavier vibrancy than I'd become accustomed to. Almost as though it was eager for this journey.

"Now, Sleg, let's go over this once again. I know you have your reasons for wanting to return to Tír Na nÓg, but I'm going to need you to stay by my side and keep my friends and I out of harm's way—without undo bloodshed. Are we in agreement?"

"Undo bloodshed may require a bit of clarity, my lady."

Its voice, though silent to anything but my mind, was cultured in a way that continually caught me off guard, if you could call a screech of wind that seemed to prick the inner ear rather than flow over it *cultured*. Of all the magic I'd been exposed to in recent days, something about this enchanted weapon was the most alien, and most sinister.

Cultured or not, I could hear the subtle attempts at manipulation via feigned ignorance in its tone and was having none of it. "I'm requesting that you do not kill or harm anything I don't specifically tell you to."

"My lady, if I may say so, you are nothing like your sire," it said, disgruntled.

"Oh?" I knew I shouldn't ask but found I could not contain my curiosity. "What's so different about us?"

"You haven't a wit of ruthlessness, and a highly retarded survival instinct as well."

"Perhaps it's because I'm a living creature with an innate sense of compassion and mercy."

"Spear givin' you trouble, Looloo?" Toxicore had come up beside me soundlessly.

"We were just discussing our game plan for... for the other side."

"Other side of what?" called Knox, overhearing us. His voice was growing increasingly shrill from nerves.

"I told you, you'll see," Hattie snapped, the threat in her voice like a club.

"Discussing?" Tox queried. "Ye're tellin' me ye're tryin' to coax and wheedle that spear into doin' yer biddin'?"

"I wouldn't say I'm wheedling—"

"Naw, you'd probably say you were politely askin' the spear, if it wouldn't mind, to just do this and do that and if 'tisn't too much trouble, blah, blah, blah. Whisha, girly! Ye're the child o' the one-time king o' the Tuatha Dé Danann. Act like it!"

I scowled at Toxicore. "You, sir, do not have any right to make demands of me."

"See, 'twasn't so hard, was it?"

"Toxicore, I'm simply being polite. It's something you're deeply unfamiliar with, I know, but there's no reason to be a, a…"

"Twat?"

"An uncivil rapscallion when a bit of manners and mutual respect will get you much further much quicker."

He sauntered up to my knees and beckoned me to bend toward him. "Now I know yer as hardheaded as that giant what squashed Fergusoni, but you can't be as much o' an eedjit as I been accusin' you o' bein'. The Morrígan, she's spent more lifetimes than you can dream of plottin' and schemin' to take o'er first our world, then this one. And the last one what stood in her way, she locked him in a cage, knowin' if he e'er got out, he'd bring such a world o' misery down on her head that she'd be smashed flat afore the echoes of her screams went quiet. And she turned his wife into a swan and tried to kill maybe his last livin' child. That would be you," he added. "So, now that ye're takin' not only yerself *right into her house* but also the t'ing she needs to ensure that world o' misery doesn't come down on her—that would be the spear—do you really, truly believe that bein' all mannered and sweet as honey when she sends the worst o' the worst monsters she can dream of—and you should trust me, she has monsters 'twould give yer nightmares nightmares—at you is goin' to be the best way o' gettin' to and from her court in one piece?"

The green of his one eye glistened balefully, like swamp gas, as he spoke. I didn't answer, couldn't really, and merely cleared my throat.

"Now, ye're the child o' a god for all intents and purposes. You best remember that and *be* that, or all yer pretty-pleases and thank-yous are goin' to drown in the blood spewin' from your throat when it gets opened up like a filleted fish." He squinted at the scarf I wore tightly around my previously wounded throat. "Again."

Toxicore had never sounded so serious before. Perhaps *grave* was the more appropriate term. "I shall take your advice to heart," I muttered, sounding too meek to my own ears. And when he put it like that, I believe I was right to sound meek, especially when I still had no answer to the question, *Was* I the child of a god? Or had Lugh given over his divinity before I'd been conceived, and I was merely playing magical games as poorly as I played poker? Sure, I'd gotten lucky now and again at both, but luck was entirely the wrong thing to rely on.

Whatever the case, Tox's speech and whatever encouragement he might have intended to be giving me, had the opposite effect. I felt deflated, even silly to be honest. Taking my friends and uncle into the lair of two goddesses who were out for my blood, with little more than determination and a well-appointed spear, seemed exactly as ludicrous and ill-advised as Orville had warned me it was.

But how could I call it off? I wasn't going for just myself. Hattie and her mother and brother had a stake in this game now too, and when I glanced at her, she was watching me with her keen, no-nonsense stare. I sensed that even if I lost my courage, she was going without me, one way or another. And just as she'd stuck by me throughout all my recent trials, there was no way that demons or dragons or three-faced goddesses of war and fate were going to keep me from doing the same for her.

"Time fer me to get that gateway open," Tox said, losing interest in me and my internal struggles. He turned toward the hoary old sycamore. "I haven't been able to do this for nigh seven hundred years. I'm goin' home!"

At least someone was excited.

15

Passing through the gateway tree was a substantially less disconcerting experience than the first time, at least for me. Once we arrived in the deserted ring-stones in Tír Na nÓg, poor Knox had as much trouble holding his stomach as he previously had his bladder. It seemed that humans who weren't acquainted with magic and the fae through their own unusual lives were ill-equipped for the experience of moving through the gateways. I had more reasons than I'd previously realized to be grateful for my heritage.

Guarded by Paddy, Knox leaned against one of the rune-emblazoned standing stones as Hattie and Tox knelt over a scrap of paper and the bottle of Orville's ink-blood and collaborated on the spell Paddy had shown them to divine his location. I stood guard, keeping my gaze roving over the gaps between the stones. I held my shillelagh in one hand, Sleg in the other, and wondered why I'd bothered to bring a rifle and two revolvers at all. Would they do any good in this world? Gunpowder and metal seemed a poor match for magic that could be used to suck the blood from a living being's body on command, as I'd done to Abhartach, or the very soul from a person, as the pixies were said to do.

I'd wager I'd get the chance to find out. My luck did tend to run both good and bad, and now I had Tox to thank for becoming ever more acutely aware of it.

It wasn't like the last time I'd been in this particular ring-stone circle in Tír Na nÓg, when the changeling who looked like my now-former (though I had not yet had the chance to break it off) fiancé. The sense of otherworldliness was still present, but now that I'd been to dimensions outside my human one a few times, I found I was much less unsettled than the first time. It was not unlike growing accustomed to the different bustle of New York City after growing up in Boston's.

Hattie and Tox spoke quietly together—a first—and the rustle of Hattie putting away the articles to create the spell for finding Orville drew my attention back to them. Knox was seated with his back pressed to one of the stones, eyes closed as though he were suffering from a migraine. For all I knew, he was.

Tox reached into his pocket and withdrew a bottle of something dark and murky. Whether the cause of the murkiness was due to the bottle or what was in it wasn't clear until he also withdrew an old, beaten wooden spoon and poured a drop of the liquid into its bowl. The substance had the quality of thick black ink, and a very fine miasma roiled off it and was whisked away by the slight breeze. It reminded me of descriptions in the *Snow White* fairy tale of the poison the witch had dipped the apple in. According to Toxicore, all the Grimm stories were derived from authentic fae circumstances, so it could well have been.

Tox said some ancient magic chant over the liquid and held it to Knox's face. "Now drink up, boyo. Time fer you to have a long, peaceful sleep."

Knox's eyes opened slowly. "What is that?"

"Just a dram o' medicine what will fix that stomach o' yers."

"Do not take me for a fool, little man." He had more vigor than a moment ago.

Tox narrowed his eye. "Drink it, or you won't like where I put it. One way or 'nother, 'tis goin' in you."

Knox believed him, as he should have, and allowed Toxicore to dribble the spoon's contents into his mouth. He then rose to his feet, apparently also believing that it was intended to help his stomach settle.

"I'd stay down if were you," Tox commented casually.

Then Knox did something none of us were prepared for—he took off like a shot between a set of stones and into the mild mist of the grassy green hillside, spitting the mouthful of potion out as he did.

Hattie instantly had her revolver in her hand, but I blurted, "Don't shoot him! We'll get him. Just wait here."

I beckoned to Paddy and sped after the fleeing man.

The hilltop tapered downward more quickly than I'd anticipated, and gray lichen-covered stones lay everywhere, making the footing precarious. The hilltop mist thickened more and more with each descending step. Worse, it seemed to absorb sound. Within just a few dozen yards, I could see and hear nothing, the feeling like what I imagined floating inside a massive nimbus would be.

And I was hopelessly lost.

Halting, I stood stone still—excuse the pun—straining my ears and eyes for an idea of where in the world I might be. "Paddy?" I tried, my voice squeaking like a hinge.

Well done, Lula, I told myself. *Have you lost your head completely? Running off into the wilds like an idiot, with no idea what you'll find.... Or will find you.*

"Hello?!" I tried again, louder.

I thought I heard someone yelling, distantly, but I could not tell from which direction. Hattie? Maybe, or maybe just a mirage.

At my feet, the whitish-gray mist swirled like tendrils, giving me flashes of the bright lichens on the rocks. It should have been cold, at least I felt like it should have been. As well as damp. But it was neither, as though I stood amid a cloud of dry ice. I shivered anyway, the sense of being completely alone, completely lost seeping into my very pores.

This would not do. Determinedly, I shrugged off my unease and turned in the direction I thought was uphill. Knox be damned. If he got himself lost or killed, or both, that was his problem. He brought it on himself. But I was not here to play hide-and-seek with a rogue and thief. We'd find another way to hold on to Hattie's ranch if we had to.

After a few steps, my confidence began to return. I *thought* I was going in the right direction. Uphill would lead back to the ring-stones and my friends. And if it didn't, Paddy's incomparably well-tuned nose would lead him to me, then us to the others. I merely had to stave off my pesky anxiety until that happened. No problem, just a matter of keeping calm and thinking clearly. Didn't matter that I was in an entirely new world.

Sleg suddenly yanked itself from my hand and began to glow like a brilliant golden sunset, so bright that I had to shield my eyes.

"What in Lincoln's beard..." I began, but then I heard something.

"We are not alone, my lady," it said, confirming my suspicion.

The noise was *slithery*, a squelching sound moving across the ground, coming toward me. Slow but deliberate and oddly *moist*. Worst of all, unwavering.

I spun around and around, trying to pinpoint the direction it was coming from. "Sleg, do you, er, see anything?"

A miraculous thing was happening. The mist around Sleg was dissipating, perhaps from the power of the blazing weapon. Nice perk, I thought, until I saw what it revealed.

Trudging, or maybe sliding, toward us was the most unsettling set of creatures I had yet seen in recent weeks. Not terrifying or abominable, like a dragon or a revenant, but grotesque and downright freakish. Still some yards distant, the creatures stood upright like humans but were slime-covered and shaped like gastropods, complete with shells that hung from their posteriors like rucksacks. Their bodies were the same long, singular tubular shape of slugs, and they even had eyestalks, but also several bilateral appendages growing from their midsections that seemed as boneless as their physiques but which waved around like arms.

"Ah, ah, ahhhh..." Weak spurts of air emerged from my throat, neither words nor screams, as my brain was unable to decide which was the most appropriate response to what my eyes were seeing.

They were moving inexorably toward me, and I could easily outrun them based on the speed I judged their sticky, wriggling bodies capable of. Yet I could only stare mutely, my feet glued in place.

"Oh thank the fates!" I heard Uncle Paddy's voice a moment before I felt the brush of wind from his wings as he landed beside me. "That fog was quite something, wasn't it? I'm glad you're... oh." He'd spotted the slug-sapiens. "I see we've encountered a slime—or is the collective noun for them *cornucopia?*—of Muculents."

"Mu-muculents?" The name was perfect, because of course it was.

"Yes, they are mostly harmless."

"Mostly?"

"Right, in that they are unable to harm anything they can't catch. Which is most things."

"So we should just leave, right?" I said, maybe with a touch of pleading in my voice. "No need to bother them at all."

"They do appear rather unsporty. Hardly worth even using as target practice," Sleg offered in a tone that could not have been more bored. Contrasted with its usual burning desire to pierce anything that moved, its statement was particularly unsettling. Its brightness dimmed some, but not enough that the sheen of slime covering the Muculents as well as the path along the ground they traveled lost its luster.

"Oh, ehm, I don't think we can go just yet. They appear to have captured our quarry," Paddy said.

The cornucopia was six Muculents strong, and the last was emerging from the dispersing mist as Paddy spoke. The appendages dangling from either side of its body extended behind it—confirming my bonelessness theory—dragging something that was partially but firmly wrapped in their sticky lengths. Well-appointed boots extended from the end, which belonged to Knox. Bumps and bulges pushed erratically against the casing of his body, showing he was still quite awake. No doubt, he was now regretting spitting out Tox's potion.

"Oh my goodness, we need to get him free," I said.

"I'm not sure what to do," Paddy said. "I don't speak Muculent."

"They speak?"

"They're as sagacious as you or I, but..."

"But what, Uncle?"

"But not entirely friendly to others."

My thoughts raced frantically as I wondered what to do. My frustration with Knox had only grown since meeting him, and each new problem he created for us increased it tenfold. I had no idea what these creatures had nabbed him for—probably not to hold him captive until they could steal back the land he was trying to steal from them—but since it would simplify matters for Hattie if he were not dead, I supposed we should find a way to get him away from them.

"Uncle, can you find your way back to the hilltop and gather Toxicore? If we're lucky, he can communicate with them."

"What will you do?"

"Slow them down, I guess." I glanced back at them. They had progressed no more than a few feet since I'd first spotted them. "More, that is."

"Don't let them get their tendrils on you. I shall be right back."

He lifted into the sky, and I gripped my spear tighter. "Well, Sleg, here's your chance to be, um, yourself. If these creatures should prove hostile, please do what's necessary to keep me from being captured. But I'd appreciate it if killing them was your last option."

Toxicore's admonishment came back to me, *Now, ye're the child o' a god for all intents and purposes. You best remember that and be that, or all yer pretty-pleases and thank-yous are goin' to drown in the blood spewin' from your throat when it gets opened up like a filleted fish.* I'd once again been rather too squishy with Sleg, a component of my nature that I'd need to get over quickly in Tír Na nÓg, I realized.

"My lady, if there any possibility that dialoguing with these worms dissuades them from malice, I shall leave it to you. Their sludge is of a variety that I find most disgusting. I do prefer to keep this golden sheen unsullied by it."

"But you keep talking about stabbing people. How would blood not sully your sheen?"

"Blood is the ultimate purifier in which I bathe."

"… Naturally."

The first of the creatures was just a few yards away. Its bulbous eyes, a marbled copper and tin mix of color, dangled from their stalks, which now pointed definitively at me.

I cleared my throat and held up my shillelagh hand, not threateningly but in a "please stop" gesture. "Excuse me? Um, hello there, kind sir—er, person, um..." This wasn't going well. "I wonder if I might delay you for a moment?"

The creatures came to a ponderous stop, their movement so languid and glutinous that I couldn't tell at first that their momentum had ceased. Now that they were all closer, I could see their bodies better. *Wormlike* was one word that applied, but so did *sluglike*. One long segment comprised the totality of their main physique, the front flat, the rear rounded. They seemed to come in a variety of hues, all falling within a range from soil brown to apple green. The smaller segments that reminded me of arms reaching from their main bodies seemed to vary, both in number and size. These seemed to be extensions that could be summoned and lengthened or shortened at will. Other than their enormity as compared with a garden slug, I had to admit that nothing about them was any more threatening than their smaller cousins.

Until one of the leader's arm segments shot out at me so fast, I didn't even see it coming. It wrapped around the arm gripping Sleg and tightened like a tourniquet.

"Oh my—!" I began, then stopped short as the creature sent another tentacle out—Great Jiminy, how could anything move so fast?!—and wrapped around both my legs. I was yanked forward before I had time to scream, and fell on my fundament, being dragged inexorably to the beast.

I'd lost my grip on Sleg when the first tentacle grasped that arm, and from beside me, its golden light blazed with the intensity of the sun. Sleg sliced through the air, its tip not only cutting through the Muculent's tendrils, first the one holding my arm and then the legs, but cauterizing the severed stumps. The smell of fried slug flesh filled the air, making me gag. The bits of tendril still on my arm and legs loosened but did not drop off.

The wounded Muculent gave out a pained noise from a dark orifice that appeared south of where its eyestalks sprouted, the sound like the burble of a backed-up open sewer. Then, remarkably, the six creatures suddenly retracted into their great snail shells and fell motionless onto the ground.

"Dear Lugh, that was abominable," Sleg complained. It blazed into its lightning form for a brief moment, and when it returned to a golden shaft, all trace of the sludge from the mollusk man had been burned away.

The one in the rear that had encased Knox still held him, but now his body was pulled tightly against the shell's opening, still wrapped tightly in slimy tentacles. If the man's fretful attempts to escape hadn't been visibly weakening within the constriction of the tentacles, there might have been something dryly amusing about the way he was crushed against the shell's opening like a gopher being slowly consumed by a python.

That's when it hit me: Was he intended to be a meal? *Hurry back, Uncle. I'm not at all equipped to slaughter man-size snails to save a thieving brigand.*

Fortunately, the wait was short. We must have been closer to the hilltop than I'd realized. Toxicore sauntered down with a sour look on his face as I slowly and with much disgust removed the amputated tentacles from my legs and arm. They were as sticky as they looked, but the slime seemed to be dissolving into a, well, muculent sludge the longer the tentacles were detached from their owner. Hattie came as well and reached my side, holding her bow at the ready with an arrow already nocked. She had a question in her eyes, and I nodded, letting her know I was fine. Paddy alighted next to Toxicore, who took me in and gave a single approving nod.

"Tox, thank goodness you're here. I was hoping we could speak with these creatures and have them release Knox, but I'm afraid the front one attacked me, and..."

"And? And why didn't you just finish the job with that spear o' yers?" he asked.

"Why? Well, I'm not sure killing them all was entirely necessary..." I stuttered.

He gave me a disapproving glare, no doubt questioning why the "child of a god" was so kindhearted.

"Can you just speak to them? Ask them to let Knox go."

Toxicore *tsk*ed but paced to the leader. He knocked on the thing's shell, which was nearly as tall as him, as though knocking on a neighbor's door, and began speaking to it in a language I did not recognize in the slightest. A fae language, perhaps?

"He's telling them, ah… we're an envoy from the Lady Morrígan—I *think*," Uncle Patrick translated, "and something about releasing our… playwright? No, prisoner. Yes, that must be it. He's also saying something about escargot," Paddy said disapprovingly.

"Toxicore," I started, "threatening them is hardly the best—"

The lead Muculent unfurled from its shell and stood over Toxicore. The movement was so abnormally fluid and sinuous that it made the hair on my arms rise in primitive alarm. Its eyestalks telescoped out of sync, and the rubbery covers of its eyeballs oozed liquidly open. It regarded Toxicore, then spoke in that same burble it had cried out in before.

"Do you understand what it's saying?" I asked Paddy.

"Not a word."

When it had finished, Toxicore took up his side of the conversation. It went on for more than a minute, and each time I asked Tox to give me an idea of what the Muculent was saying, he ignored me. It was some kind of negotiation, but for what, I was forced to remain on tenterhooks to learn.

Finally, the Muculent and Tox concluded their discussion. The creature gurgled something to its companions, and the rest slid from their shells and rose to their uncanny height. Toxicore paced to the rear one as the leader spoke to it specifically, waiting as the tendrils covering Knox's face were relaxed. Tox held the elixir he'd tried giving Knox on the hilltop once more. The look of sheer horror on the man's features as they became visible was a thing of pity. And maybe somewhere in our world there was a person who might feel that pity, but it certainly wasn't any of us present.

"Oh my god, what-what-what—" Knox stammered.

"Best you don't know. Now open wide," Tox said, and in a flash, he slid the spoon of sleeping potion into Knox's mouth. Just as quickly, the Muculent slapped a narrow appendage over Knox's nose and lips, rendering them shut. His eyes bulged as he tried to scream, but to no avail.

"Swallow, and it'll let go. Don't, and yer last breath will have been wasted on stutterin' like an eejit."

Knox's fear-widened eyes stared helplessly at Tox, then he swallowed dramatically and his eyebrows rose in a plea.

"You promise you drank it?" Tox asked.

Knox nodded vigorously.

"You mean it? Promise?"

Knox's nod was even stronger, frantic even.

"You swear on yer life?"

This time Knox bucked his whole body, as if trying to nod with a megaphone.

"All right, then." Toxicore nodded to the Muculent, and the creature released Knox. Before the last tendril had slid free, however, the land thief's eyes had closed and his body had gone limp. "That's that," Tox said.

"He's not dead, is he?" Hattie said, a little too much hope in her voice.

"Naw, just the Eternal Youth," Tox assured her.

"So be it," she muttered, a little too much disappointment in her voice despite the complications his death would bring.

"Now what do we do with him?" I said.

Tox put away the spoon and elixir and straightened his coat. "I made a deal with the Mucks that they'll keep him safe for us till we return. We'll just stop by their village on the way back to the gateway stones."

"And what do they get in return?" my uncle said.

"Eh, just some snacks."

"And if we don't return?" asked Hattie.

Tox looked at the enchanted thief pointedly. "Snacks."

16

The map to Orville drawn by Hattie and Toxicore pointed to what Tox described as a "village" about two days' walk from the gateway stone circle. The relatively close proximity was a fortunate turn of events, but we had to hope we didn't miss Orville on the trek there. Tox had explained that each of the stones in this circle was the passage to different gateways in North America. One of them would be Orville's passage back to the gateway nearest Denver, just as ours was to Abilene, so he would soon be on his way here. Provided, of course, everything had gone smoothly on his journey to the Morrígan's citadel. I had every confidence in his wiliness—as I should; he'd proven over and over again that he could be as slippery as Toxicore was rude.

The Muculents had dragged Knox off to their village as soon as our deal had been complete. It was hard to read their expressions, if one could say they had them on their sluglike faces, (if one could even say they had faces), but I got the sense that they had grown extra wary of me. Served them right, I thought, for attacking a hapless traveler with no provocation. The experience did improve my confidence somewhat though; Sleg had come through "divinely" in a pinch. Again, excuse the pun.

There seemed to be no path leading from the hilltop, as my misguided romp through the mists had shown. The mythical world we now inhabited was as foreign to me as ancient China would be, and I was keenly aware of how reliant we were on Toxicore, and to a lesser extent Paddy, to navigate for us. But, to my astonishment, once we had a destination firmly chosen, upon our stepping outside the circle of rune-covered stones, the mists parted and a road loomed before us. White pebbles lined the roadbed, really no more than a cart's width, and the path led off into the distance like the guiding light of a lighthouse.

"Well..." I mumbled. "That's something."

"Tír Na nÓg is what that is," Tox bleated and then set off at a rapid pace.

His eagerness to visit his homeland was evident in the pep in his step. After some seven centuries of banishment, it seemed appropriate. In comparison, I had not yet felt a single moment of nostalgia for Boston since this adventure had begun. I was beginning to wonder if I ever would.

As Paddy set off after Tox, I looked back at Hattie. She gave me a smile and shrug, and side by side, we followed.

Sometime after we descended the lonesome rocky knoll—though I could not say I felt any passage of time—night fell and we entered a thickly wooded ancient forest directly out of a child's fairy tale involving cannibalistic witches and man-eating wolves. We followed the cart path without deviation, having been warned by both my uncle and Toxicore with utmost severity to avoid exploring. The trees were indeed trees, but there was nothing on Earth I could have compared them to.

They megalithic guardians of the forest grew from a loamy-smelling night-black soil, yet their leaves shimmered in a hundred different vivid colors, their branches lighting up like starlight against the darkness of the night sky. Even the tree bark itself seemed to sparkle in its own way. I should have been awed by the marvelous strangeness, and I was. But there was the ever-present feeling of being in a place that was not meant for us, of being intruders. The magical lights of leaves and trees pressed the darkness away from the path, but between the trees, lurking, waiting, eager shadow ruled. Even without the warning not to stray, Hattie and I would not have left that cart path for anything.

As we passed through the strange place, no one suggested stopping for the night. Mostly, I wished to push on because I had learned not to trust things I could not explain; and I could not explain the brilliance of the trees nor the lingering certainty that we were not welcome within them. Nor could I explain the strange way my mind seemed to drift, becoming oddly detached from the experience as we drifted through that forest. I put each foot after the next, and yet never grew tired, never felt the sense of time passing, of the night growing fuller. In the quietness, all I had were my thoughts, and even they disappeared as soon as they came to me. The forest encroached and became all there was, but whether its ambiance was good or ill, I knew better than to let its wonders beguile me into complacency. Hattie must have felt the same, and we walked without speaking almost through the night under that glittering canopy, each of us clinging to our footsteps as the only metronome available to mark our progress.

After a time, the journey settled into a haze. Now and then, the forest revealed that we were not alone. Creatures of an otherworldly nature glimmered, unseen but sensed, at our periphery. Despite telling myself over and over to stay alert, the serene fugue settled over me like a soft blanket. I felt watched, but never panicked. At one point, I found my hand resting on my blackthorn club, but just resting. Hattie carried her bow with an arrow nestled in the string, but it was not raised. Perhaps we were spared from any malevolency due to having a dragon at our side, or perhaps no malevolency was there—there was no way to judge, or at least, I had no way to. And though I could not have sworn a full night passed, dawn reached us eventually, and I realized the brightness of a rising sun was visible only because the trees had begun to thin and the white path was no longer as stark against the darkness.

Finally, at the forest's edge, Toxicore suggested we step a short distance aside from the cart path and break for a while. Blinking in the daylight, though I could see no sun in the sky, I tried to recall the long night, but memories eluded me. I could only picture enormous, glowing trees and an echo of a sound that reminded me of wind chimes.

We settled in a grassy glade near a stream, and all save Paddy fell asleep. He volunteered to stand as our guard, his vigor not in the least diminished through lack of rest. I could see why he'd become so attached, as it were, to his new form. A dragon, even a small one, appeared to have few, if any, weaknesses.

Enormously awake and refreshed some unknown time later, we again set off. Our foodstuffs would last another two days, but I noted that hunger did not seem to be plaguing me as it should have been. I asked Hattie if she felt any different, and she concurred with me.

"It's funny, but I only feel like we left Abilene a couple hours ago. I don't even feel like we walked the night through, but just for a little bit. No farther than from the barn to the back pasture." The wonder in her eyes matched my own feelings.

"My uncle tells me that time doesn't pass here," I offered in explanation. "That's one of the reasons he's lived so long. Or did when he was still a man. Something like eight hundred years, though I'm not sure if I really believe it."

"I believe it," she said without hesitation. "Must be why we're not getting hungry and footsore."

I hitched my rucksack up on my shoulders and reached back to where I'd tied Sleg, tapping it for reassurance. Its silk wrapping was holding strong, though at my touch, Sleg oozed its dissatisfaction through its cover. "Let's call it an auspicious start to our quest, shall we," I said.

"Sure, Doc. It's a lot more auspicious than Knox's start, that's a fact."

I snorted in amusement, and our journey continued.

We rested briefly once more at what I would have liked to call midday if time were normal, but since there still was no hint of an actual sun overhead and the light hadn't changed at all, it was impossible to know how much "time"—whatever that meant here—had actually passed since we'd emerged from the enchanted woods, or stepped into Tír Na nÓg to begin with. This was the same sensation I'd experienced in the pocket realm my mother inhabited, so I was at least familiar with the experience if not exactly comfortable with it.

Along the way, Paddy took flight and kept a watchful eye for us on the road ahead and behind. Free of the heavy, watched feeling we'd had in the forest that had stifled any urge to converse among each other, I asked Toxicore for more information about where we were going.

"'Tis called Baile na Geasaíochta."

"...City of..." I struggled with my Old Irish.

"Spells, or perhaps Sorcery or Prophecy. English has never been capable of reckonin' with the Irish."

"Sounds... ominous," I admitted.

He gave me a sidelong glance. "Did you t'ink we were goin' to a city park?"

"No, of course not." I brooded for a moment.

Hattie closed the gap between the two of us, and we all three walked closely abreast along the narrow lane. "What else should we know?" she said.

He drew a long-suffering breath, reluctant to shoulder the "burden" of being the bearer of information, as usual. "Stay together is rule number one. And don't get lost. The city ends at the Sea o' Mists, but I suggest we keep as far from that side o' town as we can."

"Certainly, we'll follow your advice, but can you tell us why we should avoid that side?" I asked.

"Why? Why is 'cause that's where the Lady Morrígan's fortress is, isn't it? Easier for her to keep an eye on Magh Mell from there. We don't want to wander o'er there till we've found the druid and got the lay o' the land from him."

I stopped dead in my tracks, the reality of what we were doing finally hitting me. "We're walking straight into her hands. What are we thinking?" I mumbled.

"Aye, like leapin' directly into a pot o' boiling water," Toxicore said lightly, carelessly, if I was any judge of his tone. After walking a few more paces, he realized I wasn't still beside him, and he grudgingly stopped and faced me. "Accordin' to the map, 'tis where the loopy druid's still at too. Not getting cold feet, are you, Looloo?" Before I could say, he added, "Besides, the Morrígan knows ye're partly human and therefore"—he glanced at me skeptically—"not always goin' to make the wisest choice. But even she won't expect you to try waltzin' into town right under her nose. Far as she knows, ye're still runnin' scared o' her and whate'er monsters she sends after you."

I frowned, imagining walking directly into the lioness's den. With a glance at the cloudless sky and a silent command to myself to keep going, just keep going, I began walking once more. "Maybe we should prepare ourselves for chance encounters with those who may be on her"—what was the fae equivalent of *payroll?*—"side," I finished awkwardly.

"Aye, sure, but Baile na Geasaíochta is a maze of magic and illusion. The only way you can be prepared is knowin' you need to be. Worst t'ing for you to do is act like you don't belong."

"But aside from you, none of us belong, not really."

He went on as if I hadn't spoken. "We'll hide you in plain sight, make you look like just another fae wanderin' the streets. She'll never suspect, long as ye're glamour's strong and that spear stays hidden."

I allowed myself to experience in ingot of reassurance, however misplaced, until he jerked his large thumb at Hattie and said:

"'Tis the witch—sorry, witch, 'tis the *shaman*—what's goin' to be the problem."

I swallowed hard. "Why is that?"

"Look at how much iron she's carryin' fer one." He eyed me again. "You too, Looloo."

Hattie heaved a deep breath that was so dramatic it was as though she were struggling to contain a monster in her chest. I knew exactly how she felt. This was incredibly important information that Toxicore hadn't bothered to even consider telling us, and right now, she must have been having ideas on where *exactly* she wanted to stash some of that iron.

"What else, Darkheart? Spill it before I spill somethin' from you," she growled, bringing the whole party to a stop once more.

I don't know if it was her tone or the proverbial candle lighting in the dark of his mind, but Toxicore scowled, looked right and left as if searching for a way to escape this woefully unprepared troupe, and finally decided he might need to share some germane details.

"Look now, lasses. Ye're both babes in the woods here, and by comparison, I'm a wise old master. So, listen up, 'cause I don't like bairns and I don't like bein' responsible fer others, and I'm only goin' to tell you these t'ings the one time.

"Firstly, you already know not to drink or eat anything a fae offers you. You'll fall under their spell and may never leave Tír Na nÓg if they choose to keep you here. That mostly goes fer you, Dumas, as Looloo is less susceptible, what with her father bein' Lugh and all.

"Secondly, if you were to say that *I'm* not fond o' iron, you'd have to say the greater fae'd sooner turn you into toads and kick you into a viper pit than let you walk around with them guns. You best stash them well outside o' Baile na Geasaíochta if you plan to leave there in yer own skin.

"T'irdly, again, mostly in yer case, Dumas, don't look a fae in the eye. They don't trust humans, and they don't t'ink you smell particularly good. Most o' all though, don't talk to them. You can practice that art startin' now if you like."

He tugged the peak of his pyramid of white hair and nodded, as if coming to a great conclusion. "Lastly, don't dance."

We both waited for him to elaborate on this last part, but he seemed to think it was self-explanatory. "Why would we dance?" I finally asked.

He looked at me like I'd asked why breathing was necessary. "Just don't. Take me word for it."

Hattie and I exchanged a bewildered glance, but her perpetual scowl when it came to Toxicore, quickly broke through. "Last question, then, Darkheart. If I happen to break any of these rules, what would the consequences be?"

"Why?"

"What do you mean 'why'? I need to know what I'm gettin' into."

"I just told you."

She started to argue, but I gently held up a hand. "We've come this far, and I'm sure that between your wiles, my faeness, and Paddy's fearsomeness, we'll get along just fine, Hattie. We should all just try to remember"—I waited until my glare at Toxicore drew his eye to look into mine—"we are all in this together. Right?"

Tox almost dared to chuckle, but Paddy landed beside us at that moment.

"Everything all right?" he asked. "Why have you stopped?"

"The goblin decided he wanted to test his luck against my patience," Hattie snarled. "And they're both short."

Paddy's scaly brows rose in concern. "Oh?"

"He was just filling us in on some of the dangers of the city we're coming to. Are you familiar with the City of Spells?"

"I've not been there, but I do know the tales. 'Tis like any fae city, and… oh! Your guns. Yes, I had forgotten about that. It's been so long since I've been to Tír Na nÓg…"

Despite being a dragon, he sometimes seemed to be going as senile as his human age might have suggested. "Yes, Uncle, the guns may be a problem, as Toxicore explained. Did you see anyplace we might hide them until we come back this way?"

"And yer knives," Tox added.

Hattie looked like she might be about to have a stroke.

"It's just temporary," I tried reassuring her. "We'll be right back for them."

"I don't go anywhere without my Sharps."

"Ye're welcome to wait here," Tox suggested with great hope.

"No, that's not an option," I said. Compassion infusing my tone, I went on. "You'll have your bow, and I'll still have my shillelagh, but mostly, we have no intention of inviting a fight. It's up to you, though, Hattie. You could stay with our gear until we get back." Lowering my voice, I said, "I know how important your dad's rifle is to you. I'm not sure I'd be able to leave it behind if our places were reversed."

I could see the struggle in her eyes as she thought it over. After a moment, my uncle suggested, "There's a great wall of mist surrounding the city. It's close now, and I was able to explore a bit past the start of the fog while I looked ahead. Any number of mounds and barrows rise along the land that have ample caches of stones marking them. I could easily take your weapons to one of those and quickly hide them. No one who wasn't specifically looking for them would find them. The mist is quite thick," he added.

After a few more seconds, Hattie looked at me and forced a semi-amused snort. "If you think I'm lettin' you have all the fun, Doc, you don't know this Lakota woman at all."

I smiled. "I never thought for a moment you'd do that."

She jerked her chin forward and started walking again, unhitching her gunbelt as she strode on. "You be careful with this, Stowe. It's genuine buffalo and I don't want to have to buy another one."

17

What my uncle had called *mists* seemed more like walking into an opaque but permeable wall of water. I couldn't even see my own feet on the white stone road beneath me as we picked our way through. Occasionally, the mists would part enough to make out the ghostly shadows of small mounds of earth and stone in the landscape around us. These, Toxicore explained, were where the fae buried their rare and unfortunate dead. If we were to get lost in the mounds, we may never emerge. Hattie and I both grew uneasily silent until Paddy—now carrying all of our iron-based weapons in his claws and draped around his neck—pointed off to our left at a mound that had become faintly visible. He flapped over and was lost to sight when the heavy gray air shifted again, but became visible a few minutes later when he sent a stream of fire over our heads. The enchanted dragonfire, bolstered by the Orb of Incandescence that he carried in his stomach, burned the mist away long enough for us to get an idea of what the mound looked like. But only for a brief moment. The saturation closed in once more, swiftly and with vengeance. It seemed almost a living thing that resented any disturbance.

After that, we hurried on, and I forced myself to ignore the fact that it would be impossible to find that particular barrow again without Paddy. It shouldn't matter, right? He'd be with us upon our return from Baile na Geasaíochta. Of course he would.

Our consistent and dogged progression toward our destination paid off not long after when the mists parted abruptly and spilled us onto a swath of sunny farmland. This came as a great relief, I suspected even to the dragon and gnome.

Even with the mists behind us, sight of the lane we traveled along was obstructed by towering crops of a plant that reminded me of corn but had "ears" of a bright violet hue. Likewise, instead of corncob shaped, they were oblong and tapered at one end, and they smelled of fresh early springtime.

I fought with myself about plucking one, my natural curiosity making the struggle real. But by the time I'd argued that it couldn't hurt anything—there were miles of the fields in every direction, one plucked fruit wouldn't matter—we could hear the fae city. First coming to my ears as a buzzing vibration like a swarm of bumblebees, the faint sound didn't draw attention initially. But before long, it rose and crescendoed into an all-out hullabaloo not unlike the metropolitan burg I was raised in. In just a few hundred yards, we reached a wide-open area with a sweeping view of all. And I saw it—the city where the Morrígan's fortress stood, Baile na Geasaíochta.

Thoughts of the unique plant life snapped from my head as I stared in a state of slack-jawed overwhelm. While it was undeniably a large city comprised of buildings and structures of all varieties, their design was like nothing I had ever seen. Towers and spires of every color found in nature stretched upward, reaching for the sweeping blue sky and smudges of white clouds like hundreds of arms raised in worship. Yet these structures appeared to be part of the soil they rose—or grew —from. I saw not boards and nails joined together or bricks and mortar stacked up high, but growing trees the size of towers and massive boulders carved into the shapes of homes and such. And everything was covered with life: flowers, lichens, mosses, illuminated wild creatures that here and there took flight and turned the whole of the scene before me into a chaos of bright, beautiful flora and fauna.

And that was just what passed for architecture. The city stretched a great distance to our right and left and was encircled by a set of outer ring-stones, similar to the smaller circle of gateway stones, that seemed a kind of threshold. Nearly as tall as the doors of a gothic medieval church and carved with runes, these ring-stones were the only thing in sight not covered by some form of plant life, serving as stark white bastions separating country from city. Our cart path led directly through, and Tox strode past them without a second glance back to see if we followed.

Paddy landed alongside us before Hattie and I crossed the border. "Master Darkheart, one moment please." He waved a claw at me. "Your glamour, Lula-lee. Change yourself before you're noticed."

So gobsmacked by what stood before us, I'd forgotten this vital step. The only entity here who might know me on sight was the Morrígan herself, but who could tell what means the fae had of transmitting a person's likeness? I'd bet a year of my life they didn't have such archaic visual mediums as wanted posters, but instead, likely something far more sophisticated and, well, magical. For all I knew, the Morrígan could compel someone to shift their countenance into an exact replica of me based only on our single meeting, and send that person forth asking all and sundry if they'd met another me, the *real* one.

Now there was a disquieting thought; my imagination obviously had far too much fodder at its disposal. As Toxicore waited impatiently between two great ruined plinths, I poured water from a canteen onto my scarf and siphoned a bit of Sleg's vitality to keep my magic energized, making myself look as ordinary as I could imagine: cropped blonde hair; faded blue eyes; and weathered, middle-aged skin. I stayed female and human, though, unready to act the part of a fae, as I did not feel that was what I was deep in my bones, at least not yet.

Hattie looked me up and down, shrugged languidly, and said, "Bein' a redhead suits you better but it'll do."

After a none-too-confident grin, I then turned to Tox. "Is there anything we can do for Hattie to make her fit in better? Anything at all?"

"Aside from casting a spell to turn her into a mouse what can hide in yer pocket, nuttin. She's no fae, and no magic in this world or another can make her one."

"You best not even dare try turnin' me into a rodent, Darkheart."

"Remember this," Paddy said to her. "The fae are usually priggish toward humans, but few are outright hostile. Many humans have wandered into this land in centuries past, so you won't be the first who's come, nor the last. 'Tis just a matter of being respectful and quiet. Human voices tend to grate on the ears of some of the fae races."

"I agree with Paddy. Yer da did want to call you Screamin' Hawk, so yer mum says," Tox said. "Silence here will be yer best strategy. Elsewhere too, if you can do us all a favor."

"Tox," Hattie said, a bit too sweetly, as she bent to his height. "Come here. I need to tell you a secret."

Instead, he took several steps away from her. "Ye're goin' to scream in me ear," he grumbled. "I know a poison-laced sugar cube when I hear one."

Hattie straightened. "Hate to say it, but you're smarter than you look."

"Shall we?" I said with all the bravado of Napoleon before setting forth to attack Russia. I only hoped this mission fared better than his had.

18

On the other side of the City of Spells's ring-stones, the city sprang up like a fairy ring of mushrooms in an otherwise empty field. Already overawed by its looming buildings, spires, and living architecture, I was not at all prepared for the next round of wonders: the inhabitants of this Otherworldly milieu.

The majority shared a likeness with Leannan and Fiona of the Denver coven, humanlike though far more comely than typical people. But there were others. Some kinds I'd seen before: hobgoblins like Toxicore and trolls like Motherlode Mankiller and the faux marshal in Deadwood. Yet there was no end to the variety of beings populating the city. From creatures as strange as the Muculents, to others that could be cousins to Toxicore's race but were different in small yet distinct ways, greater and lesser fae teemed all around us. Some of the city dwellers even shifted from one shape to another before my eyes— cats becoming mules, birds becoming ants, and so many other things —until my mind simply gave up settling on what it was seeing and chose instead to focus on the buildings or sky, which at least stayed in one shape.

Despite growing up in a large populous city, I was not at all prepared for the City of Spells. It spread out in every direction. Small and large, round and square, every building conjoined together to create structures both beautiful and alien. Buildings were not so much constructed as grown, fused, or perhaps spun like spiders' webs into being. Towering trees, ancient as the hills, had been gently coaxed over vast expanses of time to bend and intertwine, forming an undulating canopy above the city. Their massive trunks housed winding staircases and hollowed rooms within.

Everywhere I looked, nature and artifice mingled into one, creating a veritable maze of wonders, where every stone had a secret to tell, every tree had a gift to give, and magic lurked around every corner. It was all quite dizzying.

Somehow, I shrugged my awe off. "It's been a while since we looked at the map. We-we need to figure out where Orville might be," I stammered, doing my damnedest to focus on our goal. We hadn't passed him on the road here. I had an unnerving worry that he might have been headed back to the gateway stones even if we hadn't seen him; but, in the Otherworld's peculiar way, a road of his own had appeared when he needed it and taken him there, never to cross our own.

"Darkheart," Hattie called, and I thought I detected a strain in her voice, too. At least I wasn't the only one who could barely rein in my wonder. "Get over here. We need to refresh the map."

"Need to get off the street first," he proclaimed, barely even turning back. "Remember, most fae don't take kindly to humans. Stay close, keep yer heads down, and don't speak unless spoken to, or we'll all end up prey for the Morrígan's pets."

As he said this, Tox shifted his appearance. Still a gnome, yet transformed into someone elderly with a long white beard sprouting from his cheeks and chin, bushy enough to hide his neck and half his chest. He developed a small but noticeable hunch, and the patch over his eye was hidden by a floppy-brimmed brown hat drooping over that side of his face. The hat came to a point that trailed down his back and was lost in the folds of a thick woolen cloak of the same color. He was completely unrecognizable as the Toxicore I knew, and it struck me how easily he could disappear on us in this place. He could transform into anyone and simply wander away, and we would be left entirely to our wits without a guide. I promised myself to keep any antagonistic or critical thoughts he might provoke to myself until we were back in our own world once more.

Fortunately, like any human city, the City of Spells had its own kind of commerce and entertainment, and Tox led us to an establishment not too far away that blended the two. We ducked through a doorway that was entirely covered by a net of Otherworld ivy, which parted on its own as we passed through. Hattie and I both shied away from brushing it with our hands and shoulders, distrustful of plant life that could move so purposefully.

"Tox," I whispered, touching his shoulder as he led us to a table. "We have no money, or whatever passes for such. Should we be in here?"

"Leave that to me," he said shortly.

Immediately, I was seized with the imperative to warn him not to steal from anyone here and lead danger directly to us, but I stopped myself. I'd just promised I wouldn't hector him. If I couldn't contain the impulse on the very first test, I never would. My life, and Hattie's, was in his hands. How dreadful.

The interior of the building was as exquisite as the outdoors. The walls and ceiling were adorned with intricate carvings, mosaics, and paintings depicting settings and creatures from this world, and to my great shock, mine and Hattie's as well. Clearly, just as Paddy had said, humanity's realm was no mystery to those who lived in this one.

What I was seeing paled in comparison to what I was smelling, though. The air was filled with an irresistible scent of sweet honey and spices that made my head whirl. All around the interior, Otherworld creatures moved about, eating or drinking or talking among themselves. We'd found a tavern, of course. Where else would Toxicore have led us?

We took a table, and two humanlike men—or half-men, as they were even shorter than Toxicore—clad in something similar to waistcoats approached us cautiously, their eyes wide with curiosity. Hattie and I sat stiffly, though I knew we should have done better to seem at ease.

The swarthier of them said something to Hattie, not in the least shy about engaging her, though he stood no taller than her thigh. My eyes widened right along with hers. His language was foreign, a chattering cadence with a singsong intonation that was unlike any tongue I'd ever heard. Helplessly, Hattie looked to Tox for translation.

He conversed with them in their own language, and their curiosity seemed to dull some. In a moment, they were giving Hattie side-eyed glances that broadcasted caution and not just a hint of scorn. Soon, though, they were gone, and if my perceptions were working at all, it seemed they left in a hurry.

"What did you say to those... what are those?" Hattie said. She couldn't seem to decide if she was angry or curious, and her tone wavered rather cutely.

"Brownies. Friendly sort to most humans. Occasionally they'll do one a good turn if a good turn is done fer them."

"What did they want?" she asked.

"Didn't I just tell you? They were goin' to offer you a round o' mead if you'd tell them about where ye're from. Curious about the human realm, their sort are. I warned them though, didn't I?"

"What would you need to warn them of? I'm no threat to them."

"Sure, you aren't," he scoffed.

Before Hattie could take offense, I said, "Perhaps we should get to the map."

"Naw, first, a round o' mead!" Toxicore said and scuttled away before I could stop him.

A serving bar stretched across the room's far end, and his path to it was unswerving. Despite his elderly disguise, the spryness in his gait couldn't be missed by a blind man. As I watched him go, I took in the rest of the establishment's patrons and realized the tingle of concern I'd felt about carrying the spear over the city's threshold had been unwarranted. The people of Baile na Geasaíochta all carried unusual items. Some had staves of wood, much bigger than but not unlike my shillelagh. A handful had obvious weapons like spears and swords, though the metals were different to my eyes than human steel. It didn't surprise me that this world would have natural elements that ours didn't, though. Others carried bags, but they were in shapes and materials not found in the Earthly realm. I didn't stand out any more than anyone else by having a long silk-wrapped item. It could have been anything, or even just a regular spear, and no one would have given it a second glance.

What they did glance at, and even openly stare at, was our table, their eyes drawn not to me but to Hattie.

Naturally, she quickly grew uncomfortable with the attention, but worse, she struggled with the knowledge that there was nothing she could do about it.

"Just ignore it, Hattie," I suggested. "Where's that map you started? Let's get it ready for when Tox gets back."

As she was removing the makeshift inkwell and pen from her bag along with the paper she'd originally drawn on, Tox returned, carrying four mugs. He sat them all in the middle of the table and took a seat, quaffing half of one in a single gulp.

"I can't drink that," Hattie said, giving him a cold stare. "According to you."

"Wasn't fer you, was it?" he said. He finished his first mug and grabbed a second.

Trying to fit in, I tentatively grasped the handle of one for myself. "I can't possibly drink two, Tox, and you shouldn't drink three."

"Last one's fer Stowe," he said, and swept the final mug from the table, setting it before my uncle.

"You are a capital fellow, Master Darkheart. The very finest," Paddy said, and shoved his muzzle as far into the honey-scented brew as it would go.

"Well, well, it's not normally like you to be so generous," I praised, but I could not hold back my criticism entirely. "How in the world are we going to pay for this?"

"We're not," he said. "She is." He indicated Hattie with a savage jut of his chin.

"What?" she blurted. Lucky for Tox she didn't have a mouthful of mead, as she'd have spit it out in surprise.

"Aye. The proprietress agreed to a wee wager. She'll give you a target and a chance to hit it with yer bow. If you can, drinks are on the house. If you can't, she takes the bow. Either way, we get drinks." He emphasized how gleeful this arrangement made him by taking another quaff of his second mugful.

My eyes flew to Hattie. If she did what came naturally to her and strangled Toxicore to death then and there, I didn't know if I would dare to intervene. She sucked her lips in and appeared to be using her entire body to keep her mouth under control, but slowly, incrementally, she calmed. "I'm a fair shot. So long as there's no magic afoot, and she doesn't ask me to shoot from here to the moon—wherever the moon is here—it might not be of any consequence. And if she asks me to shoot you, goblin, we'll drink free for as long as we're breathin'. *That* I am sure of."

"You shouldn't call me that, you know."

Tox being offended by anything she or I could say was a new one on me.

"What? Goblin?" she said.

He finished his second mead. "There's goblins in Baile na Geasaíochta what won't like their moniker bein' applied to a gnome. Or even a hobgoblin."

"And I don't blame them." After she took another temper-calming breath, she said, "So when's this shootin' display supposed to happen? We still have Downs to find."

As she asked this, I spied a familiar type of figure approaching our table. She was a troll. Once you've seen one, you cannot make the mistake of misidentifying them. Her overall stature and appearance were similar to Motherlode, except her tusks, though still yellowed ivory, were shorter and slightly straighter. Otherwise, she was brutish, bulky, and had the rough, pocked skin of both the other trolls I'd met. Like Motherlode and the Deadwood marshal, she looked like she could —and would—happily snap us in half with one hand.

"I think the proprietress is coming to answer that very question," I quickly warned Hattie.

She turned to look just as the troll arrived. Standing beside us, the fae towered over our seated figures like a statue carved in honor of ugliness, crossing her arms intimidatingly and glaring down. She wore leggings of brown suede under a tunic of coarse, undyed linen. Around her tree-stump-size neck hung a necklace of bone and gemstone beads. Her face was painted with ochre in jagged lightning bolts from forehead to chin. In contrast to her rough attire, a garland of wildflowers, nut shells, and fresh greenery encircled an unruly black topknot piled atop her broad cranium.

"Ach, Beatmylla, couldn't you wait till we all finished our drinks?" Toxicore complained.

I expected the troll to answer, but as with all things fae, my expectations were immediately turned on their heads. Out from the troll's topknot flew a tiny... person, for lack of a better term. No taller than my ring finger, this diminutive being glittered like pixie dust but shared not a single other commonality, besides being winged, with the horrific soul-sucking monsters. The figure had no sex that I could see at first, just the outlines of a human form, as they zipped directly toward Hattie's face. If they wore clothing, it was skin-tight as well as skin-colored, straining my sense of modesty.

Hattie shot to her feet at the winged being's speedy, unexpected approach.

"Don't strike at her!" Toxicore warned, not a moment too soon, as Hattie had just lifted an arm to backhand the creature. "Beatmylla'll cook you so hot, your children will be charcoal!"

Hattie froze, too stunned to speak. The tiny person flew up and looked her in the eye, making Hattie's own cross at how close the being hovered. I heard a microscopic voice, tinny and high-pitched, castigating my friend. Then the being backed off and flew up and down the length of Hattie's height from a couple of feet away, as if assessing her. They zipped over to Toxicore, and their tiny voice came to my ears again.

"All right, all right, fine," Toxicore gruffed. "Lead the way, Beatmylla."

Beatmylla returned to the troll's topknot, and the troll turned away from us without saying a word, beckoning us to follow.

"Grab yer bow, Dumas. Time to show the sprite yer skills." Toxicore swiped my mug from the table, apparently having decided I was drinking it too slowly to deserve it.

"What in Lincoln's log cabin, Tox?" I whispered as I walked beside him. "That lilliputian person is the proprietress?"

"Don't let her hear you call her a person, Looloo. She's a bit of a racialist."

"Everywhere I go…" Hattie grumbled.

Glancing at her commiseratingly, I said to Tox, "So she's a she?"

"How do I know? I just call everyone what has a voice pitched high as a mosquito's a girl. Easier than tryin' to tell them apart from each other."

"That's rather rude," I chastised.

"And here I thought you were the practical one," he replied.

The tavern's patrons parted to let us pass, the attention of all now gripped by the coming event. It seemed we were not the first to be roped in to such a pastime, and I began to suspect that this type of thing was common entertainment here. It fit well enough with how I'd come to see fae-human relations, with mostly the fae side looking at the mundane human race as weak simpletons who were if not to be outright shunned, at least to be pitied. A spark of pride lit in my chest then; Hattie would show these racialist peacocks and braggarts that there was nothing simple, pitiful, or weak about her kind—or was that *our* kind? My own mixed lineage left me unsure.

At the bar, the sprite emerged from the troll's hair and said something to her. The troll lumbered to the far end of the bar, and Beatmylla flew up to Tox's face, gesticulating with their tiny arms and giving him directions by the looks of it.

After nodding to her, he turned to Hattie. "You go stand at the other end there." He waved a hand at the far end of the bartop.

"Grunchya is yer target. You have one chance to hit her, and it has to be right in the head."

"Grunchya?" Hattie said skeptically. "The troll?" We all looked where the monster stood, placidly eyeing us with an undercurrent of disdain that suggested she'd never seen a human hit anything more distant than their own nose with a bow and arrow and didn't believe for a second Hattie would do it now.

"Aye. One chance, I said. You got to hit her, in the gob I say, or near-about."

"I'm not going to shoot someone with an arrow, Darkheart! That'll kill her."

"You have to fulfill the deal or lose the bow," he said matter-of-factly. "One hit. Come on, Dumas. I know you have it in you. How many times've you tried to hit me? Like that one time I collected one o' yer horses on the promise that I'd only be out of town fer three days and would pay you double when I got back. Remember that?"

Hattie was eyeing Tox closely, her expression suggesting she thought his rambling aside was proof that he'd gone completely mad. Slowly, she said, "You didn't know I'd be able to find you so easily in Junction City. I thought you were gonna spit fire when I showed up and stuck Judgment right into your cheek."

He was nodding happily, seemingly pleased to be sharing this rather unsavory memory with her. "That's right. You remember what you told me? The only reason you weren't blowin' me head clean off right then was 'cause you wanted yer payment first, but you didn't have the same qualms about gettin' yer due with yer fists if you had to."

Her eyes narrowed. "You know you're lucky you had the money or you'd still be sportin' a set of matching blinkers."

"Aye, like I said, you can hit anyt'ing you set yer mind to. And that's all you got to do here. One hit, square in her face."

Like the other patrons around us awaiting what was to come, I was positively mystified by what almost appeared to be an agreeable moment between the two. Of course, the customers seemed more impatient than mystified, but all of us had no idea why Toxicore felt he needed to give a pep talk to someone who had to shoot an arrow at a target that was bigger than a bear and only twenty paces distant.

Hattie, on the other hand, had grown solemn, serene even. Beatmylla zipped between her and Toxicore, gesticulating impatiently, apparently agitated at Hattie for taking so long to fulfill her end of the bet. Hattie, ignoring the tiny sprite, calmly laid her quiver on the bartop but held her bowshaft gripped in one hand. Without a glance in any direction, she paced up to the troll, planted her boots in a fighting stance, lifted the bow, gripped the shaft with both hands like a bat, and swung it at the creature with a roundhouse that cracked against the troll's jaw so hard that I felt it in my own.

She didn't wait for Grunchya's reaction before spinning around and walking back to the sprite, who'd gone still and hovered in place with precisely calibrated wingbeats. "That was one hit. I expect that means I fulfilled the terms of the bargain," she said.

Though Beatmylla's features were miniscule, I had no trouble seeing the anger at being bested in what Hattie must have correctly surmised was a trick. Tox's wording had been precise, I now realized, and he'd never said she had to hit the troll with an *arrow*, only with the bow. My glance shot to his face, and the smug satisfaction I saw there proved Hattie had correctly interpreted what his strange trip down memory lane had been trying to tell her.

As I digested this odd turn, I looked at Grunchya. The troll, despite the powerful blow, had not changed her rigid stance nor did she even look angry. Well, she didn't look *angrier*. It stood to reason that the strength of a human's strike would be little more than a minor nuisance to one as solidly built as the troll, for which I was grateful. Hattie might be able to throw a solid punch, but regardless of how tough she was, she definitely couldn't take one from the likes of someone that big.

Beatmylla had taken to effusing vehemently at Toxicore, but he only nodded mildly and explained that they'd followed the letter of the bargain precisely and there was nothing the sprite could do about it if they wanted to continue to be seen as a fair-minded and honest tavern owner. Beatmylla grew quiet, stared at him for a long second, then flew toward a candle that sat on the bartop. Before I understood what they were doing, they'd dipped their tiny hand into the flame and scooped up a ball of fire no bigger than a pea and hurled it at Tox.

It smacked into his cheek and puffed away in a barely-seen blast of white smoke. Tox didn't even flinch. Beatmylla returned to Grunchya, and the two of them disappeared into a back room.

Hattie looked at me and I at her.

"Guess we learned that sprites have a bit of a temper, huh?" she said.

I nodded. "And trolls are surprisingly genial about being struck in the face."

"I'm not going to put that theory to a test a second time, if it's all the same to you, Doc."

We both burst out chuckling, and the four of us made our way back to our table. The show over, most of the patrons went about their business, losing interest in ours.

Half my mugful remained, and I was not about to press our luck to order more. "Well, Tox, we've come no closer to finding Orville, but you've had some refreshment. Could you please focus now and help us find him? I don't think we'll be welcome here much longer."

"Found him," he responded blandly.

I was about to chide him for being so obdurate, but instead my gaze was drawn over Hattie's shoulder to the new patron who'd just come inside. Though the individual wore a gown of pale lavender silk embroidered with silver flowers, exceedingly pointy pale shoes that peeked from under the scalloped hem of the gown, and a short cape with a deep hood pulled over to hide their face, I knew that gait.

I looked back to Tox. "How could you have possibly known he'd come here?"

"Easy," he said. "'Tis the only tavern in Baile na Geasaíochta what serves unenchanted mead humans can drink." He downed the last of the mug he'd taken back from me and belched.

19

Hattie was still fuming at Toxicore for not telling her she could drink the mead, all goodwill he'd gained at enlisting her in what turned out to be an easy quasi heist depleted, so I took it upon myself to approach Orville. I didn't want to surprise him, but there was no getting around the fact that he would be. He'd specifically asked me to wait for his return before I ventured into the Otherworld, and here I was. But Hattie's ranch was on the line, and there was no alternative that I could see but to help my friend. He would understand. And if he didn't, I no longer had the time or luxury of caring.

Our table was near the front wall, not visible from anyone upon entry unless they explicitly turned aside to look in our direction. He hadn't, and with the hood concealing his face, his vision was considerably occluded. When he stood at the bar to place his order, I stepped up beside him casually and said in a low voice:

"Don't overreact, Orville, but it's me, Lula." I laid my hand next to his on the bartop and showed him the package of Huppman Imperiales I'd borrowed from Hattie, something that he'd easily associate with her and me.

He tensed, but credit to his comfort with subterfuge, he did not look at me, nor was his voice much strained when he said, "Doctor, I had very much hoped you'd heed my advice and wait for me to return."

"Things have grown complex, and we had to come."

"We?" he asked, sliding a handful of small shiny objects, similar to semiprecious gemstones, across the bar to the bartender, a brownie. I wondered how the short person could reach the bartop but decided to satisfy that curiosity another day. The brownie slid a mug like the ones we'd previously drank our mead from to Orville and took his payment.

"Hattie, Tox, Paddy, and me," I said.

"Four more if you would, kind sir," he said to the barkeep. Finally, he turned to look at me, and I spied his perfectly waxed mustache and dark glittering eyes deep in the hood. "If Master Stowe and Darkheart are with you, that explains how you reached the City of Spells in one piece. I look forward to your tale." He said this with an expression that appeared to be anything but enthusiastic.

The four additional mugs arrived, and I helped him gather them up, then led him to our table.

"Nice dress," Hattie said smoothly as we reached the others.

"It's a gown, Miss Dumas, to be precise. And I do take my skills at the art of disguise seriously, as you can see." With a bit more pomp than strictly necessary, he fluffed the gown and took a seat. After taking a long drink from his mug, never removing his eyes from us from over the lip of the vessel, he swallowed and leaned back. "Now, please do fill me in on why you've risked life, limb, and a fae-instigated war on Earth to come to Tír Na nÓg."

I leaned down to scratch the spider bite above my ankle, probably for the tenth time since the start of my explanation to Orville. It hadn't bothered me at all while walking through the enchanted forest, but it was now, cussed thing. I'd never tried Ghitaine's sachet, not being overly keen on the idea of mixing a paste of unknown materials with my own spit and applying it to my skin, or anything else. But now, the bite was growing to be such a nuisance that I more seriously considered it.

We're not more than halfway through our indescribably delicious drinks when I finish the tale. Brevity was easy—we had so little of a plan to begin with that my explanation could be summed up as: Hattie needed a spell from the Morrígan's vaults to save her land from a thief, and I could no longer put off rescuing my father, if for no other reason than to pass Sleg back to its master so it would quit pestering me about killing something.

"So," I finished. "As you can guess, we're hoping you'll remain behind to help us instead of returning to Denver right away. We need to get into the Morrígan's castle, and you are the man for the job." I then realized that it was not yet clear if Orville's original mission to sneak back into the castle and find the spellbook for Leannan had been successful. "Aren't you?"

Orville rubbed his heavily creased forehead with his fingers. "Lula, I've only known you for a short time, but it has been plenty of time to learn of your dogged impetuousness. I really should have expected to find you here." The mixture of bleakness and exasperation in his expression made his immaculate mustache droop. "Master Stowe, you couldn't talk her out of this?"

"Talk her out of it?" My uncle sounded genuinely confused by the question. "I hadn't considered it, to be honest. I don't see the danger as anything greater than what she's already faced."

"You don't see..." Orville was incredulous. He seemed about to argue, then reconsidered. "No, of course, you wouldn't grasp the tension here in Tír Na nÓg. The Lady Morrígan is very much up in arms about this spear business, and *her* business as well." He indicated me with a nod. "She doesn't like to be bested, not even temporarily. And as for you, Darkheart, I don't imagine you'll be too happy to know how frequently your name has crossed the sharpened tongues of the Argent Crows in these times, either."

"The Argent Crows, you say?" Tox said.

Orville looked pained. "Indeed. Your disguise will only get you so far with them on your trail, you know. Frankly, I'm surprised you haven't gotten Lula caught yet."

I felt the infrequent urge to defend Toxicore. "He's been quite helpful, Orville. In fact, we had a run-in with some creatures called Muculents, and Tox was pivotal in resolving that, er, issue." I hadn't felt the need to divulge the kidnapping of Knox to Orville, as brevity was, as I mentioned, the goal—and perhaps I felt a twinge of embarrassment about having resorted to the ways of a, dare I say it, *outlaw*. "As was the spear of course. But who are the Argent Crows?"

"The spear?" His eyes widened in alarm. "Do you mean you've had it uncovered since you arrived?"

It galled me that I actually felt chagrined at his implied scold. I really should have known better than to reveal the weapon.

"The Argent Crows are the Morrígan's personally trained royal guard," Sleg cut in. "Nasty and savage. It would be such a delightful challenge to test how many I could strike down in a single thrust." Its wistful tone lowered to a conspiratorial whisper. "But don't listen to this jackanape, daughter of Lugh. Can any human really be trusted?"

"Why are you whispering?" I asked the spear aloud. "No one else can hear you."

Instead of answering, it merely said, albeit in a more normal volume, "You are a child of the Tuatha Dé Danann. No churlish mortal should be allowed to speak to you thus. If you'd like, I can ensure he never does again."

Abstaining from giving the weapon an oh-so-deserved talking-to, I returned my attention to Orville. "It was a momentary thing. They most likely didn't even recognize Sleg for what it is. I don't know if you've met a Muculent, but they are decidedly... different."

Orville, however, did not abstain from a deeply put-upon sigh. "Maybe they knew it and maybe they didn't. The Muculents keep to the borders and don't interact much with the more urbane fae. Their dietary preferences are not one that most here approve of, which makes them unwelcome. Maybe you'll get lucky and they won't speak of it. But I must drive this point home with all emphasis. Do not expose the weapon in

Baile na Geasaíochta. There isn't a soul here who won't know it on sight, and therefore, know who you are. You may have wandered into the viper's pit voluntarily, but do you want to make it easy for her to strike?"

His dark eyes held mine, and there was nothing in them but genuine concern. I simply nodded my assent.

"All right then." He leaned back and finished his mead in a long drink. "Now, I was on my way back to the gateway before stopping in for a last pint. I hired a mount from a local proprietor to get me there, which I should be picking up now. I'll still need to visit him to let him know my plans have changed."

He prepared to stand, but I reached out and placed a hand upon his wrist. The feel of his gown's sleeve was sublimely soft, more luxurious than any silk I'd ever touched. Humans could learn a thing or two about fashion from the fae.

"Orville, wait." The moment of truth was upon us. "Does this mean you'll stay and help me? Help us?" I added, glancing at Hattie to bring her into the query.

"Of course, dear doctor. I am at your service."

20

Orville strode purposefully through the lanes in the meandering, magnificent city. Doing my best not to become overwhelmed by the wildly unusual landscape, I followed, the others behind us. Hattie continued to draw glances, but at least outside the tavern, more of the city's inhabitants had better things to do than gawk. She naturally stood out, not only due to her lack of an innate fae glow. That was just Hattie.

Distracting myself, I continued our conversation. "Orville, were you able to secure the spellbook with a—what was it? A spell to draw Quetzalcoatl from the phylactery?"

"I did. In fact, I have it here." He stopped beneath an awning. That was the first word that came to mind, but the construction really appeared to be a gigantic mushroom cap that so happened to be just above head height and provided a nice bit of separation from the main street traffic. "Actually, Master Stowe, I wonder if you wouldn't mind carrying it for me. I rather think you'd be better suited to the task with your greater agility and defensive capabilities." He patted a carrying case he'd slung over his shoulder meaningfully.

Hattie asked, "Since you're wanderin' around on the streets, you must not have had too much trouble gettin' the book, Downs. Why are Paddy's agility and fightin' skills necessary?" Right to the heart of the matter.

Orville looked cagey, in his charming way. "In case something happens to me."

"In case… Orville, I don't like the sound of that," I said.

"And I don't like saying it, but we're in a magical land, and it seems best to me that a magical entity possess the tome."

"I'll take it," Toxicore said.

Orville eyed him, seemed about to protest, then was dissuaded when Paddy concurred. "'Twill be awkward for me to carry it," my uncle said, "and if something were to happen, I could drop it or the satchel could be torn. Master Darkheart is better equipped for such a task."

"Why does everyone keep suggesting something bad might happen?" I asked, noting the edge of shrillness in my tone. The bite on my ankle flared again, and I raised my leg to scratch it.

Without acknowledging my query, Orville gave in. "Darkheart," he said dubiously, handing the bag over.

Toxicore pulled aside the hem of his cloak and slid the satchel beneath it. A moment later, his hand emerged empty, though his cloak showed no sign of the package. I had to admit having a touch of jealousy for his "pocket." It would certainly make carrying and concealing Sleg much easier.

Orville continued on down the lane as I posed a new question. "How will we get into the Morrígan's fortress to find my father's prison? The same way you've managed to on previous occasions?"

He looked at me from the side of his eye. "I'm sorry to have to tell you this, Doctor, but there's no need to seek your father in the Morrígan's castle. He's no longer there."

"What?" I nearly tripped on a slightly offset cobblestone but quickly regained my pace.

"Where is he?" Hattie asked.

"He's been exiled to an island off the coast called Magh Mell."

Toxicore had mentioned this name before. "Why? What's there?" I asked.

"Very little except danger in the form of a beast more hideous than you want to contemplate. It's the abode of the nuckelavee. A monster so ghastly and cruel that the Morrígan has master carvers working year-round affixing sigils to the barrier stones encircling the island just to keep the monster contained there. The beast works tirelessly to try to smooth the stones and break the spell, and the carvers can never stop, or it will be free."

I remained quiet, absorbing this unpleasant news. Hattie, again, asked a pointed question. "I thought Lula's pa was trapped in a cage that only the spear could unlock. Does that mean his whole cage was moved?"

"Excellent question, Miss Dumas, and the answer is yes. But you misunderstand what Lugh's, or I should say Bran's, cage is. It's not a prison of bars or walls but rather his own mind. And that has gone quite… askew. He is not the great and royal lord of the Tuatha Dé Danann anymore. He is a mere shell of what he was, all thanks to the measures he took to pass as human and live among them. He can only reclaim who he is, who he *really* is, and be free of his cage if he is reunited with his divinity. No bars or building is needed to keep him under the Morrígan's control while the spear contains the divinity orb. But more on that later. We're here."

He slowed outside a towering building with two broad trees forming an archway over the front entrance. An elegant but incomprehensible script was carved along the arch like a sign.

"Follow me, quickly," Orville said and led the four of us past the entrance and into an arched tunnel beside the building that was as pleasant as any flower-bedecked gazebo in a summer garden.

"Now, I need to go speak to the proprietor about my mount. I advise the rest of you to wait here. Snig-gnawg isn't always fond of humans, and he's never fully trustworthy. But let me tell you this before I go, Doctor. The spear—I've learned why it slept for so long and how the Morrígan was able to keep it contained. You see, before Lugh crafted it, the weapon was a wondrously renowned harp of gold. Lugh had it melted and used the gold to forge the spear. And therein lies its weakness: the music it once played will now make it sleep, and it has probably long-since forgotten its original nature. In being reformed, it went from being a thing of beauty to a thing of danger, and now, aside from the command of its master, only music like that it once played will stop it. One tune in particular."

"What tune?" I asked, fascinated in spite of myself.

"Only the Morrígan knows."

"And only the doc or someone of Lugh's family line can reawaken it, that right?" Hattie asked.

"Precisely."

"Meaning, if this tune gets played while the doc's holding the spear, it won't have any effect on it?" she pressed, drawing the important details from him.

"Well now," he said, pondering. "I don't know for certain, but it stands to reason. Lula's touch awoke it from sleep before. If it's in your hands," he said to me, "it shouldn't be prone to the spell that stops it."

"But only if it's in my hands," I said.

He looked pensive, but Hattie took this as a positive. "This is great news, Doc. Long as we steer clear of the Morrígan and you keep that pointy has-been harp close, we shouldn't encounter any trouble." She considered. "Except this knucklehead thing."

"Ye-s-s-s, that. I have to confess to a modicum of concern about that," I said.

"I'll tell you more upon my return," said Orville as he paced to the end of the tunnel.

Once he'd entered the street, the spear's wispy voice filled my head. "Do not listen to that man. He obviously doesn't know a mighty weapon of war when he sees one."

"He did say that you forgot your original nature when you were re-created. Do you know this tune that might disable you?" Hattie's curious glance found my eyes, and I shrugged and jerked my chin over my shoulder, where Sleg in its wrapping jutted up from the strap holding it to my rucksack. Awkward as carrying it was, I'd gotten used to the weight, and, honestly, I took some comfort in knowing it was there. On second thought, I might not have wanted to carry it in a magical storage pouch after all. A magical wooden club with hazardous foliage at my command was nice; but a virtually unstoppable weapon that could turn into a flash of lightning was another thing altogether. Except, of course, if I were to throw it and it was put to sleep.

"Disable me? Nothing can do that, not again. I am unstoppable and mighty!" it answered, then trailed off, perhaps uncertain of its own certainty.

We fell into silence after that. Toxicore moved near the mouth of the tunnel, his gaze never leaving the main street. He was so alert, in fact, that it was making me nervous.

After what felt like ten minutes—but who could say in this place?—my squirming nerves turned into biting ones. "What could be taking him so long?" I said.

"He may be attempting to barter with the proprietor for extra mounts for the rest of us. It might be best to have a speedier option than walking when we're ready to leave the City of Spells," Uncle Paddy offered. "These things can take some time."

I wanted to be placated, but the explanation felt wrong. With nothing else to distract me, I settled and withdrew my shillelagh, practicing the spell that sprouted vines from its serious end and then the one to withdraw them as I tried to remain patient. This did an adequate job of taking my mind off things, until the irksome bite shot another prickle into my ankle. As I bent to scratch it, preparing to really dig in and put an end to the itching once and for all, movement in the nearby depths of the archway wall's crisscrossing boughs caught my eye. Something small, mouse-size, and whitish-gray.

I stilled, leaning toward the wall to peer into the shadows between boughs. The alley's soft light glittered against something shiny, a set of tiny black beads, then another set, and another, until I realized there were at least a dozen of them. Eyes... spider's eyes, in fact, glaring at me.

"Come here, you pestiferous little—" I started, reaching unthinkingly for the eight-legged dust-mote that had bitten me. I would be damned if the creature wasn't following me, and I was going to get to the bottom of it right now and perhaps somehow glean the antidote to the incessant itch it had inflicted on me.

But then Toxicore suddenly stiffened at his post near the street and sucked air through his teeth in a manner suggestive of a sudden fright. Seeing Toxicore frightened—another first—sucked all my bravery away like a sudden yank on a corset lace.

Hattie and I instantly straightened, alert.

"Argent Crows," he warned in a low voice. "Hide yerselves!"

I shot my gaze back to where the spider had been tucked away, but it was gone. No matter; we had a bigger concern now. Hattie and I pressed our backs into the foliated alley wall. Toxicore, of course, was gone in a shimmer. Paddy, the only one among us who seemed to have no enemies, merely sat placidly, tongue lolling, watching the street.

My view was partly obstructed by dangling green and purple vines, but my ears were not. The sound of many booted feet moving at a quick pace came to our ears a moment before a troop of half a dozen armored fae passed in front of the alley tunnel's mouth. My stomach clenched in anxiety, but none of the soldiers glanced inside. Just as my belly began to relax, I heard one of them give a loud command in the local language, and the beat of the boots stopped as one. I didn't need to be a geometry scholar to know they'd halted directly before the entrance to the building Orville had gone in.

Tox reappeared beside us. "We'd best wait here till they're inside."

"Inside," I whispered. "Where Orville is."

"Aye. He's the one they're here fer, most likely. Which means, we should get as soon as we can."

"We can't leave him! What if he needs our help?"

"Help?" he asked. "You feel good about yer chances of winnin' a fight against a bunch o' fae warriors what's been usin' magic since yer da tricked Bres the half-Fomorian into drinkin' bad milk?"

"Bres the half...? I have no idea what any of that means, but my need to help a friend and my need for his help dictate that I not stand idly by if Orville is in trouble. Hattie, will you come?" I asked as I stepped toward the street.

"Does a frog bump his ass when he walks?" She was already beside me, and Paddy didn't need any encouragement either. He'd taken a liking to the younger druid.

"Ach!" Toxicore fretted, but we paid him no mind.

I peeked around the corner and saw the last of the Argent Crows already passing through the door of the apparent livery. Hoping we weren't too late, we rushed to the entrance, whereupon I took a quick glance through the doors.

The smell fuming from inside hit me in the nose like a wet feather pillow. Precisely because it smelled like feathers, though not wet. More musty, with a distinct patina of the lion's cage at the Philadelphia Zoo. After blinking to acclimate to the gloom, I saw why—instead of stalls for horses, peppered throughout the vast space were numerous round piles of sticks and foliage that could only be birds' nests. Yet these nests were big enough to be the abodes of the aforementioned lions. Scattered on the floor among them were giant splotches of a fecal matter no animal I'd ever seen would be capable of producing. This observation was supported by several winged animals milling around that appeared to have the heads of eagles or hawks and the bodies of—yes— lions.

"Ah!" Paddy said, seemingly delighted. "That's why the sign over-head says 'Snig-gnawg's Griffins.'"

"Are they dangerous?" I asked, scooting away from the doorway.

"Oh, aye, very, but only if you're cruel and they're hungry. This Snig-gnawg must be a master trainer to be keeping so many."

His admiration was obvious, but I was not sure now was the time to be praising the husbandry skills of a fae who may very well have double-crossed Orville. "Come on," I said.

Beside me, Hattie pulled her bow off her shoulder and loosely nocked an arrow. Paddy pressed close to my leg, and Toxicore... was gone. In days past, this would have been concerning, but he'd come to my aid enough times now that I believed he'd be here if needed. I crossed my fingers anyway.

The bright yellow eyes of the dozen or so creatures lazing on the ground or in their nests watched us closely as we moved into the enormous space. But the Argent Crows, along with Orville and the proprietor, were nowhere to be seen.

This wasn't surprising, though, as it soon became even clearer to me why the city was called the City of Spells. I'd noted the building was tall from the outside, but "tall" was an inadequate word to describe the interior. The roof soared overhead so high that I had to crane my neck back to try to glimpse it—yet, glimpsing it was not possible, because it soared to such heights that it disappeared into the interior's own atmosphere, complete with clouds. What I'd taken to be roof posts proved to be trees rising every few feet from the earth, their canopies lost in the cloud cover. The interior stretched before us for blocks and blocks in every direction. Some magic had transformed this livery into exactly the kind of den or aviary such creatures as griffins must prefer. Why they chose to build their nests on the ground was an unanswered question, and it would remain so at least until we found Orville.

"Puts my little stable in Abilene to shame," Hattie said, her voiced hushed. "Where is everyone?"

Her eyes never left the animals we passed, and there was a rapturous mix of excitement and a veneration in her face. I imagined mine showed only respectful fear.

"Don't look them in the eye," Toxicore snapped, his voice some-where behind us, though he was not. At least not visibly.

We pressed forward, none knowing what or who we might encounter. At least the place was well lit, even if I could see no light source. Still, the interior's depth and the visual impediment caused by the nests and trees made it none too clear where the Crows could be. Given the size of the place, we had before us an impossible search.

"Oi! Who are you?"

We all jerked our heads to spy the owner of the husky voice coming from our right. A creature strode toward us, his tone expressing clear anger at the intrusion. He'd spoken English, though heavily accented. Possibly because of Hattie's obvious human roots? Or could it be because he'd just been speaking with Orville?

"Aye, that's Sniggles, 'tis," Tox whispered. "Now you see why 'tis best not to call me a goblin."

Tox had complained that goblins would take offense at their name being applied to hobs, which I'd taken to mean they considered hobs unsightly or lowly. But the, shall we say, *unattractiveness* of Snig-gnawg was so categorical that Toxicore looked like a cute little bunny in comparison. He was a gnarled creature, about Hattie's height but twice as wide as her and I put together, with pointed ears and sharp teeth that didn't quite fit behind his black lips. His nose was mere black slits inside his wide green face. Wearing a loose-fitting tunic and leggings suited for manual labor, he trailed a cloud of dirt, dust, and grime. His hand, tipped with savagely long claws, was wrapped around a pitchfork, and his hulking shoulders promised a formidable foe should a fight ensue.

My first encounter with an actual goblin, and something warned me it might not go half as well as my first with a hobgoblin. On that occasion, Toxicore had just insulted my modesty; this creature looked like he might consider an insult a mere icebreaker.

As the only fae present, I took on the role of speaker for our party. "Pardon me, sir, are you the owner of this establishment?"

"What's that human doing here?" he demanded rudely, gesturing at Hattie with the pitchfork.

"She's with me," I said, just shy of curt, taking umbrage at his tone despite myself. "I'm here to inquire about a friend. He just came to see you, I believe."

The goblin halted in front of me. He positively exuded impatience and, what had Toxicore called it? Racialism? It definitely had an unpleasant miasma. "Two humans in one day are two too many," he spit, actually spitting. I took a step back. "If you're here, you must be lookin' for the druid. Which means you're mixed up in whatever he's done to anger the Lady Morrígan." He turned his head and split the air with a sharp, long whistle.

The griffins around us bristled and squawked at the noise. Hattie and I tensed at the shrill sound. Between two tree trunks, I caught the shadow of what I thought was another griffin loping toward us, but a second later, the shadow caught enough light for me to make out what was approaching more clearly: several Argent Crows, the entire troop that had passed, by the looks of it. Now that they were near, I caught a better view of their uniforms. They wore headdresses shaped like the heads of the blackest of crows, complete with long, sharp beaks and beady black eyes. Their charcoal-gray trousers and tunics flashed beneath floor-length hooded cloaks of black oiled canvas, and each had high boots of black leather. What their faces looked like was indiscernible beneath their headdresses, and I wasn't sure I wanted to know.

As they approached, the items that most stood out, however, were their weapons, varying from zinc-colored flails to bone-handled daggers to bastard swords. Upon the breasts of their tunics were black and red sigils and a diving red crow, claws extended like a hawk's, over a char-colored field.

In a word, they were terrifying. That might be the reason that when I heard Orville shout from somewhere in their midst, "Flee, Lula! Run!" my reactions were like those of a woman in a dream being pursued by man-eating tigers. The kind of dream where one is encased in frozen molasses.

21

I t was Sleg that saved us.

Or was it the cause of our downfall?

"I can help, my lady. Let me," it seethed in my head.

Orville had been seized, that was clear. And we'd be next if we didn't do something. But leaving him behind was no option.

I looked aside and saw Hattie readying her bow. She understood the assignment, there was no doubt about that. But what were our chances against this much greater, much abler foe? Was a fight really the best decision here, now, in this world? But if we ran, where could we go? First through a city that was capable of defying physics; then, if we made it past the ring-stone boundary, through a mist-filled cemetery where one misstep could find us swallowed in its endless fog for eternity; and if we made it through *that*, then through a forest filled with an ethereal, indefinable malice?

When measured against all those, a fight admittedly seemed the least worst option, but I hadn't any hope our small rag-tag group was a match for what was approaching. Thus, I finally gave Sleg its wish.

"Maim only," I commanded the spear, hoping Hattie and Paddy were in agreement. "Just buy us some time to save Orville and get away from here."

"As you wish," it grunted, none too pleased. Figures.

I reached for the quick-release tie holding Sleg on my back and yanked it. Instead of falling, the weapon did as the weapon was wont to do and simply hovered a foot off the ground, unwilling to be tainted by the dirt and detritus of the floor. The Crows, now merely forty feet distant, knew when someone was about to brandish a weapon and drew their own, though with Sleg still enshrouded in its silk cocoon, they may not have known what it was. Snig-gnawg had slipped away among the nests. As the Crows closed in, I caught a glimpse of Orville in their midst, hands bound behind him and a stout fellow holding a slip of rope around his neck for good measure. Another stood behind them, holding the reins attached to a bridle worn by a ferocious griffin.

The rest of the Crows lunged. I yanked Sleg's silk wrapping free and reminded it: "Maim only!"

"No, Lula!" Orville yelled. His voice was cut off sharply, and I lost sight of him as the Crows rushed toward us.

They hadn't a clue what they were getting into.

Hattie was the first to fire. Using one of the an unenchanted arrows she'd brought, she struck the closest Crow in the arch of his foot. The enraged howl the fae unleashed was all anger, no pain. He barely stumbled, withdrawing the arrow midrun as though it were no more bother than a splinter. But Sleg put an end to that.

Whipping itself horizontal, Sleg halted the Crow's forward momentum by slamming into his midsection. The Crow doubled over, robbed of every iota of breath. With lightning speed, Sleg managed to beat four of the fae into drooling, unconscious piles before any of them could reach us. It was starting toward the fifth, a woman who was holding her ground with her sword raised. She seemed to have a great deal of courage, poor thing, but what we'd all just seen proved that courage was not the winning hand today. Sleg leveled itself in the air, speartip aiming for her heart, and began to stalk forward in a menacing hover.

Wisely, the soldier chose to be led by her fear instead of her courage and turned to run back into the forested livery. It was at that moment that I realized Orville and the fae who'd been holding the reins of the griffin were gone.

I spun around frantically in search of them, but they'd escaped.

As I finished my revolution, I caught Sleg sidling craftily behind a tree trunk, as though preparing to chase the escaping Crow. "Sleg! Come back!"

In case you're wandering if a normally inanimate object can show reluctance, like a dog that's been told to stop chasing a squirrel, the answer is most assuredly yes. But it did return, and I quickly took it in hand, telling it: "Well done."

"Well done? Hardly. I am not a weapon of wound, my lady; I'm a weapon of war. Pity that I must keep reminding you."

Hattie was rubbing her chin, looking around anxiously. "Doc," she said, "I ain't gonna say you made a bad decision unleashing that thing, but we have a problem. Now they know it's here."

"… Oh." How could I have been so reckless?

Paddy knew my tone as the self-criticism it was and, in a tone suggestive of remedying a mere slip of the tongue rather than having put us all in danger of eternal incarceration, said, "But we are still free, so perhaps we should find a less obvious place for them to seek us out. I believe the term is 'go to ground.'"

"But we have to go after Orville!"

"No," Hattie said definitively. "Paddy's right. We go after him, and every fae in the city is gonna see us. Downs knew what kind of danger he was messin' with. The first thing we gotta do is make a plan, a *real* plan, and do it somewhere safe."

I squeezed my hands into tight fists, knowing she was right, and knowing I may have just done something that put us in greater danger than ever. But we weren't going to be any help to Orville if we were sharing a cell with him. So…

"Toxicore," I called, "where are you?"

"Wishin' I were bein' fed apples by the Hesperides in Hera's garden, but I'm still stuck here," he grumbled, appearing before us.

"What…?" I began, then cut myself off. "No, don't answer that. I really don't want to know. You're familiar with the city. You must have some ideas about where we might hide? Old friends, perhaps." I was truly grasping at the hollowest of straws, but I could think of nothing else.

"Friends? I been gone a long time. And all those what used to associate with me probably left town when the Morrígan got tetchy about me not givin' her yer whereabouts last time I saw her."

"Is there no one you think you can trust?"

"I know we can't trust that back-stabbing Snig-gnawg, and Beat-mylla's likely to hold a grudge fer a while." He paused thoughtfully. "But there might be someone I can t'ink of."

"Yes?" I prodded.

Without answering, he squatted down and began removing the cloak from one of the unconscious Crows. The man moaned and twitched, and his helmet came off. I could see his face, which was similar in features to Leannan and Fiona—that is to say, humanlike and not monstrous. But I was not naive enough to think that the Morrígan didn't have plenty of those she would happily throw at us if given the chance.

Before I could scold Toxicore, he held the pilfered cloak out to Hattie. "You'n me need to change our looks, Looloo, but sure the witch will have to use mundane chicanery. You need a disguise, girly-o."

"Don't call me 'girly-o.'" Hattie was clearly torn about taking up the mantle, but Tox was right. We'd be harder to find if we weren't who they were looking for. She reached for the cloak. "Is there anything you can do to change it? I'll stick out just as much if I look like one of them. And shorten it?" I could see the struggle it took for her to ask the gnome for his help. If Toxicore gloated, I doubted it would go well for him.

Fortunately, he was too distracted by the insensible Crows, who had begun showing signs of life, to bother. "Color change is the best I can do." From within his pocket, he withdrew a flask, removed the lid, and waved his free hand at her. "Put it on and make yer choice."

"Green," she said without hesitation. "Like Lula's eyes."

While Toxicore splashed her with his alchemical magic, I blushed a bit, flattered not only by her preference but by how readily she knew my eye color.

"Shall we?" Paddy said and led the way to the entrance.

I quickly re-covered Sleg and tied it back to my rucksack. As we huddled inside the doors and Paddy checked to see if it was clear outside, I shifted my glamour to appear more faelike, instantly growing a foot taller and now in a male disguise.

"'Tis safe," Paddy said, and we all tramped out, doing our best to look like we belonged.

Toxicore moved purposefully down the street, making turns here and there into alcoves and side streets that I could have sworn weren't there moments before. Few passersby noticed us, as Hattie had chosen to pull up the hood of her borrowed cloak and hide her lack of fae light. Best yet, the Argent Crows who'd escaped were nowhere about. Probably off to sound the alarm.

"Where are we going?" I whispered to Tox, but he ignored me.

Shortly, we came upon a wide canal that flowed through the heart of the city, its waters glittering like diamonds. Along its length, delicate arched bridges decorated with mother-of-pearl inlays and mosaics of shells spanned the waters. Toxicore led us along a walking path beside it toward the city's edge, now coming clear in the distance.

We'd gone maybe a mile total when I spied the castle at the end of the canal. It had to be the Morrígan's lair. And we were moving directly toward it.

"Tox, wait. Didn't you say we should avoid—"

Before I could complete that sentence, the noise I'd been hearing but paying no mind finally pierced through the outer layers of my awareness—a sound that I knew not with my mind but with the part of me, instinct or something more primal even than that, that devoted itself to recognizing things that could well kill me. It was a shrieking, bestial sound like the cawing of crows, but crows that swallowed souls instead of carrion.

It began as a faint murmur, barely audible over the cheerful water of the canal running up to the castle walls. But it grew louder with each step, escalating into a piercing, bone-chilling cacophony of chittering screeches.

The Morrígan's pets, the pixies, were behind those walls.

The thought had no more than entered my mind when a black mass arose over the top of the castle walls, billowing up and up like a rising tide of darkness incarnate.

The whispery, creepy sound of the creatures flapping their leathery wings filled the city, and their untold numbers blotted out the sky behind them. My heart seized in my chest. As one, the teeming pixie horde issued deafening screeches as they took flight in all directions, circling out from the castle and dispersing wide. Their gnashing teeth and rending claws glinted in the light as they bent their hideous heads towards the ground, searching. Hunting. A voluminous cluster turned their attention forward, rushing with claws outstretched and fangs bared toward our group as we stood like terrified statues on the canal path.

Just as I turned to flee, finally heeding Orville's suggestion in the livery—but much, much too late—I felt Toxicore's rough hand on my wrist, holding me back.

"What are you—" was all I said before everything around me was black, cold, and as airless as a strychnine-filled syringe.

22

This was a new kind of blackness I'd found myself in, one filled with objects both sharp and dull and mostly indeterminate.

Except for one thing—I reached out trying to get my bearings and found another hand, warm and rough and completely unexpected.

Jerking away with a soundless shriek, I discovered the worrying lack of air. To worsen matters, I was hit with a nauseating sense of vertigo, as though I were moving at great speed. And it was bitingly cold.

I forced myself to hold still, to not panic.

My self-control was effective for all of ten seconds before the panic won.

I began flailing at the space around me, knocking things over and battering my arms against the unseen objects surrounding me. The rough hand brushed me again, reaching out, and when our fingers touched, the other hand clasped mine tight. Oddly, the grip had the opposite effect of horrifying me. Without thinking, I gripped it back, tight as I could, finding it to be the only solace in this dark, airless cell.

And then, out of nowhere, someone else gripped my free hand and yanked it—hard. I flew from darkness to dimness and landed on my back on a floor made of polished wood.

With eyes as wide as one of Aunt Ada's Blue Willow chinoiserie plates, the first thing I noted when I turned my head aside was that my hand was still clasped within my shadow-world companion's— Hattie's, of course. She lay on her back beside me, staring at me with equal surprise.

"What in the blue hells?" she seethed.

"All right there, Looloo, Dumas? Still breathin', are you?" Toxicore stood before us, wearing no glamour, and leaned down to get a good look at my face. His bumpy nose had three curly hairs growing from one nostril that might have been used as fishing wire, they were so thick.

"What-what just happened? Where are we?" I managed, sitting up.

Hattie did the same, pulling her hand free and immediately reaching over her shoulder for her bow and quiver. They were not there. "Darkheart, you better start explainin'," she growled. "Beginnin' with where my bow is."

"Ach, left it behind, did you? Just give me a—" His hand went into his pocket and came out with Hattie's bow and quiver. "And yers," he said, retrieving my rucksack and the spear the next instant.

That's when it became clear. "You pulled Hattie and I into your pocket?" I breathed.

"Aye. 'Twas that or leave you to have yer spirits sucked dry by the Morrígan's flyin' pets. Or is that pests? Either way, not a good way to go, believe you me. Ye're heavier than you look, you know, but I got you here anyway." To his credit, he was only gloating a bit. Apparently satisfied we were no worse for wear, he looked around. "Now then, where is she?"

"Where is who? And where are we?" I repeated, standing and taking a better look at our location. We appeared to be inside a foyer, but a foyer of what was not clear. The walls around us were curved and wooden, though not made of planks. Our surroundings appeared to be the actual innards of a hollowed tree trunk, though one so massive you could have parked a horse and buggy where we stood. Yet the ceiling was too low to stand fully upright. Hattie, an inch or two taller than I, had to hunch uncomfortably to stand beside me. Before us rose a staircase of stone, disappearing somewhere overhead into the dark of the tree bole. Now that I was getting my bearings, I detected a strange bubbling sound coming from above.

Before Toxicore answered, an urgent scratching came from the front door. Then Paddy's voice: "Lula, are you in there? Master Darkheart?"

I scrambled to the door and opened it. My uncle stood there, and the moment our eyes met, we both nearly gasped in relief. "Uncle! Thank the heavens you're here." I spun on Toxicore and demanded, "How could you grab Hattie and I and leave him to the pixies?"

"How many hands do you t'ink a gnome has?" he said.

"No matter, Lula," Paddy said. "Pixies are no match for a dragon's speed. 'Twasn't but a moment before this splendid snout of mine caught your scent and led me here. It really is quite the talent."

Stepping back to let him inside, I couldn't resist a pat on his head. "Now, then, Tox," I said, "you were about to tell us where we are."

"We're in the home of Nebulux Spellscourge, me ex."

"Your... did you say 'ex'?" The words *ex what?* were on my lips, but I didn't really want to know, did I?

"Bit of advice afore we go up to the lab," he said. "Don't mention any o' the other colleens you've seen me with. And don't let her make you drink anyt'ing. She's always brewin' up somet'ing or other, and 'tisn't always easy fer her to find willin' testers." With a contemplative look, he added, "Or unwillin' either."

He turned and started up the staircase without another word, but Hattie grabbed him by the shoulders.

"First, tell us why the heck you brought us here."

He smiled mischievously. "Told you already. She's me ex, but she's still got a soft spot for ol' Darkheart, believe you me."

As it turned out, that only softness Nebulux Spellscourge had for Toxicore was the carpet of fat toadstools that sprang up from the floor before him, spored from an enchanted potion she flung at him the moment he entered the upstairs chamber. The three of us were far enough behind that we were spared, though Toxicore sidestepped the potion just in time.

"Get out or I'll have yer ears for soup!" the resident hobgoblin yelled at Tox, who was now hiding behind me.

Paddy quickly translated her threat as I stepped away from Tox, not wishing to be misused as a target in her next barrage. What was it with hobgoblins and throwing potions at people, anyway?

"You missed me and you know it, Nebby!" Tox yelled back, shoving himself into my shadow again.

Switching to English, Nebulux warned, "Move over, girly-o, afore you become as blighted as that fecker." She brandished something in a pink glass vial. "I'll show you how much I missed you, goblin!"

"See! Goblin *is* the right word for you, Darkheart," Hattie crowed.

"I'm sorry, excuse me, madam. Toxicore, could you please stop being a coward and using me as your human shield?" I chastised, adding indignantly, "Everyone, please, can we be civilized for a moment?"

The diminutive lady hobgoblin squinted unpleasantly at me. Her bushy brows arched over eyes that were the brightest orange I'd ever seen, showing the near-incandescent gleam in Toxicore's green one was innate to their kind. Her bark-brown hair was piled atop her head in an elaborate series of knots and whorls, fixed in place with an inspiring latticework of carved wooden pins. She dressed in a haphazard, eccentric style, preferring function over form, with a dark, ragged corset over a loose-fitting black dress covered in pockets and pouches, along with stains and burns from some kind of chemical—or perhaps alchemical—experiments. The hem of her skirt appeared singed, as though she often stepped too close to the large stone hearth burning at the edge of the room. Around her neck hung a pewter pendant set with a large ruby-red stone.

"Why are you here, half-blood?" she demanded of me. "And with a whole human too? Hmm?"

"Sure they're with me, Nebby," said Tox.

"Still haven't told me why ye're here, either!" She threatened to throw the vial once more, and I finally managed to scoot close enough to the wall that Toxicore was fully exposed and could not get behind me.

"Because we're goin' to Magh Mell and need yer help," he blurted.

This finally had the opposite effect of riling up Nebulux. For the first time, she lowered the vial and didn't immediately reach for another one. This gave me a chance to better take in the chamber's interior.

The stairs had twisted three stories up and deeper into the ancient tree—or perhaps into another one, it was so hard to get a grip of this world's construction—ending at this chamber of table after table of unearthly wonders. Crystals of amethyst and amber jutted out from the walls and low ceiling, bathing the room in a soft enchanted radiance. The wooden floor was engraved with arcane symbols and circular patterns. Furniture shaped for hobgoblins grew from woody living vines and tree boles and provided surfaces for Nebulux to work. And the kind of work she did was easily discerned.

The woman was a magician or, more likely, an alchemist. The tools and apparatuses aligning the tabletops were a whimsical assortment of twisted glass and precious metals, decorated with mysterious symbols. The bubbling sound I'd heard below came from glass vessels containing strange-colored liquids and gasses. Filling one was the tell-tale argent liquid of quicksilver. Drying herbs and unusual plant specimens hung from the ceiling. To make the slightly odd interior actually alien, withes wound throughout the room, budding and blooming with flowers and pods that released strange fragrances and pollens. Their tendrils wrapped around even more tools of the alchemical trade, holding them in the air in place of a normal shelving system. Though none moved now, I sensed they had the same sentience as the vines that adorned the opening of the tavern where our adventure in the City of Spells had begun, and would do as commanded (and not, I hoped, as they pleased).

"Magh Mell?" she asked appraisingly, her hand going to the ruby at her throat. It was perfectly smooth, the size and shape of an egg. "Home to Tír Na nÓg's only source of chimera stone? That Magh Mell?"

"None other," he assured her. "And I'll bring you back some o' the stones in exchange for your help gettin' us past the nuckelavee."

"Why would I help you?" she snapped, but the waspishness had dulled some. Tox may have as much facility with nettling his ex as he did everyone else, but he also knew exactly what to say to calm her (I'm sure much deserved) ire toward him.

"Chimera stones," he repeated.

Nebulux's citrine eyes appraised me more closely. "So she's the one, is she? The half-blood that calamitous crone's been after."

Taking that as my cue—after all, it was clear I could no longer luxuriate in anonymity—I stepped forward with my hand extended to shake. "I am Lula Cullen, Madam Spellscourge, and it's a pleasure to meet you."

She stared at my hand as though it smelled bad, so I withdrew it. After scowling at me some more, she shifted the look to Hattie, then gave one firm nod. "Sit, all you, before yer necks get bent that way permanently."

As our luck would have it, Nebulux was not fond of the Morrígan, which made her as eager as she was willing to help us. No one said why, but apparently the feeling between the fae queen and the lady hob was mutual. Whatever the rift between them, it seemed that it wasn't great enough to have forced Nebulux to leave the City of Spells. As she and Toxicore talked matters over, I spied through one of the chamber's windows and found we were still in the city. In fact, we weren't a great distance from the castle itself, and Nebulux's lab had a direct line of sight to the castle's main tower. A way for her to keep an eye on her nemesis, and vice versa? In the short time we'd been exposed to her, Madam Spellscourge proved to have a streak of cantankerousness to rival Toxicore's, and I wouldn't have put it past her to set up shop in a place the Morrígan couldn't help but see day in and day out, just to be spiteful. The window was paned and its frame hinged, allowing a stick propped against its base to hold it open. I caught the strong salty scent of the ocean blowing in from beyond the castle. But as soon as a small flock of pixies flew into sight, I ducked away.

"They're still hunting for us," I whispered to Hattie.

"Right!" Nebulux bleated, startling Hattie nearly out of her stool. "What you need is two doses of me own brand of vanishing cream, each. 'Twill help you slip about with the nuckelavee none the wiser, both coming and going. Nuttin what's used me cream can be seen nor heard nor smelled. But there'll be no slippin' out till after you get the chimera stones—three, Toxicore, and not a chip less."

"I can't take yer vanishing cream," he protested. "Makes me itchy."

"T'ink the nuck's talons'll be any less itchy, is it?" She dismissed him as if he'd ceased to exist and went on to explain, "I haven't any on hand, but I can whip some up afore long."

I replied, "Thank you, madam. Just a question: Hattie and I haven't yet been given a good explanation of what this nuckelavee creature is. Could either of you explain?"

"And what's a chimera stone?" Hattie added wisely. Neither she nor I would put it past Tox to involve us in a caper to collect some magical artifact that might, in fact, kill us. I knew what a chimera was, in the Greek sense, and was definitely reticent to be involved with anything concerning one.

None of us missed the glance shared between Toxicore and Nebulux.

Finally, with a dismissive shrug, Nebulux responded, "The nuck's a horseman, ugly as the harridan of havoc's pixies, and has foul breath." Pointedly, she began rummaging through the bottles and potions held by the vines dangling from her ceiling, as absorbed as if she'd been hunting a particularly elusive potion all day.

"And?" Hattie pressed.

"And we don't want to tangle with him," Tox said. "That's the most important t'ing."

It was Hattie's and my turn to exchange a look. We'd get more information when we needed it. I hoped. "And the chimera stones?" I asked.

"Gastroliths, not so hard to find out on Magh Mell," Nebulux said. "Just don't want to be trying to take one from a living chimera. They spit them up every now and then."

A gastrolith? The stones some birds and other creatures swallowed to help their gizzards digest food? That sounded suspiciously, well, mundane. More of a job for Charles Darwin. But then, I had always admired the naturalist. Wouldn't he be in absolute heaven to get to explore a place like this? Chimeras being real was anything but mundane, however. I supposed it all came down to one's perspective, and mine had widened quite a bit lately.

"Madam Spellscourge, we'll be incredibly grateful for any help you can offer us," I said, using my most congenial tone. "But as you might imagine, our reason for traveling to Magh Mell is a matter of both danger and urgency. We may have to vacate the island in great haste, and I'm not sure if we can promise to find these gastroliths. Is there anything else we could offer in exchange for your assistance? Something we can get before we go, perhaps?"

She'd gathered several containers and two small cauldrons. The ingredients to the vanishing cream covered the top of a table, and based on the way some of the liquids in the transparent jars seemed to move on their own, gelatinous and sinewy like slugs in slime, a tiny bit of worry about what this concoction might do to us bubbled in my belly. If we were meant to drink whatever came of these things, I wondered if I might not prefer to face the nuckelavee head-on.

"What I need are chimera stones. You lot can get them fer me, or you lot can go back to yer world and quit darkening me door."

"This is me world," Tox trifled.

Nebulux huffed. "And I'd like to have a word with whoever lifted the curse what was keeping you out, but since you going to Magh Mell and you being gone fer eternity are the same t'ing, I'm not pressing the matter, am I?"

I looked back to Hattie again, and she raised an eyebrow speculatively. This was not shaping up to be the adventure I was most looking forward to.

"Now get out o' me lab while I work," Nebulux said, waving us toward the staircase once more.

23

Following Toxicore down a hallway at the stairs' base found us in a hobgoblin-sized sitting room, filled pell-mell with scraps of beautifully colored cloth and half-finished needlepoint projects. Nebulux seemed to be a fidgety one, the type of spirit who was always busy with one project or another. I supposed that when living in a world where time didn't pass, one had to find ways to stay occupied. Hattie and I cleared some seats to wait while Paddy paced around the room, absorbed in sniffing everything, and Toxicore wandered off to find some refreshments, or so he claimed.

"How long do you think this will take?" I called after Tox as he paced away. I expected no answer, and that was what I received.

Sighing, I tried to make myself relax on the pint-size furniture.

"Well," Hattie said, reaching for her pipe and tobacco. "Think we'll ever see Downs again?"

I tried to be matter-of-fact. "Of course. As soon as we save my father, we'll march into the Morrígan's castle and free him. From what I understand, Lugh is not one to be trifled with. And once he's reunited with this"—I patted Sleg—"he'll brook no more injustice, I'm sure of it."

She held her eyes steady, but by now I could feel the doubt she hid. "If you say so. He's your pa, after all."

I fingered the embroidery on a scarf draped over the back of my chair. The thread was silky and strikingly vibrant. "I have to keep my chin up and focus on one goal at a time, or I'll become far too overwhelmed to so much as remember my name."

With a tight smile, she nodded.

Absently, I scratched at the spider bite on my ankle.

"Still not healed, huh," she said flatly.

The time had come to tell her of my suspicions. "I'm afraid this is no ordinary spider bite."

"You don't say."

Lifting my eyebrows, I said, "You suspected as much?"

"Doc, we've all seen how injuries with you just don't take."

"Of course." I shared my suspicions about the bite and its giver being part of some kind of enchantment that allowed the creature to follow me. For what reason, I didn't have more than a guess.

"That explains it," she said, blowing pipe smoke through her nose. "I didn't tell you because I didn't want to worry you, but I'm pretty sure I saw those three hobs when Downs was takin' us to the griffin stables." She stared off for a moment and muttered to herself, "Is *stables* even the right word for that place?"

"Oh?" I asked, not in the least surprised. "How could you tell it was them?"

"They're just as weird lookin' without their glamours as they are with them. I'm assumin' they had dropped their glamours, anyway. They're not an easy trio to miss."

"And you miss very little," I said, but even through my admiration for her, my frustrated worry about Motherlode's minions resurfaced. "I don't know how she thinks having those oddballs follow me is helping matters."

She drew from her pipe and blew out the smoke. "I bet if you killed that spider, they couldn't anymore."

I chewed on this. "If I see it again, I'll try." Internally, however, I liked the idea of trying to catch the little thing better. It wasn't its fault it had been used in this way. And perhaps the creature would come in handy at some future date.

Clanging and clashing echoed down the hall, and Toxicore came into the sitting room, carrying several bowls and spoons balanced on plates. The precarious stack looked ready to topple if any of us so much as exhaled, and I jumped to my feet to help him set the dishes down on a coffee—or whatever similar drink they had in Tír Na nÓg—table.

Next to a bowl he pushed over to Hattie, he set a bobbin-size vial. "Swallow that first if ye're hungry," he said. "'Twill keep you from gettin' fairy-bound."

Her eyes narrowed at him. "Why are you bein' nice to me, Darkheart?"

"Tryin' to buy some goodwill, aren't I? If that nuck catches us out, 'tis goin' to take more'n a half-blood and a hob to get away."

"Will a dragon have better luck?" Paddy said, now attentive to our conversation.

"… About that." Tox took his serving of soup and began to slurp it straight from the bowl.

At that ominous phrase, I couldn't even look at mine, even if the bittersweet steam rising from it had been more enticing. "What about that, Tox?"

He licked the dribbles from the few scraggly white hairs sprouting over his top lip. "Paddy'll have to stay behind. The wards what keep the nuck in also keep his kind out."

If my heart could have dropped out of the soles of my boots, the force with which it fell would have sent it straight into the Earth's core. "Paddy… can't… go."

"Aye, but you needn't have a worry, Looloo. If worse comes to worst, your golden stick shouldn't let any harm befall you."

"Tell the hobgoblin that if he calls me a stick once more, I shall puncture each of his organs with fire before skewering him to the tallest tree in Baile na Geasaíochta," Sleg seethed.

I should have been relieved by Tox's assurance that Sleg was all the protection we needed, but I knew his next words would do something to shatter it. I was not, therefore, disappointed when they did.

"'Course, that supposes the Morrígan hasn't set up a spell to put it back to sleep."

The wavering of my resolve was like the first tremors of a city-leveling earthquake, and I opened my mouth—not sure if I was yet ready to admit I wanted to give up and go home, but Toxicore hadn't stopped speaking.

"So, all that bein' as 'tis, 'tis a good thing ye're a Danannín what can probably knock the nuck right off his horse." He paused and looked off to the side inquisitively, as if trying to solve a riddle. Later, I would realize the puzzle was how to knock the nuck off his horse, given the nuck's nature, but I could never have guessed it at the time. "If you feel so inclined," Tox finished and reached for my bowl. "You goin' to eat that? 'Tis some o' the best mandrake and mushroom soup this side of the gateways. Shame fer it to go to waste."

With numb fingers, I waved for him to take the soup. "W-why would you call me a Danannín? I thought we had no way of knowing if I was fathered by Lugh as Lugh or Lugh as Bran."

His apparently not-to-be-interrupted slurping made me want to scream, but everything in me had stilled. Tox was many, many things, most of them unsavory, but I could fathom no reason he would lie about this.

When Tox didn't answer, Paddy pressed him for me. "That is a wild assertion to make, especially at a time like this, Master Darkheart. What possible reason could you have for such a claim?"

Tox set the bowl down and stared at me keenly. "How you feelin', Looloo? Sick at all? Poorly in any way, even a wee bit tired?" Before I could answer, he said firmly, "No! And yer neck? Healed right up, didn't it?"

I reached for the scarf I'd worn without fail since Quetzalcoatl had used Sophia Carter to slit my throat. Truth be told, I'd forgotten about the wound, given my remarkably swift healing skills, especially with the aid of the magical energy of Sleg. Now though, I slowly unknotted the scarf and pulled it free.

Paddy and Hattie drew closer to me to get better looks. Her eyebrows rose appraisingly, and she nodded. "Not even a scar." With her customary scowl for Tox, she looked to him. "But that doesn't mean much. You said yourself the fae are harder than average to kill. Plus you brought her back from the dead in her own body. Just means she's resurrected, not a demigod."

"But she's half-*human*," he stated, as if that cleared it up. When it was obvious from our confused expressions that it didn't, he went on, miffed but for once articulate. "Bein' half-human means that even if her da was a greater fae and she could survive t'ings most humans couldn't, her human blood's still weak as ditch water. Don't you know math? Weak plus strong equals meh. Means she'd fade like Paddy did when he was a cat steak and soon die again. So, like I asked you once already, Looloo, how you feelin'?"

All eyes fell on me. "Quite well," I admitted. "Better than ever, to be honest."

"See," Tox said, satisfied. "Danannín."

"But this could just be the effect of being so close to the spear. It is a vessel of remarkable magic. Couldn't I just be siphoning my longevity from it?" It hit me suddenly that if Tox's statement was true, and necromancy on humans was only a temporary resurrection, I might very well be dead right now, again, if not for Sleg. I looked at my rucksack, where the canteen holding cauldron elixir was packed way. Was I being a fool not to drink it? Tox's continued explanation gave me reprieve from that consideration, though. I was not comfortable with the idea of immortality, not after the things my mother had told me.

"Naw. Can't take a power like this from somet'ing unless 'tis innate in you. For example, I can't shapeshift like the Morrígan or Lugh 'cause I'm not a greater fae. I can only wear a glamour."

"... Are you saying I can shapeshift?" I asked wonderingly.

"Don't get full o' yerself just yet. You might be a Danannín, but you'll have to learn yer powers first and harness them."

"But how!" I was frazzled. This was all so simultaneously exciting and terrifying—and there was one other problem. "Orville warned me that knowing what I was without knowing how to control my... er, self could lead to something terrible happening."

"Then I wouldn't recommend tryin' anyt'ing too terrible," Tox advised.

"Thank you. The way you're so free with your deep wisdom is truly inspiring."

"Not me fault ye're too big fer yer own britches," he said. "Besides, we have other t'ings to sort out. Such as how to get to Magh Mell."

"A boat might do it," Hattie said, attempting to mock Toxicore.

The trouble with mocking someone who has no self-awareness to begin with is that they simply assume you're the dumb one. "You might find this hard to believe, girly-o, but there are no boats what will take us to Magh Mell. It might have somet'ing to do with the monster horseman you heard mentioned."

"So you're admitting the nuckelavee is more than an ugly rider with bad breath," I jumped in.

"He isn't called the nuckelavee fer nuttin," Tox said matter-of-factly. "Don't you worry though. You've faced plenty o' monsters. This one's just on horseback."

I didn't want to let his comments divert my need to inquire further, but I'd learned that pushing Tox to speak when he was busy, or eating, or really just existing as himself was futile.

Hattie had likely come to the same conclusion, because she said, "Then we steal a boat."

"Steal one? Ye're a sailor too, are you?"

She clenched her jaw and tried to stare him down.

"I may know a way," Paddy said.

"Really?" I asked. "You mentioned having never been here in the City of Spells before, though?"

"Tír Na nÓg has but one sea on this end of the world. I have an, ehm, colleague of a sort who may be able to give us—you—a ride. Master Darkheart, I shall need a bellowing conch. Might Madam Spellscourge have one?"

"I'll ask," he said.

"While you're at it," Hattie said, "can you see if she has some of that Ink of Influence?"

I turned to her, alarmed at what she was implying. "But we'll get the ink when we rescue Orville. I promise we won't leave Tír Na nÓg without it."

Stone-faced, she said simply, "Just in case..."

Though not hungry, Hattie and I retained the habits of our own realm and finished off our soups—after I made Tox bring me a clean bowl. Soon, Nebulux called Toxicore up to her laboratory while we waited below, then sent us off without a goodbye or a good luck. Tox doled out two smaller potions to Hattie and I, a marvelous magenta glass conch shell to Paddy, and noted that the alchemist had said, Toxicore quoted, "How could I have any Ink o' Influence? The last t'ing Fergusoni made was a stain what took three brownies and twenty buckets o' water to scrub off the cobblestones."

Hattie took this news stoically, and I knew better than to mumble further assurances that we'd get the ink. She was in no mood for platitudes. I kept my chin up with the promise to myself that we'd find a way to stop Knox, no matter what, with or without magical ink.

The skies of the City of Spells still harbored a handful of flying pixies on the prowl, but those who could donned our glamours and Hattie her cloak, and we kept our presence hidden, creeping through alleys and along covered walkways relentlessly toward the sea spreading away from the city's eastern border.

Shortly, we reached a system of docks and piers extending out into the silvery bay like the delicate fingers of the city itself. Rather than being constructed of wood, the piers appeared to have been woven from supple tree branches, interlaced with strands of ivy and rope bridges. They curved into semicircles around the shoreline, lined with creatures of all description fishing from their sides.

Boats glided from pier to pier and out beyond the harbor, their sails billowing in the breeze. The ships were crafted to resemble sea creatures of kinds I'd never seen, with shells, fins, and tentacles extruding from their hulls and creating seagoing craft straight out of some fae-touched dream.

Orbs in shades of topaz and amethyst drifted over the piers, like Faraday's hydrogen balloons, lit by an unseen source and throwing illumination over the tangled strands of seaweed and schools of tiny silver, gold, and rainbow-colored fish that swam below. The orbs seemed to respond to the movements of the fishers, following them as they went about their business.

Hattie remained behind me, trying to look as inconspicuous as she could. Toxicore and I went unnoticed in our glamours by the folk around us, and Paddy just remained a dragon. We'd passed others of his ilk on this adventure, making him stand out no more than a dog on the streets of Boston might.

As we drew close to the piers, Paddy told us to follow him and surreptitiously slipped down to the sandy shore beneath one of them. Underneath the woven structure, tiny creatures the shapes of stars but wearing shells like hermit crabs scuttled away from our footsteps. The calm lapping noise of the water against the shells and pebbles amassed at the water's edge was inviting. If I could wish myself away from danger and into a vacation, this was the type of seashore I might venture to. But nothing in our current predicament could push the imminent dangers from my mind.

"You all wait here. I shan't be long," Paddy said. He nodded to Tox, who handed him the conch, and waded out into the water.

"Careful, Uncle, don't go too—"

My statement died on my lips as he reared back and leaped out, catching a few feet of air before diving under the waves.

"Hope the starjellies don't eat him," Tox said without a trace of concern in his voice. He turned away from the water and looked back toward the city. For the first time I'd noticed, his expression did not make me think of someone who was about to either rob a store or insult someone. Upon closer inspection, he looked pensive, afraid even.

"Something bothering you, Tox?" I asked.

"No. I just don't like boats."

I nodded, doing my best to show some sympathy in my expression. It was trifling of me, but I had trouble believing that an individual who'd faced down as many horrific monsters—and more—as I had of late was afraid of traveling by watercraft, but I supposed we all had our foibles.

Paddy emerged and shook himself like a wet dog after handing the conch back to Toxicore to stow. "Shouldn't be long now," he said, looking inordinately pleased with himself.

For what? I wondered. "Should we go up and wait by the docks?" I asked. It seemed unlikely any boatman he may have summoned would want to slide their craft up onto the stony beach.

Paddy looked at me askance. "No, no. This will do. She's a bit shy."

She? I thought but didn't question.

Some minutes passed, and I know I wasn't the only one getting impatient. Paddy didn't elaborate on what type of ship to keep a lookout for, and not even the most modest of rowboats veered in our direction beneath the pier. We were quite hidden, and I began to wonder if his method of hailing assistance had failed.

That's when the nearest wave spit out something that had my lungs seize and heart nearly stop in my chest. A mass nearly the size of a handsom flopped gracelessly onto the strand, bearing a shell, four flippers, and a beak-nosed head that reminded me of a parrot—but a parrot the size of a dinosaur.

"What in Lincoln's name?" I squealed, reeling backward and smack into Hattie. She held steady, keeping us both from falling over.

The creature, some type of gargantuan sea turtle I saw now that I had enough distance to get perspective, rested benignly where the wave had deposited it. It stared at us with fishbowl-size eyes, beautifully aquamarine and luminous if utterly alien. The scales covering its head and flippers were a mute emerald color, and its powerful flippers measured almost half the length of its body. The broad shell could have sat Hattie, me, and Toxicore, with room for another—and I suspected that was exactly what was about to happen.

Paddy paced to the creature's head and, inexplicably, their noses touched the way it was said Eskimos touched noses in greetings of affection. They stood face to face silently for some moments before Paddy turned to us.

"Lula, Miss Dumas, Master Darkheart, please meet Coralthys, a long-time friend."

"A-a pleasure," I stuttered. "Paddy, does your associate understand English?"

"She does."

In acknowledgment, the creature snorted at us, sending saltwater shooting from her slitted nostrils, which were large enough to hold a hand mirror.

"Coralthys often travels to Magh Mell to dine on some of its unique aquatic offerings."

"Any chance she eats nucks?" Hattie said. I applauded her boundless hope.

"Alas, no. But the good news is, the nuckelavee doesn't bother her kind either. She'll get you there quickly and discreetly beneath the ocean's surface. Lula, I believe this will be your chance to truly put your water powers to the test."

As I gaped, his meaning slowly came to me. "I'm going to have to keep us from drowning, aren't I?" I said.

"Indeed," said Paddy.

"You can do it, Doc. You're only gettin' stronger, the longer we're here. I believe in you."

But the trick, at least according to Orville, is that I must believe in myself, I thought but didn't say aloud. What was I afraid of, anyway? I'd used my water magic numerous times, and had in fact even harnessed my powers over it to suck the last drop of blood from an ancient vampire. Surely if I could draw water to me, I could push it away as well. I could easily imagine creating a bubble surrounding the three of us atop Coralthys's shell, keeping us dry and protected with plenty of air, and keeping the sea at bay around us.

"Perhaps I should practice first," I said hesitantly.

"I kinda doubt Downs has all that long for you to master your magic, Doc. Maybe we should just hop on and you can figure it out as we go," Hattie pressed. "It's not like we'll get that far from shore before we know if you're powerful enough. We can just swim back."

Her confidence in me was encouraging, but I struggled to push away my concern that it was unwarranted. "I... yes, I suppose you're right. Let's—" I cut off when I noted that Toxicore had slunk away inconspicuously, now nearly halfway up the long row of pier supports that led up the beach. "Tox? Where are you going?" I asked.

He peered over his shoulder, squinting. "Told you, I don't like boats. You t'ink someone what doesn't like boats is goin' to like ridin' atop a sea turtle any better?"

"Well it isn't as though we have many options."

"Sure we do. We have the option of stayin' or goin'. And I'm stayin'."

"Darkheart, wait," Hattie said. "I wonder if this might persuade you to come along."

She had reached inside her satchel, and her hand came out holding up something too small to see from even just a few feet away.

"What d'you have there, girly-o?"

I too was curious, overwhelmingly so, and I stepped closer to Hattie for a better look. Toxicore did the same, though his feet dragged a bit reluctantly. He'd learned quite well that harboring a touch of reluctance to get too near his frenemy was wise.

"It's just a bauble Madam Leannan thought you might like," she said. "See?" As she said this last word, she flipped her hand like a magician doing a trick and said something that sounded like "Mo rún, do ghníomh."

The item in her hand suddenly blossomed with tiny moonlight-colored flowers like a cherrywood tree, and a narrow withe virtually grew in thin air from her hand, whipping outward and wrapping itself around Toxicore's arms and torso like a rope. Speechlessly, I watched as he went as limp as the kelp fronds we'd seen from the pier.

Hattie, looking immensely pleased with herself, said, "All right, I suppose that will do. Now, you walk on over to that turtle and hop on."

"What in the worlds, Hattie?" I breathed as Toxicore, with no muss no fuss, walked with staccato footsteps up to Coralthys.

"Leannan gave me this, told me if I ever needed to compel the hob to do something he refused to do, it would make me his master."

So there'd been a bit more to the discussion about Hattie staying with the coven, and potentially becoming Leannan's sweetheart, before we left Denver. My jealousy—still not admitting that's what it was—had been for entirely the wrong reasons. "That's truly marvelous. I wonder why she gave it to you and not me?"

"I don't think she figured you'd ever be impolite enough to use it."

I thought it over. "That may be right. What happens if you remove the vine from around him, though?"

"All I need to do is leave a single bud or flower petal on him, and he'll do whatever I say." She got a conniving look. "Think I should make him swim to the island?"

I relished this consideration for a moment longer than was seemly —I'm not *always* polite, at least on the inside—but finally said, "I imagine that will take a bit longer than it should."

"Yeah, you're probably right. Maybe when we have some more time to kill, huh?"

Grinning wide enough to hurt my cheeks, I said, "I shall count the hours until then."

24

We both laughed a bit too hard as Toxicore, arms bound to his side, attempted to climb up onto the turtle's shell, which peaked at a height exceeding his own. Surrendering to our time considerations, Hattie finally plucked one of the white flower petals from the viny branch and placed it into a pocket inside his cloak. Speaking another phrase caused the rest of the binding to sprout in reverse, and it condensed into a tree nut, about the same color as a lime but slightly smaller. She palmed the magical pod and returned it to her satchel as I helped the freed but still pliant Toxicore to Coralthys's back.

Turning to Paddy, I said, all levity gone, "I wish you were coming with us, Uncle."

"As do I, Lula-lee. Just remember, you are greater than your enemies because you are you—a woman stronger in spirit than anyone I've ever met. You and Miss Dumas both. 'Tis but an angry horseman that you'll face, and soon, I have no doubt, you will see your father again, almost as if for the first time. Let the joy of that reunion encourage you, and let nothing stop you. I've never seen anything capable of doing so yet." He extended his wing so that its tip touched the spear on my back. "And if all else fails, don't be afraid to put some holes in things."

I knelt and hugged him with all my might, then quickly scrambled onto Coralthys before I got weepy. Hattie had hunkered down by the great turtle's head and was speaking in low tones to the creature, patting one of her flippers companionably. She'd shown time and again that she thought of horses as more than working beasts, and it seemed she was developing the same rapport with Coralthys. This seemed more than appropriate, as it was clear the creature had much more wisdom than even horses, among the most intelligent of animals. Hattie's respect for beasts was a trait we shared, and it made me feel even closer to her.

With the help of Coralthys's flipper, Hattie climbed onto the turtle's back and sat behind me. We'd instinctively taken a back-to-front seating formation, with Tox in front of me and Hattie behind me. But the turtle's shell was so wide that we could have all sat in a circle. With a bit of arranging of all our cloaks, weapons, and baggage, we managed to get somewhat accommodated, only for me to realize that we had no reins or handholds as Coralthys turned lumberingly toward the water.

"How will we hold on?" I asked, really to anyone who might provide an answer.

"Use your magic to keep yourselves in stillness," Paddy offered.

As I stuttered over all the ways I feared I might not have that power, Coralthys propelled her body into the surf. The cool water hit our boots, then our knees, and I began to panic. Hattie's warm hand on my shoulder and her calm words "You can do this, Doc" were the reassurance I needed.

Sweeping my hands out as Coralthys dipped below the surface of the foamy waves, I centered my thoughts on the magical energy within me that governed water. Feeling its cool, flowing power, I willed it to expand away from us, encapsulating us in a bubble of air that ended at our boots so we could breathe. It was exhilarating. Not yet had I immersed myself in water and tried to control it, and being fully surrounded by it now changed me at a cellular level, making me feel both in command of and part of the sea at once. I fancied I could almost hear the creatures swimming around us, their voices foreign but clear. If I listened closely enough, could I understand them? Anything seemed possible with the power surging through me. Spreading my arms to their full width, I touched my fingers to the bubble's inner membrane, remaining in contact with the sea and all its might. The water parted before us as Coralthys fully submerged and dove deep down under the ocean's surface, until the light from above faded and shimmered into the mere memory of sun.

Hattie let out a marveling sigh as a school of colorful fish swam by. Leaning over my shoulder and peering through the transparent walls of our watery conveyance, her eyes widened at the spectacle of an entire underwater world we passed by. Knowing that somehow, beyond all expectation, we were safe, I closed my own eyes, letting the tremendous feeling of oneness with my element engulf me.

But, naturally, after a few minutes of peaceful travel, a disturbance in the currents vibrated against the membrane. At first it was subtle, but it rapidly increased.

"Can you feel that?" I asked Hattie.

"Feel what?"

I shook my head to show my uncertainty and focused both on what my fingertips were sensing and what I could see in the watery world surrounding us. A large shadow was approaching, displacing huge volumes of water with powerful undulations. Coralthys continued on steadily, though I know she must have sensed the creature's approach as well.

Even as I fought back the fear welling within me, the creature became clear: an enormous serpentine shape looming out of the gloom, all glittering scales and razor fangs.

"Darkheart, what is that?" Hattie breathed quietly, as though to speak too loudly would draw its attention.

"A makara," he answered mechanically. "A sea creature what guards thresholds."

"Is it friendly?" I whispered.

Proving that Hattie's enchantment could only change his will, not his nature, he said, "Is anyt'ing with teeth that size?"

I envied Toxicore at that moment. Whatever control Hattie's enchantment had given her over him, it seemed to have also made him utterly fearless. He sounded bored even, as though facing leviathans of the deep was a mere happenstance that could be ignored if one were so inclined.

I strained my powers to strengthen the bubble, turning it into a glasslike shell that was still somehow liquid, hoping its magical field would deter the beast. But its yellow eyes were fixed with fascination on what it must have seen as a strange object moving through its domain. Aggressively, it closed the gap and butted its draconic head against the bubble, testing its surface with its curved horns. It seemed only to care about the three of us and ignored Coralthys, who continued at a pace that suddenly felt much too slow. When the makara's first attempt failed to pop our protective pod, the creature tried again, thrashing around us with its eel-like tail and gnashing its teeth. Hattie gripped my waist as Coralthys was pushed about in the tumult. Her firm hold kept me steady. The makara struck again, and the impact weakened my control. Hairline fractures began to appear in our protective shield.

"Should I shoot it, Doc?" Hattie said. "Loosin' an arrow in here might do nothin' but bust this bubble and spill us into the ocean."

Calm, almost in spite of myself, I said, "No, just give me a moment." I swept my hands against the bubble's skin, channeling my fright and desperation into the water outside. Thinking of wind and water, cataclysm and danger, I willed a vortex to form and spin the nearby seawater into a whirlpool.

"Well, would you look at..." Hattie whispered, trailing off in wonder.

The vortex spun from no more than a sapling's width into a great redwood's in seconds, lengthening as well until it was like a colossal screw reaching for the ocean floor. We could feel its powerful tug on Coralthys, but it caught the makara first. The creature thrashed its long tail, now nearly fully caught inside the tunnel of swirling sea trying to drag it down and away from us into the depths. Its great maw opened and a stream of bubbles shot out, their volume enough to engulf us completely. As each bubble burst against our own shell, I heard tinny little roars like ant-sized thunder. The beast was bellowing its rage, but each bubble-roar was so petite and dainty that I couldn't find it in me to be afraid. Whatever it was in the fae environment that allowed bubbles to contain sound would have to wait till we were not under threat of death to be equally marveled at. At last deciding we were too much trouble, the makara gave a mighty undulation and pulled its sinuous body free of the vortex, fleeing from both our bubble and the treacherous waters that had almost trapped it.

Shaking from both fatigue and exhilaration, I almost missed it as Coralthys, calm and steady as could be, slipped between two white stone pillars rising from the ocean floor beneath us. The light of day above us grew stronger as the turtle brought us closer to the surface, and in a few moments, we emerged in a peaceful cove surrounded by a sandy shore. The moment our heads crested the water, I released my hold on the protective water shell. It splashed away from us, leaving droplets of white foam on the cove water's surface.

Hattie's warm hand lay on my shoulder. "You did it, Doc. We made it."

Gratefully, I patted her hand as Coralthys came to a stop, floating a few feet from the beach. She'd brought us as far as she was willing.

Toxicore and I clambered into the surf and then onto the damp sand. Hattie stayed behind and exchanged some words with the sea turtle. Her giant, luminous eyes and sharp beak could not possibly bear any kind of human expression. Nevertheless, I sensed she was smiling at Hattie, as though they'd become fast friends. Hattie once again patted her flipper, and the turtle sank beneath the water and was gone.

Joining Tox and I, she removed her cloak and started squeezing the water from the bottom. "I asked Coralthys how to use the conch if she was willin' to shepherd us back to land when this is over. Not sure we'll find a boat out here any easier than back there," she said.

"You think of everything, Hattie. I hardly know if I'd get through a day in Tír Na nÓg without you."

She shrugged, giving me a light grin. "That's what partners do."

I had a nearly overwhelming desire to take her hand and squeeze it, but instead I smiled back. The stock-still figure of Tox caught my eye, and I grew serious. "I suppose he's more useful to us as himself than as this docile creature you've created. Do you think you should release him?"

"I think we should toss him to that makara and see which of them is ornerier—my money's on the makara, by the way—but my ma would probably scold a few years off my life for that." She wasn't serious. I could tell by now that she'd developed a grudging if not like for Tox, at least an acceptance of his usefulness. She stepped up to him and took the magical petal that held him bound to her will from where she'd tucked it in his cloak.

Instantly, Toxicore's blustering, cantankerous manner asserted itself. "You wily witch! If you e'er cast another spell on me, I'll turn yer toes into earthworms and make them dig you down to Dubnos to roast on Arawn's own cook fire!"

"Weren't scared of the water, were you?" she countered without an ounce of concern.

"'Tisn't the point," he groused.

"Oh, and what is?"

"You made me do t'ings what weren't me own will."

Hattie reached in a pocket and pulled free the small glass vial Toxicore had given her in Nebulux's home. I thought she'd swallowed its contents before eating her soup, but light shone through it now, sparkling off the undrunk liquid inside. "Is that right? You mean things like whatever this was supposed to do?" she said.

Toxicore nearly had the humility to look abashed—but not quite. "Don't see yer complaint. That was just goin' to make you stronger'n faster. Could use that when we face the nuck, we could."

"'We'? You mean you're not gonna skedaddle the second this ugly cuss shows his face, like usual?"

"I'm not goin' to run. I'm goin' to practice selective visibility to maximize my strengths."

I raised my eyebrows, impressed at his command of nonsense.

"Then why didn't *you* drink it?" she countered. "Besides, you didn't ask me if I wanted to be stronger or faster, did you?"

"You t'ink folk with arms this short is much fer fightin'?" he asked, lifting his below-average-length—if average is measured in human lengths—arms. He had a fair point.

"That don't make no never mind. You're a pretty good pot at callin' the kettle black, goblin."

Hattie gave him the full effect of her hard stare for a moment longer, then huffed and let the matter go. The usual fuse that had been lit between them ebbed, thankfully. The broader issue was:

"Hattie, you ate Madam Spellscourge's soup. This will mean you're fae-bound now."

She gave me a warm smile, one I was not quite able—or ready—to interpret. "Well, Doc, I reckon I already am." Her eyes held mine for several beats, not a waver or doubt in them.

My insides grew unusually warm, and I looked away.

"You have no need to worry about that now, anyway," said Tox, giving me something else to focus on. "Nebby doesn't know you had her soup, and Dumas passin' through Magh Mell's threshold stones afore me ex could marshal the magic means the spell is broken."

Projecting my next words to our general surroundings, unready to meet Hattie's eye again, I said, "We... ahem, we should probably get out of the open. There's no telling where this nuck creature might be, and we don't know where to begin our search for my father. Do you two think we should take our vanishing potions now?"

My worst fear had been realized when Nebulux handed the bottles of vanishing cream over—they were to be drunk, not spread over our skin or misted into the air. I had some serious doubts about whether I would be able to force myself to swallow the strange gelatinous mix. Fortunately, Toxicore's next comment meant we'd be able to put it off for a bit longer.

"Don't suppose we'll have much trouble findin' yer ol' man," he said vaguely.

When I looked at him, he was staring up the strand, which ended abruptly at the edge of a wild forest. It took a moment of pointed focus for me to see what he was seeing. A simple cottage built with rough, lichen-mottled stone was nestled among the overgrown roots of a ganglion of sycamorelike trees. The deeply sloped, moss-covered roof almost hid the cabin from view, explaining why I'd missed it to begin with.

The instant I realized it might indeed be my father's, I went numb. Head to toe, my body seemed to have detached completely from my mind, and I was just a floating bundle of thoughts, all of them dithering and anxiety-ridden.

"Do you think that's his home?" I nearly whispered.

"Not likely anyone else would be livin' on an island with the nuckelavee," Tox said.

I looked around helplessly. What to do? This was the moment I had been waiting for, yet I realized I hadn't planned it. I was not a woman who plowed ahead eagerly without first considering my path. And I should have been eager at this moment. Shouldn't I?

"I'll go with you," Hattie said.

"Oh, yes, thank you. That will be lovely." There it was. I was eager for her help more than for the moment at hand. I could no longer ignore that Hattie was a rock on which I'd come to rely nearly more than my own common sense. Instead of it being a worrying revelation, it soothed me. "Shall we?" I said.

"I'll just wait here and try not to get... ehm, in anyone's way," Tox stated. His pause was suspicious, and the way his eye darted around the cove, seeking out something that clearly had him on edge only added to it. Mostly, though, Tox was never one to be concerned with whose way he might be in.

Trying not to let his obvious nervousness affect me any more than I already was, I took the first step—the hardest—toward the cottage. Hattie and I approached cautiously. Seeing it from up close revealed an assortment of garden beds interspersed among the tangle of roots, order in their disorder, filled with thriving plants of all varieties. There was no sound from within the cottage, and no trace of fire in the chimney. Then again, the day was mild, even the hint of breeze from the ocean a temperate and comfortable one.

As I reached the door, Sleg spoke up. "Ah, finally, the master and I reunite. No offense to you, my lady, but here is a lord who knows how to dispense a good skewering and slaughter as much as I. It will be a joy to be back in capable hands."

"Believe me, Sleg, I take no offense at the confirmation that I'm not a mayhem-hungry murder monger."

Sleg tsked, in no way peeved by my subtextual critique. "Indeed. Not all can be as splendid as the Tuatha Dé Danann."

Raising my hand to knock, I strenuously pushed down the implication that my family history and patriarch were as violent as Sleg said. If I didn't make myself believe this reunion would be a happy one, I'd stand in front of the door forever, second-guessing my reasons for coming.

After barely one rap with my knuckles, the door was pulled open and for the first time since I was an infant, I came face to face with my father.

The fae glow he emitted was the first thing that leaped out at me, nearly as strong as the sun but muted enough that his visage shown through clearly. Perhaps it was due to his flaming red hair. Lighter than mine, but the same in thickness and falling with slight waves. It reached his shoulders, and he'd tucked it behind his ears the same way I did when I left mine down. His features were far more youthful than I'd expected, making him look barely in his late thirties. He was dressed simply in a tunic of green-dyed linen under a sleeveless leather jerkin, with leggings and boots of brown suede. His face and bare arms were painted in swirling blue woad patterns, similar to Madam Leannan's and many others I'd seen in the City of Spells. Despite the oddness of the dermal accessory, something no human I'd ever seen would flaunt, I felt I was the outsider here, the strange one.

His greeting was in Old Irish, abrupt and not necessarily friendly. It was obvious he didn't know who I was.

Not trusting myself to articulate clearly in the old language, I responded in English. "H-hello. Er, I should... that is, I wanted to, um, introduce myself."

His blue-green stare didn't change as he waited for me to find my courage. If anything, he looked disinterested, even distant. His glance kept lifting to take in something distant over my shoulder.

Sleg had its own ideas about how this meeting should go. A flash of bright light blinked momentarily behind me, then the spear was hovering at my side, nearly close enough to push me away from the door. The smell of burned silk conveyed that the impatient weapon had incinerated its wrapping.

"Master, you appear in good health, though such a proletariat garb is not quite befitting of you, I must say," Sleg prattled. "It is with great pleasure that I return to your divine company. And if I might make a suggestion, the first item on our agenda should be dealing with that harbinger of horror, Lady Morrígan, for her many infractions against our persons."

If a pole made of gold could actually puff out its chest in indignation, Sleg would be doing so. Yet, for its grandiloquent reunion speech, my father barely acknowledged it. Instead, he looked at me.

In thick, heavily accented English, he said, "I don't know how you came to be here and got past the makara, half-blood, but I'm not fond of unannounced visitors or their talking trinkets. You've come to my island without permission, and I suggest you leave immediately—or face eviction."

I was taken aback at his brusqueness. Hattie subtly pressed her elbow into my arm encouragingly.

"Bran, or Lugh—I'm not sure which name you prefer—you don't understand. It's me. It's your daughter. Lula." I held out my hand awkwardly, a gesture of conciliation.

He scowled, and the expression pulled ominous clouds over his face. "Did you call me Lugh?"

"... Yes? But I'm happy to call you Bran if that suits you best." Why was I feeling like I'd done something wrong?

"Master, I agree that you should always be referred to using your noble titles. For instance—"

Lugh raised his hand in annoyance, and Sleg fell silent. "You demean the lords of the Tuatha Dé Danann with your cheekiness, half-blood. And worse, you're taking up my time when I should be pruning the moonbloom and sweetpea vines. If Lord Lugh heard you suggest I might be him... well, he's not known for his forgiving temper. And whoever this Bran is, I'd guess he's not part of whatever practical joke you think you're playing. A daughter, you say? If that were true, you would think you'd know your own father, and he, you. If you don't leave now, I shall call my steward to escort you away. He's a..."

My father kept speaking, but I ignored the words, refusing to accept what the sinking feeling in my gut was telling me. There was something wrong with his mind. That had to be it. The other option was unthinkable—that he would refuse to acknowledge me out of spite or, worse, indifference. Either he'd lost all his memories through natural means, or the Morrígan had taken them somehow. He had no idea who I was, and apparently, no better an idea of who he was. And I couldn't entertain the idea that we had the wrong person, as Sleg clearly recognized him.

Desperate to make him come back to himself, I grasped Sleg. The spear gave out a grunt of disapproval at suddenly being handled. Dispiritedness often had the effect of making me speak bluntly, and this situation was no exception. "Look, I'm not playing a joke on you. This is your spear. Just take hold and... and I don't know. Sleg?" I looked at it. "What does he have to do to take his divinity back?" The practical side of my mind had already made the leap that all it would take for my father to be returned to himself was to once more fuse his two sides: mere fae of the greater variety and Tuatha Dé Danann of the noble kind.

"It's quite simple. The master just has to—" Sleg cut off, and I turned back to my father.

Lugh was brandishing a long blue-lit digging trowel, magic enough in the metal to ensure I was not going to mistake it for a mundane tool. The edges appeared radically sharp, more an oddly shaped dagger than shovel. He held it at waist height, not quite a threat but close to one.

"This is the last time I'll tell you," he warned. "I don't want to have to call my steward—it will play havoc on the garden—but I've had enough of your mischief. Tír Na nÓg gets no peace these days from you human and half-blood vagabonds. I came to this island to be rid of your kind and—you know what, I'm just going to call him. Be rid of you once and for all." He placed a hand around his mouth to amplify his voice, but Hattie stopped him before he could summon the "steward." We did not need to be frequent vacationers to Magh Mell to have guessed this was the nuckelavee.

"No need, sir. We've obviously got the wrong man, and we'll be on our way right now." Her hand on my elbow tightened, pulling me. As I stepped reluctantly backward, I dragged Sleg along too. "We didn't mean any harm, and we're sorry for the trouble. We'll be off your island and outta your hair fast as a quick-draw who stepped on a cactus."

My father scowled and lowered his hand. Her tug on my arm was relentless. I wanted to fight it, but wrenching defeat had taken all the fight out of me. My father watched us retreat and said nothing more, his eyes growing distant and unfocused again. Was he going to forget this moment, too, just as he'd forgotten me? We'd come so far—for nothing. This man, my own father, had been a stranger to me my whole life. And now it seemed as though he would remain so. To top it all off, he was really quite rude.

Hattie, being the wiser of the two of us, got us far enough away fast enough that my last sight of him was him turning back inside and slamming his cottage door.

25

We reached the beach, some hundred yards distant from the cottage, before Hattie released me.

"That did not go as I'd expected," Sleg said. The spear had the nerve to sound even more affronted than I was.

"Well, Sleg, I never expected to have something in common with you, but here we are," I grumbled.

"Hey, don't give up yet," Hattie said. "Clearly the old rawhide is under some type of enchantment. It's not personal, you know? We'll head back to the city, hide out, and figure out some way to bring him back to his senses."

I sighed, feeling the slump in my shoulders and hole in my center as an indictment on my character. Who was I? I'd always been so stalwart, defiant, even stubborn some (most) said. And I was already willing to throw up the sponge, after one minor setback? Hattie was right; I was not this person, this milksop.

I straightened my shoulders. "Yes, of course. I don't know what I'm moping about. I should know by now not to expect things to be easy. Toxicore, can you retrieve the—" A horrible stench assaulted my nostrils then, as if an entire herd of cows had dined on carrion flower and emitted a collective bout of flatulence. "Good Lord, Tox, what have you been eating?"

"'Twasn't me, Looloo," he snapped. From nowhere, he produced a green and brown scarf made of some luxurious cloth, which I recognized as having lately been sitting in Nebulux's sewing basket, and wrapped it around his lumpy nose and mouth. "Me own skin would rip itself from me bones to get away from me if it were."

Emulating his excellent idea, I held my hand over my nose and mouth, breathing shallowly. Not even the Dead House on North Grove Street in the height of summer was more noxious than whatever this heinous odor was. When I looked over, Hattie's face had gone the color of chalk, and her eyes bulged ever so slightly. Not with the expression of someone about to be sick, even if I thought I might; it was the expression of someone on the verge of horror.

"Speakin' of skin..." she muttered and raised her hand to point to the northernmost arc of the cove.

A figure emerged from the trees, towering and nightmarish, and not one of us had any question about what it was.

The nuckelavee, a hideous abomination, stood before us. As it passed from the brush to the cleared beach, its equine body became more visible. A grotesque parody of a horse finally appeared. And *grotesque* was the nicest possible way to describe what it was: a horse, technically yes, but just its skeletal frame beneath layers of exposed muscles and veins that pumped black ichor, not a shred of skin covering it. One lidless eye gazed at us from the center of its forehead, bloodshot and baleful. But that was hardly the worst thing about the monstrosity.

Upon its back was the smaller torso of a man—a man with no legs, who sprouted from the horse like a mushroom on a corpse. Its head was obscenely large—my anatomically oriented mind immediately diagnosing the worst case of megalocephaly ever; prognosis, unfavorable—and on it spread a truly pestilent human face, with leering bloodred orbs and blackened teeth set in receding gums. I probably don't need to mention that it had no lips, just those abhorrent teeth gaping from its face. Like graveyard mist spreading over forlorn and forgotten graves, from its mouth spewed a virulent breath that reeked of decay and worse. It plumed into the air, caught by the breeze and blown toward us. Within the plume, plants turned brown and wilted like boll weevils sprayed with Paris green. Lugh had every reason to be concerned about the state of his garden.

The grotesque skinless feature of the horse bits were shared by the human bits, and every sinew, tendon, and vein of the monster was visible, if not strictly human. The things arms, like its head, were disproportionate and reached nearly to the ground. Its ragged talons clenched both a deadly black-bladed sword and a morningstar, hefted easily in its long-fingered fists.

As it moved toward us, its breath rattling and limbs jerking with a hideous grace, the nuckelavee threw back both its heads and unleashed an unearthly howl that echoed with madness and malice. The sound alone threatened to rend our minds asunder.

I felt as if every muscle in my own body were turning into water. Beside me, Toxicore whisked from sight, and Hattie drew her bow. Quick as lightning, one of her arrows hit the human torso dead center. The nuckelavee screeched, almost splitting my eardrums. But instead of dropping dead under the might of the magical arrow, it leaped into a gallop. It would be upon us in a second, and none of us could fight such a nightmare.

Well, one of us could.

"Sleg, do your thing. Kill it," I gasped.

With the force of an anvil dropped from a steeple, the spear ripped from my hand, pulling me to my knees with its momentum. In a glorious flash of golden light, it angled into a javelin arc that ancient Greek athletes would have envied. Sleg had no sense of hesitation, and none of mercy either. It bayonetted the nuckelavee's horse portion in the chest, piercing the beast and traveling deep until over half its length was buried.

This time, the monster didn't scream. It reared on its hind legs, its gangly humanoid arms thrown over its head, reaching for the sky, then toppled backward. Writhing in agony, it heaved one great feculent breath, then settled into its eternal—*merciful fates, let it be eternal*—torpor.

Everything grew still around us. There were no birds on the island, and even the peaceful sound of the waves was muted. Though I'd just commented that I should know better than to believe anything about this journey would be easy, it seemed this triumph was. The creature didn't even twitch in death's final dance. Finally, I looked at Hattie and tried to give her the kind of victorious smile I thought befitted the moment. My trembling lips did their best, but I gave up when it became clear they weren't up to the task.

"Hell of a shot," Hattie said finally. "Couldn't have done better with my Sharps."

"Yes, you could have, and we both know it. Don't give me that false modesty, Miss Dumas."

Her smile had more luck than mine. "No, you're right. It's not like me to pull a punch." She eyed the dead monster, considering. "That solves one of our problems at least."

"Indeed."

By unspoken agreement, we approached the nuckelavee. I really didn't want to. Each step closer revealed even more details of its hideous features: the glistening slickness of whatever supernatural ooze covered its exposed flesh; the yellowed and chipped cartilaginous composition of its hooves; the fact that it had no nose in its human head, just black holes with thin fleshy flaps surrounding them. Even dead, the reek of its breath permeated the air around it, forcing both of us to raise our scarves and tie them over our faces.

We stopped several feet distant, taking stock. It lay completely inert. Diagnosis: definitely death. Whatever Sleg's faults, it got the job done.

"Sleg," I said. "You can, um... come out now."

The tearing sound it made as it reversed from the carcass was nearly as repulsive as the nuckelavee was. Upon emerging, Sleg lifted vertically, and noxious black sludge dripped down its shaft, puddling beneath it.

"Ahhhh," Sleg gloated. "That was magnificently refreshing!"

It took some effort not to gag, but I owed the spear a thanks, no doubt about that. "You did well. I'm sorry for the mess you're covered in, though."

"Mess? You mean the elixir of victory? No, no, no, no, my dear lady. This is the gore of glory. I shall revel in its resplendence, displaying my might to the world!"

"… Whatever makes you happy. I'll just need to ask you to transport yourself until you decide it's time for a polish, if you don't mind." The thought of touching that vitreous sludge had my stomach turning. "I suppose we'll have to find something new to wrap you in before we go back to the city."

Toxicore blinked into sight beside us, holding his wood-handled stone mallet. I wondered what he expected to accomplish with such a perfunctory weapon when even Hattie's magic arrows hadn't harmed it but held my tongue. "Uglier than a selkie what's had her skin used fer a saddle blanket, that is. Can we go now? Me nose is a bit tender."

I looked longingly toward my father's cottage. The stout door was still closed, the metaphor of an unbreachable obstacle very obvious to me. "I suppose it would be best."

I felt no such need to give the rank carcass a second look, and we began our trudge to the water's edge, moving farther down the beach before calling Coralthys in order to put distance between us and the nuckelavee.

So when its putrid breath wafted over us again, I was at a loss at first about why that would be. The sound of a horse's grunting, however, cut right into all our awareness, and we spun as one to witness the creature rising to its hooves once again.

"Tox, you didn't…" I groaned.

"Course I didn't! I might be a necromancer, but I'm not lookin' to be a dead necromancer."

Preternaturally calm, I did the only thing that I could think of. "Sleg, would you mind killing that thing again?"

I'd hardly completed the request when it yelled, "Herald the coming of the mighty Sleg! The bane of the cowardly and the skinless, the slayer of the foul-breathed and fouler-faced, the one true… *point* of interest!"

I wondered if the spear was always like this after a battle or if perhaps the divinity stone was giving it an overinflated sense of grandeur. This time I was ready when Sleg ripped itself from my hand and thrust its length fully through the nuckelavee's side. Its divinity-orbed tip appeared on the converse side of the horse's ribcage, and the nuck shrieked again. This time, we had all prepared by pressing our palms over our ears. It toppled like the first time and went still, leaving us in the uneasy silence once more.

"How was that, my lady? Another battle fought and won!" Sleg cried, the rapture of murder deepening its screeching-butterfly voice into something even more alien. "Just say the word and I shall continue to seek out our enemies far and wide, blasting them from this mortal coil with my ferocity, sending their spirits to—"

"Thank you, Sleg! You're truly a wonder of mayhem."

"No, my lady, thank *you*. Such compliments are entirely unnecessary but completely accurate."

I turned to Hattie and Tox. "It looks like we have a new problem. If I remove the spear, the monster returns to life. But I can't very well leave it here."

Hattie chewed her lip. "Here's what I'm thinkin'—if we can leave the spear right where it is and have Coralthys get us out past the boundary stones, then you can call it back from there. The only question is, how far is too far for it to hear you?"

"Aye, should work. Let's go," agreed Tox, looking very ready to be gone, despite his phobia of the sea.

Reining in his impatience, I said, "Let me ask Sleg." Hattie quirked an eyebrow at my use of the name, but I'd explain the weapon's and my relationship later. Or maybe not; its unconventional nature induced a smidge of embarrassment I preferred not to spend much time considering. "Sleg, if we travel out past the barrier stones surrounding the island, will you still be able to hear me if I call you?"

"Distance is immaterial to our bond, child of Lugh. We are one, you and I, now that your father has fallen several swords short of a full armory."

I most definitely did not wish to be "one" with the spear, but its words were encouraging nonetheless. "Good news, we're free to go," I told them.

"Free to go? My dear sister, you are in my domain now. And thus I will decide your fate."

As one, the three of us spun to face whoever had spoken. But I could have been as blind as Gloucester and known immediately.

The Morrígan had found me.

26

"You leave her alone, lady, or you're gonna have to deal with me."

Hattie had taken half a step forward and lifted her bow. She was planning to protect me at any cost, and I could have wilted in gratitude.

The Morrígan stood twenty feet from us on the pale sandy shore. My one encounter with her before, through a magic mirror, left me with a solid memory of her appearance: a darker-skinned woman with sapphire-blue eyes and wild black hair. But up close, in the flesh, I realized that a magic mirror was a woefully inadequate tool for capturing the essence of a living goddess in her domain.

The outline of the goddess before us radiated like heat shimmers from the mouth of a volcano. This black-clad queen of the Tuatha Dé Danann seemed to burn with a controlled savagery that was utterly inhuman—utterly *divine*. The arcane symbols and patterns adorning her dark skin seemed to shift and twist before my eyes, as though her flesh were a canvas for the strange workings of unseen magics. The copper diadem upon her brow was abloom with little verdigris clovers, metallic looking, with oh-so-sharp leaves. Her eyes held us, nearly hypnotizing us with their depth—gateways into an endless indigo sky where something primal and untamed lurked.

When I'd spoken with Brigid in the Dreamlands, I'd felt in the presence of beauty and majesty incarnate. And though the effect of coming face to face with the Morrígan was similar, she left me feeling cold and insignificant, no more than a pawn in the schemes of uncaring, ineffable destiny.

More than anything else could have, the awesomeness of her presence confirmed to me one thing: the great god Lugh was no more. The man I'd spoken to was diminished in a way that seemed impossible to recover from. If he'd still retained his innate majesty, he'd have been as otherworldly and even frightening as the Morrígan was. Oddly though, despite the biting hurt his rebuff had caused me, it stoked a white-hot desire in me to reunite him with his divinity, now held in stasis within Sleg's citrine orb, blocking out all else: my fear, my impulse to flee, my sadness at being fatherless still. If the gods had shown me anything, it was that their ideas of justice were, at best, skewed. But the worst injustice seemed to be their fall.

Lincoln's log cabin, I was beginning to sound like a brainwashed cultist. Back to the issue at hand.

The Morrígan didn't even look at Hattie. This was more of a threat than if she had, as I saw the way her eyes narrowed and her lips thinned. If there was any patience in her, it was already used up, and I needed to do something before those I cared about were caught in a crossfire they shouldn't have been.

"My lady"—I put a hand on Hattie's shoulder to keep her from doing anything unwise—"whatever you think you want from me, it's too late. My blood is a dead end." A tremble at the thoughtless use of "dead end" worked its way up my spine.

"You seem to think me a simpleton," she said, and her voice had the ominous beat of a far-off thunderstorm. "I've tolerated enough inconvenience at your hands. Now, give me what I've been seeking this unacceptably long turn of time, and I will consider..." Her glance wandered aside as she tried to find the word she was thinking of. When she found it and said it aloud, though, it sounded like a lie.

"Mercy." She could have at least tried to repress the wicked grin that teased the edges of her lips at her promise.

"I will not," I swore in foolish, badly calculated bravery.

From the corner of my eye, I saw Hattie's free hand rise to her face and her head tilt back. I didn't know what she was doing; all my concentration was focused on two things: estimating how fast I could get to the sea and harness the water to mount some kind of defense of me and my friends, and trying to guess what exactly the Morrígan was going to do.

Could I have been more unprepared, more naive?

Before I knew it, a hand was about my throat. It was as hard as granite, cutting off my air with the strength of a vise. The Morrígan had moved with a predatory grace that betrayed her true nature as something not quite human. Her hair and limbs seemed to flutter as though blown by a spectral wind. I was caught in her clutches like a fish on a hook, and might have been throttled to oblivion of not for Hattie. Hawlike in both her own grace and speed, she threw a punch that struck the Morrígan in the jaw. No bare-knuckle street fighter ever hit with more ferocity, and to both my and the Morrígan's amazement, it knocked her back. With my throat free, I stumbled aside and reached up to ensure the tender flesh was still intact.

As though this were a barfight in Deadwood and the stakes were all the gold in the Dakotas, Hattie did not relent. She followed the Morrígan's backstep and punched her again. The fae queen flew back —to my astonished eyes, it appeared she actually flew—and got enough distance that Hattie couldn't close the gap quickly enough. I could barely believe what was happening as they squared off on the sandy beach, grim determination on Hattie's face, sublime disgust on the Morrígan's.

"Hattie!" I whisper-shouted through my bruised throat. Surely she didn't think she had the strength to beat this goddess in a hand-to-hand fight? Then it struck me—she'd been drinking, that's what I'd caught in the corner of my eye. She'd taken Toxicore's potion and now had strength and speed surpassing any mere human's. Did that mean she had a chance?

The answer, which shouldn't have needed to be elucidated, was clear. Not only no, but if it had been anyone but Hattie in this fight, I'd have felt the hubristic foolishness of mortals almost deserved the drubbing about to come.

After throwing another strike at the Morrígan, moving almost too swiftly to be seen, Hattie swept up a handful of sand and flung it directly into the Morrígan's face. The Morrígan let out a shriek like an enraged crow as she turned aside and clawed at her eyes, only to receive a swift kick in the backside from Hattie's boot.

Just as I got my bearings enough to consider how best to join the fray, the chance was lost—and lost in a truly extraordinary display.

Hattie lunged toward her again, and the Morrígan shot her hands before her as if to ward Hattie off. But her palms didn't connect with Hattie. Instead, a gust of air so blunt and hard that I felt its impact ten feet away blew my friend backward, lifting her from the ground and depositing her like a felled tree by the water's edge. Undecided about whether to attack the Morrígan myself or run to Hattie's side, I hesitated too long.

The afternoon air began to swirl around me and kick up a maelstrom of white sand as the Morrígan arched her back and raised her arms overhead. I threw my hands up to protect my eyes, and while I watched in mute horror from slits between my fingers, her limbs elongated, and gloss-black feathers sprouted from her stretched skin. In mere moments, where she had been standing now loomed a giant raven, the creature's beak so sharp and formidable it might have cut through diamonds.

The monster bird stared into my face. Her indigo eyes were still the Morrígan's, like twin galaxies swirling in the infinite cosmos, burning with an all-consuming flame that outshone the fire of stars.

If Hattie was going to escape from this world—if any of us were—I had to find some way to stop this monstrous creature. And I could think of only one thing that might do it.

Breaking into a sprint, I shot to the fallen nuckelavee's side, my hands gripping Sleg's shaft before a rational thought could cross my mind. As I set my feet against the slimy, noxious hide of the nuck, ready to yank with all my might, I felt a strong wind and a moment later heard the flap of mighty wings. The musty smell of feathers filled my nose, despite the scarf still covering it.

"Sleg, I need you!" I cried.

"No, lass! Don't do that." Rough hands gripped my shoulders as Toxicore appeared behind me, trying to pull me away from the spear and nuckelavee.

"What? Let go, Tox! This is the only chance we have of stopping her!"

"The Morrígan knows how to make the spear sleep, remember? If you remove it, the nuck'll melt us with his ungodly morning breath, and the spear'll be back in the Morrígan's clutches. That what you want?"

No, that was most definitely not what I wanted.

"Stay put, Sleg." I released the spear and spun around to face the Morrígan crowmonster.

Toxicore, for once, stayed in plain sight. He'd grabbed the nuckelavee's morningstar and brandished it comically overhead. If he swung it, he'd just as likely be pulled off his feet by the momentum. I drew my shillelagh, sending thorn-encrusted vines to wave around my head menacingly. The thought whispered in my mind, *You're a Danannín, Lula. Use your power.* But how?

Before us, the Morrígan filled the air with a harsh staccato caw. There was no mirth in it, but she was clearly laughing at us. We held our standoff, Tox and I against the Tuatha Dé Danann queen, even as I snaked a glance to Hattie. Much to my relief, she was sitting up and carefully checking herself over for wounds. Her bow had flown several feet distant, but the quiver was still on her back.

"Do you really think you can fight me, sister? You and your paramour?" The Morrígan's voice had a raspy, biting edge, alien and avian.

"Toxicore is most definitely NOT my paramour," I protested with the most affronted sense of propriety ever felt.

The winged goddess ignored this completely. With one flap of her enormous wings, she lifted to the air and soared to a height I couldn't hope to reach with my well-intentioned but woefully inadequate thorn vines.

"I will deal with the *you*, Toxicore Darkheart, later," she crowed, "but this fight is between the daughter of Lugh and I. Go and join the paramour."

A whirlwind burst forth from the air, catching Toxicore within its clutch. He was helplessly spun round and round, hollering in panic as the ground fell away beneath his feet, the spiked ball of the morningstar whipping around his head in a truly violent spiral. In a moment, he lost his grip, and the weapon spun off into the sea and plunged out of sight. I struggled against the rushing air, vainly trying to reach out for him to stop his flight. But it was no use—he rose nearly high enough to be gripped in the Morrígan's talons and was then flung like a ragdoll toward Hattie, who was flattened back into the sand with the savagery of the maelstrom.

The Morrígan cackled cruelly as the whirlwind ceased. Toxicore sat up, his face the disturbing green of someone about to be motion sick. Hattie tried to scramble to her feet as I launched myself to them, no plans forming in my panic-stricken mind except to shield them both from the Morrígan.

Then a chill and ominous silence fell as the Morrígan swooped inland without explanation, disappearing into the blue skies over the forest. I knew better than to believe she was leaving.

"Come on, Hattie," I urged, taking her hand and pulling her down the beach to the shallower cove where we'd disembarked from Coralthys's shell. "You and Tox need to get out of her. Call Coralthys and go."

"You're plum crazy if you think I'm leaving," she said, coming to a standstill.

"We can't possibly defeat her. You saw what she did! I'll have to try to bargain... something... just please go."

"If you t'ink she'll let Dumas go after a fight like that, ye're..." Toxicore trailed off, for once realizing his unfiltered observation was not the thing that was needed here.

But it didn't matter a whit. Our eyes were immediately drawn to the sky once more as shifting black shadow bloomed above us, then shot toward us with the actual precision of a sharpshooter's aim. The musty smell of feathers hit my nose again, this time like a tidal wave. The next moment, we were engulfed in a sheath of crow's feathers, hundreds—millions! They struck our bodies with the force of a hurricane, their edges slicing across our exposed skin like tiny knives. Everything was pitch-black. If we'd opened our eyes, they'd have been cut to corneal ribbons. If we'd opened our mouths, we'd have choked to death on the world's most malicious featherbed stuffing. I flailed blindly with my empty hand, trying to keep the shillelagh at my side. I didn't want to strike the others inadvertently. Hattie's strong grip closed on my upper arm, and I stepped into her, wanting to shield her body with mine, and mine with hers. I couldn't tell if Toxicore was still with us or had blinked off to somewhere safe.

Then things got worse. The feathery shroud rattled and hissed like locusts, utterly impenetrable, and then it began to *squeeze*. As if we generated the gravity of the sun itself, the feathers closed in around us, tighter and tighter, their rustling growing quieter and quieter as the onslaught condensed into a dense, impenetrable mat. Hattie lost her footing first, and I followed, the two of us toppling to the side. I landed on a bony body, too short and angular to be Hattie. So, Tox was as caught as she and I. We could not hope for a rescue by him, what little hope there might have been. We were utterly confined and slowly buried under solid, concrete-heavy plumage in a stygian grave. There was no sound coming to us, and no air. Did the fae queen mean to suffocate us?

I expected Hattie and Tox to survive—they had, after all, drunk the elixir from Dagda's cauldron. I, on the other hand, had not.

Moments passed like an eternity as we all wriggled and twisted in vain, and I didn't know whether the darkness closing in was just the Morrígan's casket of feathers or my mind using up its last molecules of oxygen. Our struggles grew frantic, then... more subdued. We were as fixed as time, and time was nearly out.

I thought of my father, mere yards away. The only emotion I could summon was regret—for the sacrifices he'd made to save me, and for the sacrifices I'd made to try to rescue him. All of it for nothing. Would he ever know his daughter had died just outside his cabin? Would he ever even realize he'd had one?

As I swallowed the acrimony of these thoughts, the unexpected happened. A song broke through my fugue, so beautiful and lilting that it could have come from nothing but the most fantastical song-bird to ever exist. The only bird I'd seen on the island was the Morrí-gan's monstrous crow. This sound couldn't be coming from her, surely? The cascade of harmonies spilled forth in a gentle rain of sound that washed over me, immersing me in a tranquil sea of enchanted bliss. The melody carried for no more than ten seconds, but its sheer beauty was enough to make me momentarily forget I was suffocating. Then it ended, but another miracle took its place.

Fresh, clean air tinted with saltwater brushed over my face. My eyes flew open the second I realized the feathery cocoon was slipping away like a cover being withdrawn. I was free, but as soon as I twisted to the side to grab Hattie, I saw that she was not. Attempting to plunge my hands back into the dense plumage was useless. The feathers remained locked around Hattie's and Toxicore's forms as tightly as a corset, holding them where they lay back to back on the sand like a sculptor's poor-taste rendition of a human-gnome statue.

The Morrígan's voice came from over my shoulder. "Yield, sister," she said. "Your half-blood powers are as newly sprouted saplings before an ancient oak."

I spun around to face her and saw she'd returned to her human form. Well, not fully. The enormous wings still sprouted from her back like the angel of death.

She spoke again, unhurried and slow, as if mocking my urgent need to help Tox and Hattie. "You needn't bother trying to free them. There is nothing you can do. You're a half-blood. I'm a goddess. What frailty of reason makes you believe you can best me? And that one"—she waved a hand at Hattie, and I saw that her fingers were still tipped with stiletto-sharp bird's claws—"what absolute *madness* drove her to assault me?"

Though she sounded more baffled than angry at Hattie, I flexed my grip on the shillelagh, prepared to battle her if I had to. "I'm not just a half-blood. I'm a Danannín," I seethed, going for threatening but probably just sounding peevish.

"*A Danannín,*" she mocked. "Should I cower? Should I kneel?"

That's when I realized that all my advantages had evaporated, for in her other hand was the spear, inert and unalive in the way a weapon really should be. She had been the songbird, thus proving beyond all else that there was no way at all to predict the whims and wonders of the Otherworld.

Her eyes followed mine. "Yes, it sleeps once more. No longer yours to command." She looked toward the cottage nestled in the trees and swung Sleg's point toward it. I thought I saw the inside shutter of one of the windows snap shut. "Nor his."

I tried to reach out to Sleg, but the mental summons went nowhere. Near the driftwood log where the nuckelavee had fallen, the skinless horror once more stood on his own hooves. He didn't charge or attack, apparently under the Morrígan's command to stand by. Slow flaps of the Morrígan's wings kept his fetid breath away. One nice perk of having shapeshifting powers, I supposed.

I dug deep then, hoping against hope that my cleverness would offer some idea, drawing all the powers of my practical mind to bear on this knotty problem. I had done nothing yet to prove to myself—or anyone else—that it was true, that I bore within me the power of a god. If anything in my life had given me a reason to attempt to wield this unknown power, this moment was it.

I lifted my arm slowly, dangerously, as though about to cast a spell of earthshaking power.

But what if I fail? The thought burst to mind like a firework. My extended hand began to shake.

Who am I kidding? I'm not a goddess. Look at her. She has wings, for criminy's sake! I have a piece of wood. What am I thinking? My arm, suddenly so heavy, dropped.

It wasn't the prospect of my own suffering that stood in the way of my resolve. My failure would hurt those I... loved.

Orville's words came to me: *Belief in magic, you see, is easy if you're born with it and raised among others who wield it. But for those who come to it late in life, and especially come to it from a life of rejecting it as folly… discovery has a certain level of inherent volatility.*

Belief—that was what I lacked. And without it, Orville's foretold "inherent volatility" could be worse than whatever the Morrígan might do. Or I could just embarrass myself, which would do my friends no good either.

So what did that leave me, then? Obviously, capitulation and maybe risking the truth. Some of it, anyway.

Drawing a fortifying breath all the way to the bottoms of my lungs, I said, "I already told you, Lady Morrígan, my blood is useless to you. My father returned the cauldron to Dagda, who has now locked it away in an unreachable world and installed a dragon to guard it. If you use me to find it—well, I doubt even you are more powerful than a dragon."

Especially when that dragon had a bone the size of the Tower of London to pick with her. But I saw no need to tell her *my mother* was the cauldron's guardian. If she didn't believe me about the cauldron's keeper, she could find that out for herself. And I hoped my mother lined her nest with the Morrígan's bones.

"So, that's that. I don't care if you believe me. Take my blood and go find out for yourself, or send another one of your ghoul-adjacent lackeys to do it for you. But leave my friends alone. Haven't you already taken enough from me?"

Of everything I'd just said, the thing she focused on was: "Ghoul adjacent? Do you speak of the chief, Abhartach?"

"I… well, yes. He wasn't alive before I met him, and believe me, he was more than dead after I was finished with him."

She donned a coy grin, as though she knew something I didn't and found my ignorance amusing. "You really should stay here in Tír Na nÓg, sister. Can't you see who your real friends are? The things you and I might achieve if you could conceive of what you're missing." Her eyes strayed from my face to the divinity orb housed in Sleg's tip. The orb's inner fire flashed, reflecting from her indigo eyes like a comet.

I felt breathless at this unexpected turn in the conversation, my throat locked between a derisive laugh and a disbelieving gasp.

She saw my, likely comical, expression and snickered. "Did you think a mere common fae could exsanguinate Chief Abhartach? Yes, I know what you did. That was your innate power, sister. It's what makes you one of us instead of one of them." Her bird-clawed finger pointed to Hattie and Tox again.

Before I could speak, the Morrígan glided toward me, and I could have sworn vapors of darkness trailed in her wake. Her expression had settled into something I did not trust at all: cold, calculated appraisal. I held firm in my stance.

She stopped near me and narrowed her eyes, then leaned close and sniffed. I tried not to jump away, but it is rather unsettling to have one's odor so casually assessed. Dear Lord, I hadn't showered in days!

"Ah, so that is why you are so blind to your own possibilities. You've been cursed," she said. "By my wayward husband, if I'm not mistaken. He does have such a peculiar odor."

Inadvertently, the strong smells of sweat and Chinese food that had clung to Dagda came to mind. Yes, the cad had cursed me. Now, I wondered if she planned to do the same. Refusing to rise to her bait and even consider the idea of allying with the woman—she'd sent soul-sucking bat-monsters after me, for goodness' sake!—I returned the conversation to where I'd started it: "If you can tell that, then you know I'm telling the truth. I've spoken with Dagda myself. He's the one who told me everything. The cauldron is out of your reach."

She went on, dizzying me with a new change of subject. "Your father cannot see or hear you for who you are. He's blind to your very existence. It's ironic, actually—the both of you being so oblivious."

Trying not to let her rattle me, I responded, "Well, how would he know me? He hasn't seen me since I was a month old." It was my bravery speaking again, but it was silly. I could see plainly that even if he'd raised me to adulthood, at some point, my father had forgotten I existed.

She seemed to follow my train of thought, not dignifying my defiant yet meaningless comeback with a reply. "You must wonder how you might recall him, remind him who you are. I can tell you. Would you like me to?"

"Does a bear do literally everything in the woods?"

Humorlessly, she said, "He simply needs to be reminded of your true name. Can you tell him that?"

Had I really been worried she'd curse me? Because if curses were knives, what Dagda had done cut deeper than anything the Morrígan could. She had taken Lugh from me, but by rendering me ignorant of myself, it was Lord Dagda who'd taken my *father*.

And I could see that she knew it. Yet, at the same time, something else caught my eye. Scuttling at great speed across the sand behind her was a bedraggled gray ball of many-legged, spiky fur, about the size of my hand. That damned spider? Had it truly swum this far? Tenacious beast, but not my biggest concern at the moment.

I snapped my attention back to the Morrígan. "How did he forget? Was it your curse or his own choice?" I suspected that Lugh may have lost more than his godlike powers when he sundered his divinity from himself and made Sleg its carrier.

"Does it matter?" She shrugged, and the motion caused more shadow filaments—or were they feathers? it was hard to tell given her grim ethereality—to take flight from her hair and shoulders. "Gods! Your breath, beast!"

Without a hint of warning, she flipped the hand holding Sleg so that she had a good grip on the shaft and slung the weapon straight at the nuckelavee. The creature, speared for the third time this afternoon, collapsed in a slow-motion manner that suggested disgusted resignation at yet another death. I wanted to feel sorry for the thing. Well—no, I didn't.

Nervously, I glanced at the dense mat of feathers encasing my friends. Nothing had changed. I worried they were terrified, or worse, somehow dead. But, as I knew Hattie would tell me, right now I had to focus not on what *might* happen but on what *was* happening. "What do you want, Lady Morrígan. I've told you, the cauldron is out of reach. Would you—would you want to make a trade? My life for theirs?"

"Your life? Why would I want that? Have you nothing better to bargain with, after the trouble you've caused me?"

"I've caused you?!" I clamped my mouth shut. Instigating her ire further would be dumb, irredeemably so.

"However," she crooned, "you seem to be deeply misguided about me. I am no wanton, bloodthirsty killer. In fact, I'm but the harbinger of death, not the bringer of it."

I imagined Tox mocking her in my thoughts, *'Binger or Bringer, 'tis a distinction without a difference.* Glancing back to the nuck, I bristled at the nerve of her trying to persuade me she wasn't a cold-blooded murderer, but I repeated, "Then what do you want?"

She looked to the sky, her expression wistful as though she were remembering some great event that had long-since passed. "I want a war. A grand, sweeping clash of ages that will once again see me brought to the forefront of the minds of all mortals. I want to hear their prayers rising on the wind like the thunder of worlds, beseeching me to grant them victory, to be their savior from the eternal darkness they fear more than they fear me! I want to smell the blood of struggle washing across fields of mud and fallen carcasses, and taste the mixed sweat of agony and triumph borne on the storm of battle."

Well, that was admittedly more specific than I'd expected, but at least she was being honest. And now I knew a bit about the Tuatha Dé Danann that I might have surmised sooner if I'd given it thought: their deepest fear—or if fear wasn't something they were capable of feeling, then aversion—was obsolescence.

But she wasn't done. "Don't you see, sister? Here, in Tír Na nÓg, war is wasted. There are only two of us left who care enough to fight, me and my supercilious stepdaughter. And neither of us can raise an army that has the spirit-deep, abject fear of death your mother's kind does. Mortals are so willing to worship a goddess who can turn their fate at a word. It's their greatest quality! But we fae, we live too long to fear anything or to even know when to cower before greatness. Look at you, for example. You stand before me, not kneeling, not even wheedling. I miss that—standing amid those who know well enough to cower when I walk onto a field of combat."

She actually grew melancholy, a faraway look in her tear-shined eyes. I mean, really, was this supposed to be moving, this sentimentality about mass death? Maybe I am at least half god, but it was clear that I'd never get any closer to being full god, not with my tendency to be a touch more opposed to needless suffering.

But... if it meant we could all go free—something Hattie had said back at Leannan's boarding house came to me. Maybe there *was* something I could offer the fae queen.

"My lady, I can't declare a war on your behalf, but I can get you across the gateways to the mortal realm." The moment I said the words, I regretted them. But there was no going back. And based on the gleam of elemental fire sparkling in her eyes, I could see they'd had the right effect.

That fiery gleam fell on me and held me in its inferno. "There is so much of the essence of mortals tarnishing you, sister, but you can lie almost as well as the Tuatha Dé Danann. How could you know how to open the gateways, hmm?"

"I can't open them, but I can get you through them. Do you know what a phylactery is?"

By the squint of her eyes, she appeared to be considering equivocating. But the bait was too enticing.

Great Jiminy, what had I started?

"I am familiar with the magic, but none have perfected it."

"Someone has, and not only perfected it but created one. And I can get it for you. With the phylactery, you can come to Earth in essentially any form you wish, and do... whatever it is you want to do. Though, I really feel obligated to add that there are far better ways to get attention than starting a war."

She gave a condescending chuckle, the kind one reserves for the woefully outmatched that one is toying with for their own amusement. "Tell me, what human has even a tenth of the wit it would take to create such a thing?"

"I won't tell you that, but I will tell she's not a human." Leannan Sídhe had not created the phylactery we'd taken from Havóq, but another witch had in the past, and it made sense to surmise that witch was most likely fae. But I didn't feel the need to go into specifics, not with the intensity of the Morrígan's stare nearly burning through my skin.

She sneered, and I nearly flinched from the threat in that look. "You'll tell me, or they'll hear my judgment." Her eyes flicked to Hattie and Tox.

This was the moment in negotiations when I knew I had to call or fold. If I gave so much as a hint of weakness or uncertainty, she would play all four aces and sweep the table of every last coin. "No. I won't. It's your choice now. Believe me and get what you want, or don't and watch your biggest wish swirl down the drain." I'd promised the phylactery to Motherlode already. But I'd lost the spear, so even if I didn't give Motherlode the phylactery and instead gave it to the Morrígan, I'd happily let the troll come collect her prize for herself. I chose not to think deeper about what our magically sealed oath's price might be with this new twist in the terms. As it would turn out, I didn't need to.

The Morrígan almost had me then, her next words so tempting that I came close to giving in. "I can tell you how to break your curse and retrieve your father. Don't you want to know who you are, *truly* are?"

"All right"—I struggled to keep my voice steady—"tell me then."

"First, the name of she who keeps a phylactery."

"I must say, my lady, it's almost physically painful that you think I'm that dumb. Do we have a deal or don't we?" In fact, it *was* physically painful to have to step away from her offer. But did she really know how to break the curse Dagda had laid on me? She'd just told me how good the Tuatha were at lying. I couldn't risk it, no matter how hard my heart felt squeezed inside my chest, like a snake beneath a wagon wheel.

After eyeing me darkly for a few more beats, she stretched her lips in a parody of a smile. "Then this is our deal. You will bring me the phylactery, and I will free them."

I remembered the deal she'd made with my father—his freedom for my mother's. But the Morrígan had released my mother as a swan, keeping the agreement but leveraging a ruthless twist that hadn't been discussed. Fine. If she wanted to bluff, then it was time to raise my bet. "You'll let them go with me back to Earth to get the phylactery, and you won't harm or change them, or me, in any way. Also, you'll let me take my father back with us."

"Your father stays with me," she snapped. And, as though she'd heard my thoughts, she teased cruelly, "And how is your mother, dear sister?"

My hand clenched tightly around the wooden grip of the blackthorn club I still held. I wanted nothing more at that moment than to tempt fate and use it to teach her some compassion, one whack at a time. "Deal or not? I'm done asking. You have my father"—I knew I'd never win his freedom in this negotiation—"so you know I'll be back with what I'm promising." *Once I figure out how to break this curse. Dagda and I are going to have some WORDS.*

"What you're promising? So you do promise to bring me the phylactery?"

"Yes, I said as much already."

"You swear?"

"I swear! My goodness, do you realize that you have serious trust issues?"

She glared at me as though I'd insulted her mother. Without knowing what else to do, I paced closer and held out my hand.

"Shall we shake on it?" I'd just done the one thing that was guaranteed to turn Leannan Sídhe against me, and she was not a greater fae to trifle with any more than the queen before me was. But what else could I have done? I'd simply have to find a way to win this game by playing both sides of the table. I wanted to laugh at myself. Pretending to be a master poker player—had I lost my last marble? Where was Orville when I needed him?

My hand remained untouched in the air for an uncomfortably long minute. I might as well have been trying to hand her a dead fish, the disdain on her face was so great.

"No?" I said. "Fine, and I'll be leaving with the spear as well. We both know it's mine, since Lugh is... not himself."

She snorted. "You'll be leaving with nothing of the—"

We'd both turned to look at the object in question—and were both equally shocked to see the nuckelavee once more upright and, well, *alive* isn't the word I'd use, but you know what I mean. Notably, Sleg was no longer stuck through him. In point of fact, Sleg was no longer visible anywhere.

The nuckelavee tensed as we stared at it. Then, being a creature of at least some sagacity, it spun on its hooves and galloped off into the forest. I couldn't blame it.

"How..." she screeched and morphed before my eyes into a killer giant crow once more. "HOW!"

Her wings unfolded and lifted high at the shoulder as if she was about to launch—or about to batter me to death with them.

"It wasn't me!" I protested. "How could it have been?" Her uncanny indigo eyes shifted to Hattie and Tox. "And it wasn't them either!"

"Then who?" she crowed at me.

"I... I don't know!" But was that true? The little tracking spider I'd just spotted once again, the three hobs following it across worlds, and their avaricious master, Motherlode Mankiller—she'd had them follow me this far, and I'd been fooling myself all along if I really believed the were simply "keeping an eye on me." It was the spear, she'd intended to steal it all along. And what better time than when it was inert, and no one was paying it any mind? Hobs could appear and disappear with otherworldly stealth—Tox had taught me that much—and even if Knob and Bob had, to put it charitably, *questionable* intellect, Dorkus was no idiot.

Speaking of idiots, now was a good time for me to play one. If the hobgoblins got the spear out of Tír Na nÓg, and that was a monumental *if*, then I knew where it would be—with Motherlode. And more importantly, it would *not* be with the Morrígan, and she would not be able to go after it herself. So, my tack on the subject was to remain mum, giving her my best confusion-filled: "I have no idea at all where it could have gone."

Maybe I *was* learning to lie as well as the Tuatha Dé Danann, because she croaked an enraged, "The fate of this thief will be like a mouse to an eagle! Creature!" she yelled at the distanced nuckelavee. "Do not rest until you've searched this island for them. If your breath is the last thing they smell, so be it!" And she flapped off without another word to me.

"Wait!" I cried and chased after her, struck with horror at Hattie and Toxicore's continued entrapment. "What about our deal?"

She disappeared rapidly over the water. There was no way I would catch her, not even if I could swim like the makara. Instead, I veered toward Hattie and Toxicore. Just as I reached my hands into the plumage confining them to attempt to peel it free, their feathery coffin exploded, sending midnight-black plumes hither and yon like an erupting storm cloud. The slight ocean breeze caught most of them and lofted them away, and Hattie and Tox lay on the beach like marionettes with cut strings.

I fell to my knees beside them, afraid I'd have to force air into their lungs to bring them back to life—struck anew with horror at the thought of having to put my lips anywhere near Toxicore's—but they both sucked in oxygen on their own almost as soon as they struck the ground.

"Oh thank fate," I panted. "I was afraid this day was about to get so much worse."

27

At the sound of the conch, Coralthys returned with all haste. This time Toxicore grudgingly climbed aboard her shell without being spellbound by Hattie. Though he did retrieve a stash of pixie dust from his pocket and snort enough to choke a horse before we dove beneath the surface of the sea. His demeanor became nearly pleasant after that, if a bit too flirtatious. As we left Magh Mell, I filled them in on all that had occurred.

Toxicore's take on hearing my suspicions that Motherlode's three hobs had stolen the spear was... unique. "See, this is why I call meself a *gnome* instead of a *hobgoblin*. You just can't trust those hob feckers."

No argument from me. Our journey back was thankfully makara-free, but the moment we reached shore, the tables turned once more.

Paddy eagerly awaited us—escorted by several well-armed and very disgruntled Argent Crows. Most of the group was composed of those we'd tangled with in the griffin stables and still sported the shadows of their wounds. The one who'd lost his cloak to Hattie yanked it back angrily. We were informed that they'd be our escorts out of the City of Spells, and once we crossed the city threshold, it would be enspelled against us until I returned with what the Morrígan and I had agreed upon. I should have known better than to entertain the idea that she would simply allow us to walk free upon her flight from Magh Mell.

This meant we had two bitterly awful pills to swallow: Orville Downs would remain the Morrígan's prisoner, and we had no further opportunity to seek out the Ink of Influence to save Hattie's ranch.

At least Toxicore managed to find the positive side: "Least now Nebby won't get all up in me mug about not bringin' her the chimera stones," he said as we were unceremoniously shoved through the threshold markers.

"Wha—oh! I'd completely forgotten about that." I stared back through the ring-stone boundary, distracted by the guilt of leaving Orville behind.

"'Twasn't as if I was goin' to anyway," he continued. "Even though I have them right here." He withdrew an orb from his pocket about the size of an ostrich egg. The strange artifact seemed utterly unremarkable at first glance. Its surface was dull and weathered, marred by scratches and dents from whatever else had been inside the chimera's stomach with it. Yet when the light struck it just so, it flashed with a surreal inner radiance, a brilliance lurking just beneath the tarnished exterior, straining to break through.

I shook my head, trying to make sense of his deceptiveness. "You mean you had them all this time and didn't just give them to her in exchange for the vanishing cream potions?" The potions which I noted none of us had taken. I reached into my pocket and let my finger roll over the cork of the one I carried. If given the choice, I'd never have traded Sleg for the ability to become imperceptible, but, I reasoned, any artifact of magic was a good one. If nothing else, I could use it to steal the phylactery from Leannan if it came to that. A new wave of guilt washed over me at the very thought of such unconscionable deception. But I had made a promise, and this time, with a member of the Tuatha Dé Danann.

"Why would I do that?" he asked, genuinely baffled. "'Tis a game she'n I like to play. She gets to pretend I need her help, and I pretend right along with her. Women love t'inkin' others need them, so I gave her a reason to. She ne'er really wanted me to get her the stones to begin with."

I looked at Hattie, needing confirmation that what I was hearing was one of the craziest things a man had ever said aloud. She was eyeing Toxicore with a look of equal parts hopeless pity and dumb-founded scorn.

It was Paddy who tried to impart the oh-so-needed practicalities to him. As the two began walking back up the white-stone cartway to the gateway ring-stones, he said, "Toxicore, as a man who's been married myself, I feel I must tell you…"

Their voices faded as they stepped into the thick mists surrounding Baile na Geasaíochta. With a heavy sigh, I turned to look one last time at the city. Giving in to a deep temptation, I lifted my hand to touch the nearest threshold stone.

"Do you think you should do that, Doc?" Hattie asked, ever reasonably.

"You're right. Maybe it isn't the best idea." I was now playing the long game with the Morrígan; no reason to make a win that simple for her.

We waited another beat in silence, then she said, "Let's hope those guns are where we left them, or it's gonna be me givin' Darkheart a first-hand lesson on what women are really like, and it's gonna be a hard one."

"They will be," I promised. And, fortunately for Tox, they were.

All in all, reversing our path through the enchanted Otherworld forest was a long, glum affair. Everything we'd come to Tír Na nÓg for had been snatched away. In my case, right as I'd found it; and in Hattie's, before she even had. We were heading back home empty-handed and worse off than before.

To make matters worse, Hattie's customary brusqueness turned into downright discourtesy. Toxicore made the mistake of saying how inconvenient it would be for him if Hattie's family lost their ranch.

Hattie's response was to pull out Judgment and fire a bullet into the ground next to him. Toxicore whisked into absence at the threat, and she squinted in pain at the loud shot.

Paddy and I stopped in our tracks, speechless. I finally asked, "Are you all right, Hattie?"

"Yeah, that was a bit uncalled for, I admit. I just have a mighty bad headache. Feels like the mother of all katzenjammers, like I swallowed a whole bottle of hooch on my own."

Tox reappeared. "'Tis the vitality potion what made you dum—I mean brave enough to fight the Morrígan wearin' off."

"That right?" she said. "I'll admit that I never felt better than while it was runnin' through me, but I think I prefer an old-fashioned hang-over to this kind."

"Would you like to rest for a while?" I asked. The sky was bright enough to suggest we'd have plenty of daylight to make it all the way through the forest before dark, and it bothered me to see her so distressed. I removed the water canteen I wore hanging from a strap over my shoulder and handed it to her. "Have some. You can use it more than me."

She took it and had several sips, then passed it back. "I reckon I'm fine. Just don't need you wobblin' your jaw any more about the ranch, Darkheart."

Tox's lips parted, but I clamped my hand on his shoulder and he fell silent. Soon, we continued, and finally, a spot of brightness found us.

Paddy was soaring in lazy loops above us, keeping a lookout, when suddenly he shouted something too garbled in his excitement to make out. Before I could ask what he'd said, he zipped behind us. Hattie and I turned and spotted something in the sky—a griffin! It flew at great haste in the same direction we were traveling. At that speed, whoever it might be carrying would be on us before we could possibly run and hide.

But that wasn't going to be necessary.

"I'd know that mustache even if I was blind in both eyes and lost my ability to smell beard wax," said Hattie. "It's Downs!"

She was right. There was no mistaking Orville's distinctive, handsome jaw and oiled black mustache, or the tell-tale women's clothing he favored as a disguise. This time, it was a lovely pink-and-black ensemble flowing behind him in the wind, which would have been admired by every woman in Boston, despite its distinctly unusual cut and shape. They did have their own fashion sense in Tír Na nÓg.

He saw Paddy first, and the two exchanged an in-flight greeting before Orville directed his mount to the earth.

I ran toward him the second his boots hit the ground. "Am I imagining things, or is it really you, Orville? Did the Morrígan let you go?"

He laughed dismissively. "Let me go? I know you haven't met the matron of murder, but she'd sooner spend her long life as a scullery maid than let me go free. I believe I've mentioned to you on many occasions that I'm quite skilled at getting in and out of places without detection, and once again I've proved my skills." He must have seen something in my face at his comment about the Morrígan, because he paused, then asked speculatively, "Or have you met her?"

"It's a long story, and one I'd rather tell you when we're back on the other side of the gateway. Given your direction, it appears that's where you're headed as well. There's just one last stop we have to make."

Hattie and I had discussed leaving Knox here, though were undecided yet, but we did at least want to face the Muculents. A deal was a deal, and we still owed them some "snacks" as Toxicore had arranged, and which he said he had in his storage.

As it turned out, delivering these wasn't necessary.

28

"What do you mean, they ate him?" I didn't know whether to be furious or relieved as Toxicore explained what had become of Truman Radamus Knox. The four of us waited outside the ring-stones as Toxicore went to the Muculent village a short distance down the grassy, windswept hillside to retrieve our quarry—but he'd returned with the bad news.

"I'm not as good with the Mucks' language as I thought, am I?" he explained. "They got their snacks, though, didn't they? And they're happy enough not to bother us again, so sure we can all get goin' afore the Morrígan knows the gambler's taggin' along with us."

So, the thief was dead. At least he'd been in an enchanted sleep and wouldn't have known what was happening to him. I wondered briefly if the Muculents had taken his life before consuming him, then pushed that thought away so fast that it nearly strained a muscle in my mind. Unsure what to say next, I turned to Hattie to gauge her reaction.

She merely shrugged in her laconic way. "Doesn't much matter one way or the other. Without the Ink of Influence, it wasn't gonna be easy to save the ranch with or without him."

Orville, now on foot with the rest of us after sending his stolen griffin back to the City of Spells, asked, "Are you speaking of Fíne Fergusoni's Ink of Influence? Why would you need such a thing?"

I remembered that I'd only told Orville we needed a spell from the Morrígan's vaults for Hattie, but hadn't mentioned exactly what. Now, Hattie briefly sketched out the predicament with Knox and the Dumas ranch. Orville donned a grin halfway through her explanation, which only widened as she finished.

"My dear Miss Dumas, remind me never to bet on a hand against you. Your luck is too good."

"What do you mean, Orville?" I asked.

"I know how to create the ink and the spell to make it work. I simply need to gather a few items when we get back, and I'll have it for you in a couple of days."

"You know how to make it?" I asked, flabbergasted.

"How?" Hattie added.

Putting the smallest of lids on his self-aggrandizement, he said, "As Darkheart just mentioned, I am a gambler, and a very fine one. Fergusoni, fates rest him, was not. He lost the spell to me in a game of... oh, what was it?" He tugged on his mustache as he tried to recall. "Oh, yes, Glimmer Gambit. He was nearly as bad at bluffing as he was at avoiding giants' very large feet. Saving your ranch will be a simple matter of creating a real deed in your mother's name and presenting it to Sheriff Dickey. And in the meantime, Darkheart can don a glamour of this Knox fellow, fates rest him as well, and tell Dickey he withdraws his claim, it was all a silly mistake, and so on."

Suddenly the brightness that had begun to breach the dark when Orville arrived grew even brighter. Hattie's ranch was all but saved, and therefore, as far as I was concerned, this misadventure had been worth it after all. Maybe I'd lost the spear and hadn't had quite the rescue and reunion with my father I'd hoped for, but so what? I'd had neither spear nor father for the whole of my life. What did it matter if they were still gone—at least for now? And the Morrígan was no longer hunting me, either. Now that something good had happened that nudged my perspective a bit, I realized I'd overlooked that great fortune until now.

Orville, taken with the challenge of a good deception, was deep in the throes of planning the ranch caper. "If we can stop by Motherlode's shop in Denver when I drop off that spellbook at my wife's, I believe she'll have most of the ingredients I'll need for the ink."

That comment stuck like a well-thrown dagger into my newfound optimism.

Motherlode had betrayed me. Whether the laws of magic, if there even were such a thing, agreed with me or not, the laws of inheritance were surely on my side. I was going to get Sleg back. Besides, for all I knew, Motherlode had pulled a magical sleight of hand when we'd made our agreement in the first place, absolving her of her own responsibilities to and the consequences of breaking that agreement. Regardless of how deep a hole I'd dug myself by promising the Morrígan the phylactery, what was mine was mine, just as what was Hattie's family's was theirs. Knox had gotten his payback for trying to swindle them. It was time for me to get some of my own.

"Yes," I responded dryly. "I think a trip to Motherlode's is a wonderful idea. I have some business with that treacherous troll myself."

DID YOU ENJOY FAE PLANES DRIFTER? KEEP ON THE LOOKOUT FOR MORE BOOKS IN THE SERIES. COMING SOON!

To my treasured reader, I'm deeply grateful for your readership your presence in my wordy world. If my book has touched your heart with magic or transported you to another realm, would you consider sharing your thoughts through a review on your favorite retailer? Your voice carries immense value and can guide fellow readers to a tale that resonates with them too. Together, we can build a community of kindred spirits, connected through the power of storytelling. Thank you for your kindness and support.

Don't forget to join my newsletter at www.tammysalyer.com/news letter to stay up to date on new releases and receive a free collection of stories. Cheers!

ABOUT THE AUTHOR

Tammy is an inveterate verbarian, who spends her days surrounded by the written word, both hers and others'. As an ex-paratrooper with the 82nd Airborne Division, her stories are often as gritty as a grunt's pile of three-week-old field gear. When not hunched like a Morlock over her writing desk, Tammy runs and bikes silly miles with her super-cool weirdo partner in the playground of Southern California and spends an inappropriate amount of time watching Henry Rollins videos on YouTube. Contrary to whatever ideas her last name might conjure, she's never really been much of a Slayer fan.

Fantasy, space opera, satire, and snark fans will feel right at home with Tammy. Learn more about her and her books by visiting www.tammysalyer.com.